THE WOOKEY HOLE

Henry R. Harvey

The Wookey Hole is a work of fiction. The characters, events and dialogue are products of the author's imagination and are not to be construed as real.

Copyright © Henry R. Harvey 2019
All rights reserved under International and Pan-American Copyright Conventions.

ISBN: 978-0-359-86067-8

Library of Congress

This book is published in the United States of America by *Lulu.com*

The Wookey Hole is also available in e-book format and paperback format at henryharveybooks.com, harveygallery.com and Amazon.com

Cover design by Henry R. Harvey
Author photograph by Pamela Lynn Harvey

About the Author

After majoring in philosophy at Franklin and Marshall College, Henry Harvey trained at Columbus AFB, Mississippi, where he became a jet pilot. He was also a launch-enable (LES) officer for the Titan II missile program at Davis Monthan AFB in Tucson, Arizona. He was recruited two years later for top-secret training at Keesler AFB to become a Tempest Officer, handling top-secret and black programs, dealing with debugging as well as locating spies in the Pacific Theater.

His sculpting career began while he was stationed at Yokota AFB in Japan and flourished upon returning stateside with galleries in Arizona and Pennsylvania.

Schiffer Publishing has published two books about his life as a sculptor as well as a book of short stories: **37 Cents a Fart and Other Infamous Animal Stories.**

PBS has filmed a special about his life at CrossBow in Bucks County, Pa.
He publishes weekly essays on his site:
henryharveybooks.com and lectures on a variety of topics.
He also has an expansive sculpture site: **harveygallery.com.**

His novel, **Playing on the Black Keys** is currently optioned for a major motion picture in Hollywood. Harvey has won an award for his screenplays and is a patented inventor. He has written numerous books and novels listed below.

Harvey lives with his wife, Pamela and their Boston terriers in Old Fort, North Carolina, where they reside at *Dragonfly*, their twelve-acre estate with sculpture gardens and a 60-ft. black treetop schooner, *Moon Dancer,* which occasionally hosts bluegrass concerts.

Books by the Author

Playing on the Black Keys

The First

The Saphos Assassin

Lord of the Mill

A Universe of Metal Sculpture

Pissing in the Wind

Carver's Mill

I'm Only Two People

Requiem for a Small Planet

Peace Sign

A Passion for Metal

Poontango

The Antlers Inn

The Wrong End of the Telescope

Monsters of the Id (this fall)

Time Bubbles (this spring)

Black Dog Gallery

37 Cents a Fart and Other Infamous Animal Stories

The F**ket List

For Pamela

Pamela and I met in 1968 and in what is now coming up on half a century, she has been my lover, my friend, my wife, my editor and co-conspirator.

Somewhere along the line our literary relationship grew from writer and editor to that of a writing team. Candidly, she knows my writing style so well, that sometimes she'll offer an alternative that is more me...than me.

In short, there would be no writing, without Pamela by my side. Thank you, my love!

Quotes That Have Shaped My Life

"It's not the bridges burned that bother me, but the ones that I never crossed." (Lyrics from "Look at Me. Look at You" by The Association)

"Do unto others as you would have them do unto you." (The Golden Rule) This works for me when all else fails.

The harder I work...the luckier I get.

Words on a t-shirt at the Black Mountain Tractor Supply: *Sweet as Sugar...Cold as Ice...Cross me Once...and I'll Shoot you Twice*

Non futuis vobiscum: A famous Latin phrase mounted over our doorway.

"I was so much older then; I'm younger than that now." Bob Dylan, *Back Pages*

"I would rather have questions that can't be answered than answers that can't be questioned." Richard P. Feynman

Sorry 'bout that...

At the precise moment that Mrs. Davis's casket was being lowered beneath the grass, there was a small but pronounced *Clink*.

Everyone attending the funeral heard it and for a moment, time stood still. Apparently, the top-half of Mrs. Davis's casket was still fighting the good fight, much as Mrs. Davis, herself, had struggled for the last thirty years at Carver's Mill Elementary, trying to corral each K-through-Eight student toward an exciting and productive life.

Though Charley Blair's eyes were wet, he suppressed a grin. It was just so damned appropriate. He pictured her inside the coffin in one of her power colors, red or black...probably black today, and one of those Hermes knock-off scarves she got from Rice's farmers' market, grinning with eyes closed and thinking, *I still got it!*

But then, it looked like Father Lowell and his boys were actually experiencing technical difficulties and so Charlie slipped off his jacket and hung it on the back of the metal folding chair. It was midsummer in Carver's Mill and they were all sitting in what was essentially a field of overgrown weeds and wildflowers. He and everyone else were already sweating and at least it was a good excuse to remove his jacket. He trotted over to where the pastor and his helpers were fumbling with some rope covered with black velvet to make it fancier.

He squatted down next to them and peered into the hole. "She's still fightin' ya?" he whispered. One of the altar boys chuckled. He'd probably been one of her last pupils. He looked to be about twenty and Mrs. Davis hadn't taught in eight years.

"Okay-- Looks like ya got the ropes twisted," Charlie said. "It shoulda been turned one-eighty before you lowered it." He looked around at the three young men. None of them wanted to look him in the eye. They just kept staring down in the hole as if Mrs. Davis, herself, might open the top of the casket and offer to help.

"Do we have to raise it up again?" Father Lowell asked.

Charlie stared down at the black box. He was probably one of the few people who actually understood Mrs. Davis. She'd always been a no-bullshit-kind-of-person and they had that in common. In this last moment of her symbolically being in sunlight, he didn't want to embarrass her. "Nah... I can push down on the top half and you go ahead and lower. It should go in. Just wait till I tell ya."

Charlie Blair went into an old football position as if he were in the line and as the crank started turning, he put his shoulder into it. "Okay...now!" The casket bumped and nudged into free space and lowered without further complaint.

"Well... Goodbye again, Mrs. Davis," he whispered to the casket. It bit the back of his throat having to say goodbye at point-blank range.

As he stood up, the young pastor said, "Thank you, my son. God smiles upon you."

"You're welcome," Charley said softly, "but I'm not your son. I'm old enough to be your uncle. Next time, check the ropes before you do any lowering. This isn't right, not for Mrs. Davis."

He turned around and looked at the small number of people at the tiny graveyard. It was disappointing. Mrs. Davis had been his teacher in eighth grade, as she had probably been everyone in the county's teacher at one time or another. He'd always liked her because she was the only teacher he'd ever met who wasn't full of crap.

She was also the one who taught him the correct way to change the oil on her lawnmower, when he'd mow her lawn and the correct way to remove a nail with a claw hammer without messing up the wood. And she knew what a torque wrench was for, as well as how to use it. How many school teachers even knew what a torque wrench was? But then, there was all that other stuff she could do...not so much for him, but for some of the other students. She had said a couple of times that her *raison d'etre* was to be a lens to focus other people. He chuckled again. He hadn't taken French in high school...barely passed Spanish, but because of Mrs. Davis he knew two words in French, *raison d'etre*...reason to live.

Yeah, but there you are now, like everybody else, lying in a box and about to be covered up with dirt. Sorry 'bout that...

He scanned the pasture where everyone had parked. He knew most of the cars. Carver's Mill was a very small town. The guys from the newspaper, about five cars from the school, the superintendent, the president of the bank, the guy who runs the Texaco station...

But then he saw two women, one he barely recognized. Well... that wasn't exactly true. He recognized her all right. Susan had just moved away a long, long time ago. She was possibly the only person to escape Carver's Mill and make something of herself. The other woman was Becky, who had a little artsy-fartsy shop in Sterling Center. He'd had on-again, off-again crushes on both of them over the years, though never to any avail.

He stared just a fraction of a second too long. They'd been looking in his direction anyway, probably noticing that he'd picked up a couple of pounds...probably recalling some stupid incident that was best left forgotten.

Becky, the brunette, popped her hand up in the air and it just hung there pointed at him. At that point, it would have been rude not to wave back and so his hand slowly rose in the air and hovered for a second. And for that second, he felt strange, as if he were communicating with her telepathically somehow...touching her hand across the expanse of overgrown field. And then...*sonofabitch*...Susan's hand raised as well and seemed somehow a bit more...*friendly*. She waved it back and forth slowly as if she were a queen of England waving to her minions. It was friendly but distant as she had always been. He mimicked the light bulb-turn wave and unscrewed his own light bulb in return.

He lowered his hand first but then the three of them just stood there staring at each other. *Fuck...what am I s'posed to do now?* his mind wondered. *If I turn away...that says something. If I start walking over...that says something else. Fuck...I hate this shit...*

He did a little pantomime which was equally stupid. He held up his hand like a puppet and made it talk. Then he pointed to himself and then over there. Becky nodded to him. Susan gave her little queenly wave again.

"...shit," he whispered at the ground. *If I'd just kept my goddamn head moving...* He made a point of not appearing too eager. He meandered in their general direction, making a point of wandering close to the newspaper group. He nodded at Sam and Delta Harper, the owners of the paper, then at Cubby Miles, the roving reporter for the *Patriot*. Cubby was gay and had been in the class of '67...a year after his. He'd always had an inkling that Cubby had a crush on him. No matter when he'd looked in Cubby's direction, he was staring back, wistfully.

Sure enough, as he wandered by, Cubby separated himself from the clot of people and waved him down. "Hey, you're just the man I want to see!" Cubby said just a bit too eagerly.

Charley stopped. His eyes went flat. He'd wanted to *not* appear too eager to see Becky and Susan. But he didn't want to derail entirely either. "What's up, Cub?" he said making it clear he wasn't interested in a long conversation.

Cubby was a quick study. "Okay...not now, but the Patriot is putting together an article on Mrs. Davis. And you...and Becky...and Susan are to be the lead interviewees."

Charley hesitated. It sounded like a trick. "I can understand Susan. She made it big time...well, at least for Carver's Mill. Becky... well, she's just plain weird so I guess that fits. But where the hell do I fit in? I didn't do shit. I'm still stuck here in scenic Carver's Mill, workin' and repairing garden tractors."

"She was writing a book, Charley," Cubby said.

"Who was writing a book?"

"Mrs. Davis."

"Really? About what?" He glanced in Becky and Susan's direction. They were still watching him now...actively. "Hey, look, I gotta go. Go back and check. I think you got me mixed up with somebody else. It was probably Jon Prescott. Wasn't he the valedictorian?"

"No mistake," Cubby said. "Can I stop in, or would you rather I call first?"

Neither option sounded good. "Call."

Like most of Carver's Mill, the fields had just been allowed to go back to nature. Just walking the eighty yards or so over toward the parking area, Charley had managed to pick up some cockleburs and the golden rod was turning his dress pants yellow. He hadn't worn them since...since the last funeral he'd been to...his father's and that had been five years ago. They were now his official funeral pants.

He thought about stopping to brush himself off but it was too late. They were watching him now. They looked like they'd linked-up again...just like old times. Becky was the crazy one...the one with the mouth, the one who got into trouble. And Susan was like Cinderella or...take any blonde from any storybook that was perfect and never made a mistake. Thank God in the twelve years since he'd seen them, they'd both gotten some crow's feet and Becky looked just a bit more buxom than the good ole days.

"Hey, Mr. Super Stud, quarter back, class of '67!" Becky called out. "How they hangin'?"

Charley stopped in his tracks. She was exactly as annoying as ever. "Well, except for the fact that I wasn't the quarterback, I was a *full*-back and I graduated in '66...barely...I'm doin' fine."

"Well, I got the super stud part right...Right?"

Charlie made a face like he was about to throw up. He hugged Susan first, in as Platonic and avuncular a manner as he could muster. Becky...he barely touched at all. He treated her like she was a burn victim and just patted her lightly on the back. Then he patted her on the head. It was meant to put her back in the one and only thing he had on her. She'd always been a class behind him. Sixty-six just had a sexier ring to it. Sixty-seven...what kind of number is sixty-seven?

When he broke the embrace, for a long moment they all just stood there awkwardly staring at each other. He looked more closely at Susan Sorato. She'd always had that patina of royalty, every hair in place, and her shoes just so. That part hadn't changed. If anything, she was even more perfect. Her handbag probably cost as much as his Silverado. She looked like she maintained her body now like people in California...something else to schedule-in, only she didn't look terribly happy. At least that was *something*.

"I bought your book," Charlie said.

Susan flashed a smile.

"Which one?" Becky said. "What do you have now, Suze, like ten?"

Susan shook her head. "No, just three. And it's not like it sounds."

"Well, it *sounds* pretty impressive," Charlie said. "Sorry to say, I wasn't able to read it. I never got the hang of keeping a dictionary in my lap when I read."

"Which one was it?"

"I think it was the first. It was some kinda play-on words... I was younger than... something."

"*I'm Younger Than I Was*," Susan said.

"That's the one. Wasn't that the words to a song or something?" Charlie said.

Susan's face dropped. "As it turns out, it was part of the chorus to a Dylan song only, it was, "I was so much older then, I'm younger than that now."

"Hey, I remember that. It was pretty cool at the time."

"I swear to God I didn't remember the song or the lyrics. When it came time for vetting, the lawyers at Conifer Publishing caught it...and changed it to what it is now. It just doesn't have the punch."

"Hey, but you're not in court, right?" Becky said.

"Right. So how are *you* doing, Charlie?" Susan asked, changing the subject.

"Me?" Charlie grinned. "Oh... I'm writing a book, too. I think I'm gonna call it, *How I Graduated High School and Went on to be Rich and Famous...Fixin' Lawnmowers*. I think it's got that grass-roots appeal."

Becky touched his arm for the second time in thirty seconds. "Hey, you know the three of us outta get together and get drunk and compare notes or something. It might be fun! Is that little pizza shop still down behind the A&P?"

"Burned down. They're sayin' it was Italian lightning. Now, it's a dry cleaners or something. I don't go down that way very much anymore."

Susan tapped him on the arm in just the same way she used to when they were in homeroom together. "Well, you live here. Tell us, what's new and exciting?"

Charlie looked deeply into her eyes. It wasn't meant to be a flirtation. It was meant to be sarcastic. Her eyes were just the same as they were twelve years ago, only there was a different look behind them. It was impossible to read. "New and exciting? Well, now, let me think." He paused, staring off into space and then he just kept staring off for effect.

"Okay..." Susan said. "I get it. Is *The Gent* still around? It didn't burn down, did it?"

"Nah, it's still there."

"How 'bout *The Wookey Hole*?"

"It's still there, too. But neither one of them are what you'd call new and exciting. Speaking of which...I really gotta get back to my new and exciting repair job on a gang mower for the golf course."

"Hey, c'mon. That's no fun," said Becky. "Did you forget already? The three of us used to be..." The words just lingered there.

Charlie finally allowed himself a smile only it was more cynical than happy. "Yeah, we used to be...*something*, though for the life of me I can't remember what." He looked at Susan.

"Congratulations. You did what you wanted to do...and you got the hell out of Dodge. Those are two biggies. And that was the plan, wasn't it?" Then he looked at Becky and the back of his throat tightened despite himself. It was as bad as looking down at Mrs. Davis's casket. Becky had always had that way of just staring into his soul like no one else on the planet. Then she'd fuck it up by opening her mouth... "Oh and by the way. I ran into Cubby. You remember him."

"Short, gay, a little chubby," Susan said.

"Yeah, that's Cub. He's still all those things. Only he's the reporter for the Patriot now and he drives a freakin' Audi. He said he wanted to do a story on you two...something to do with Mrs. Davis. She was writing a book or something."

Susan's eyes went *strange* at his words. As kids she'd always just been the perfect princess. Things were different now. She had horsepower...a presence. And it wasn't that it was unattractive, it was just odd to see it. She said, "It wasn't the *two* of us, Charlie, and you know it. It was the three of us."

"Okay. I stand corrected."

"And the name of her book was *The Milk Stool*. She had written to me about it. Do you know why she called it that?"

"Nope," Charlie said. "As far as I can remember, Mrs. Davis never even saw a milk stool, much less, milked a cow." Then he looked at her eyes. She had him

"Okay, I know what a milk stool is. I get the symbolism."

"Well, I'm not getting this joke," Becky said. "Could somebody fill me in?"

"It's not a big deal," Charlie said. "A milk stool...well, it's got three legs. That's all."

"Yeah? And?" Becky said.

Susan said, "When you have three legs, the stool can't tip over. It can't even wobble, no matter what." She looked at Charlie. "The three of us were the three legs."

The First Interview

Cuthbert, "Cubby" Miles and Susan Sorato sat in the bay window of the new addition to The Country Gent. It looked out on a spanking new stone patio with wrought-iron tables and chairs that still had the price stickers on them. There was also a new ceramic fountain in the middle with three verdigris goldfish spitting water down into the basin. The Gent had come a long way since it had been a watering hole...almost literally in the 1700s. Since Lou Terkel had finally gotten married...the place was changing, tripping over itself attempting to jump into the 21st Century.

    Cubby wore freshly ironed jeans, penny loafers, a blue work shirt and a corduroy blazer...hold the socks. He'd always thought socks made his ankles look fat.

    Susan was casually elegant, a black V-neck cashmere and a skirt. She had her hair pulled back into a bun and her big glasses which broadcast: *I'm in work-mode now.* If Princess Grace had a younger sister raised in Carver's Mill, it would have been Susan.

    Cubby pulled a small, black, plastic box from his jacket pocket, opened it and propped it open on the wooden table. Then he hesitated. "Hope you don't mind... It just helps when I get back to the paper."

    By way of an answer, Susan reached in her pocketbook and pulled out a device that was silver plastic but otherwise not that different.

    Cubby glanced at it. "Oh, goody! We could do a mutual interview if you like, sort of like a circle..."

"Don't go there," Susan sighed as she slipped the recorder back in its pocket. "Fact is, I've used that exact disclaimer when I interview someone." She looked at Cubby's expression. "Background for a book. I don't write for a paper or anything. I don't think I could handle taking orders."

Cubby grinned with his mouth, but his eyebrows were in high-arch on top of his forehead. *Prickly*, he thought. He'd always remembered her as quiet, cerebral, and a little glacial. The prickly part was something new. Maybe that came with being an instant success. Maybe *Susan Sorato had actually turned into an asshole. Gee, that'd be nice*! He pressed a small button on the side of the recorder and a tiny red light began blinking. He kicked-off with, "I understand Mrs. Davis was communicating with you as well." It was meant to throw her off guard.

She sat up a little straighter. "Uhm, yes. That's right. She's writing... She *was* writing a book. She wanted to *confer*."

"She wanted to confer about writing? Getting published?"

"I don't think she worried about the writing part." She glanced across the table. "Did you have her in a class?"

Cubby grinned off into space. He was accustomed to this type of snotty treatment at the gay bars in New Hope. That or she was just oblivious to him. "Yes, my dear. We were in the same class together. I sat three seats behind you. I'm *really* familiar with the back of your head."

"I'm sorry. It was a long time ago." Susan opened up the menu and began scanning. "Boy, this place has changed. I remember when it was a tacky little bar that had good ribs and hamburgers."

"Still does," Cubby offered. "And the getting published?"

Susan looked at him. "No, it wasn't that either. I don't think Mrs. Davis was one to worry about..." She looked at him more closely. "You already know what her book was about, don't you?"

Cubby gave her one of his winning smiles. He reached beneath the table and pulled up a battle-worn attaché case that looked like it should be pasted with stamps from around the world. He reached in and pulled out a sheaf of equally battered typing paper.

Susan looked at it. "That's it?"

Cubby nodded. "It's why we're here."

"How far did she get?"

"Oh, it's finished. She was in the middle of line editing when... And when I say in the middle, I mean that's how they found her in her bed...with a red Bic pen in hand, slumped over page 257. She'd had a stroke. Lots of red ink. Lots of red blood in the bed. There's blood on some of the pages. For being a peaceful way to go, it looked pretty gory. What was weird though, once you get past the blood, she was as unmerciful editing herself as she was on her English class. When she proofed, she really ripped the crap out of her own sentences, even her own observations." He flipped open to one particularly marked-up page and turned it around on the table.

Susan mouthed Mrs. Davis's editing marks, *Trite!!! No! Who the hell cares? Redundant!* She took the extra second to try to scan the content of the pages. It was a Halloween pageant from when she and Becky were in the fifth grade...only through Mrs. Davis's eyes.

"Interesting," Susan said, not wanting Cubby to see her interest. "Have you read the whole manuscript?"

When Cubby saw her eyes he knew he had her. "No, I just started it."

"Do you think it's *appropriate* for you to be reading it?"

"Interesting you should ask. I talked to Sam about it. He said that it wasn't a diary but a manuscript...meant to be published. That and the fact that she'd called me up to talk about it getting published...I figured it gave me *some* license. But then there was a note stuck in the pages. When the police came over, it fell out." He pulled a folded sheet of notebook paper from his jacket pocket and slid it across the table. It was a list. *Make Five Copies: Becky, Charlie, Cubby, Susan, Me.*

"She wanted four of us to have copies."

"Did you make a..."

"Yup, they're in the car...sans blood stains. I figured all three of you would want to at least take a gander before I do any serious interviewing."

"Oh. I thought *this* was the interview. I was only planning on staying a couple of days. I have...other commitments."

"Of course that's up to you," Cubby said. "I guess we could e-mail each other. Or we could *text*...your entire childhood. That might be challenging. Your call."

The waitress arrived. Susan looked at her. She looked vaguely like someone she had known. *Gym class* floated through her mind. Fortunately it was a one-sided revelation. "I'd like a vodka martini very cold, very dry. Two olives."

Cubby thought, *The perfect drink for you.*

Blair Lawnmowers and Repair

Charlie was lying under the three-blade cutting deck of a zero-radius John Deere garden tractor, attempting to loosen one of the tensioning pulleys He was on a creeper so he could move around easier and at the moment, he was taking turns between swearing under his breath and putting his shoulder into a 3/8ths-drive socket wrench.

"Are you for real?" he said to the mower, though he was actually addressing the guy who'd brought it in. He had one of the new Mc Mansions atop Buckingham Mountain and a portion of the five acres had been left wild and wooded. The problem was, the asshole who owned the mansion...and the mower, had been trying to clear brush and apparently grind down the tops of the boulders with the mower. That, and the guy had apparently never cleaned the underside of the mowing deck...not ever...not never. What had once been blades were now bent scrap metal, threatening to become shrapnel. The deck was so clogged it looked like green dryer lint only six-inches thick. The topside, of course, was waxed and shiny and the guy had *Armoraled* the seat so that you couldn't sit on it without sliding off the side.

"Friggin' Bozo..." Charlie muttered under his breath just as the front door to the shop swung open. Without knowing who it was, he took an instant dislike to the shoes and trousers heading in his direction.

"Hellooo..." came a voice from the still unknown trousers. It was a guy's voice...so it was a guy.

Charlie wheeled the creeper out into the light and looked up at Cuthbert Miles. *Well, I was half-right,* he thought. "Oh, it's you," he said and wheeled back in beneath the mower deck. From the safety of all the sharp edges, caked mud and mowing blades, he called out, "Didn't we agree you were gonna call first?"

This stopped Cubby, but only for a second. "Oh, yes we did," Cubby almost purred, "though I didn't come in to talk about Mrs. Davis...or her book. What I came in for was..." Cubby looked around at Charlie's shop. It would have been very much at home in a *Leave It To Beaver* episode from the 50s. The Coca Cola clock behind the cash register. The calendar next to it with drawings of Chevy trucks. He peered around at the grey pegboard walls, festooned with green-and-yellow garden clippers, hedge trimmers on one wall, and screaming-orange Husqvarna chain saws on the other. Like he had at every gay bar he'd ever been to, he opened up his mind to try to think what line would best serve him to pick up a likely date for the evening. "I was thinking of chopping down a couple of trees," he said tentatively.

Charlie rolled back out on the creeper and looked at him.

Cubby looked back at him. "What?" They stared at each other for another second. "You're not buying it?"

"C'mon, Cub. We've been down this road before. You're barkin' up the wrong tree...hugely the wrong tree."

"Hope springs eternal," Cubby said.

"Not in my world. Look, I wasn't interested twenty years ago and I wasn't interested ten years ago. I've never been interested even a tiny bit...and I'll never be interested. I can't think how to make that concept any clearer."

"But, you're not married. And as far as I know, you aren't dating anyone."

"That may be, "Charlie said, "but that doesn't mean I'm gay. Trust me on this one."

Cubby went into a small histrionic pout. "Well, if you ever change your mind..."

Charlie allowed himself the smallest hint of a grin. It was hard being pissed with someone who was infatuated with you. "If I ever change my mind, Cub, you're at the top of my list...that is, assuming I don't blow my friggin' head off first. Okay?"

"Okay. By the way, I have something for you out in the car."

"It better not be an apple pie or something weird."

"Not to worry. It's a manuscript."

"Cubby..."

"No, it's not like that. It's Mrs. Davis's manuscript, the one she was working on when she died. You're in her book. You're in it, big time. You and Susan and Becky."

Charlie went over to the sink and began washing the grease and dirt from his hands. He had a surgical way he did it. He used his elbow to push the faucet lever on and then he tapped the soap dispenser with the top of his knuckle. He lathered up to his elbows and pulled down a blue shop towel to dry off. It bought him a little time to think. He didn't want to appear too interested. "So, what's it about?"

Cubby looked around the shop. Straight men were soooo transparent, soooo straight. You could see the way their minds were moving probably before they even did. He wondered what it'd be like to live so linearly. "It's about...you and Susan and Becky. That's what it's all about."

Charlie chuckled at the words and he flushed a little. "That's great, only it doesn't make any sense at all. I barely know Susan now. I barely recognized her at the funeral. And whatever crap we did as kids, well, how the hell would Mrs. Davis know any of it anyway? It's stupid. It just doesn't make any sense."

Cubby listened to the words...the logic of a straight-arrow heterosexual man...and decided to pull his chain...just a little. "I noticed you didn't mention Rebecca Pierce."

Charlie's eyes went flat. "Yeah, well. Mrs. Davis really wouldn't know anything about that. Plus there's nothing to know."

"If you don't want me to bring the manuscript in, I understand."

Charlie looked at him. "You're playin' games and you know how I love people who like to play games."

Two minutes later, Cubby returned from the car with his attaché in hand. He seemed to walk a bit taller when he was carrying it. He was Cuthbert Miles, now mild-mannered reporter for the Daily Planet...The Carver's Mill Patriot. Still, Charlie understood pride, no matter how small or how strangely practiced.

He decided to go easy on Cubby now that he had his professional hat on. He poured out two coffees and they sat down in the tiny back room that was his "office." It consisted of one metal desk, one metal chair with arms for himself, and a metal chair with no arms for whoever was going to be sitting there bugging him.

He had a very old computer on one side of his desk, a filing cabinet, a bunch of papers and Post-It notes attached to the wall with nails, not tacks and a photograph of his one claim to fame, a '65 Vette, Nassau metallic blue, black leather interior and the "cool" wheels. He'd bought it used and then spent several years bringing it back to like-new condition. Usually, he'd just go out in the back of the garage, turn it on and listen to some music.

It was such a bitch keeping it pristine that he hardly drove it on the road anymore. It was just easier and made a whole lot more sense to sit in it and listen to...the good ole days.

Cubby sat down and looked around at the small office. It was like fifty other offices of that type he'd been in. He wondered how Charlie could live that way, day in, day out. A floor lamp, a little carpeting, maybe a mirror, a couple of nice prints. It wouldn't be all that hard or that expensive.

He pulled the original manuscript out and slid a copy of it onto Charlie's cluttered desk.

"The Milk Stool," he read aloud.

The first page was a dedication. It said, "For Becky and Charlie and Susan. I hope I'm around to see the outcome." Charlie grunted, then sighed at the words. He was aware that Cubby was watching him, but he'd figured that out in advance. *Just...what the hell was Mrs. Davis doing, writing a book about the three of them? What the hell does she know that I don't...that we don't?*

He turned the page. It was a note to the reader. It said:

> *It's important that you know that this isn't a novel. The three main "characters" here aren't characters but people, whom I've watched from fifth grade to adulthood. There aren't any heroes or heroines in this account nor are there any monsters or mass murderers. What you do have, however, is an interesting division of labor, three distinct and separate attempts by three very different people to cope with LIFE.*
>
> *My observations are my own and if Charlie or Becky or Susan are reading this now, I apologize in advance. I never let you know*

what I was doing...that I was observing. The reason is simple. First off, you seemed to be doing a pretty good job of coping all by your lonesomes. More importantly, I didn't want my observing to interfere. In truth, I love all three of you like my own.

Charlie put the cover sheet back on top of the one and a half-inch pile and tapped his fingers on top. "Okay... Well, this is a little different than what I was expecting..." He looked at Cubby. "You're not expecting me to read this thing right now are you?"

Cubby was still a different person now, neither a reporter, nor a gay man. At least that wasn't uppermost in his mind. At the moment, he was another member of the unfolding story. "No, not at all. I'm only about five pages ahead of you as it is. I didn't feel right."

Charlie leaned forward on his metal desk. There were half a dozen repair bills that were in various stages of completion, all in a semi-circle around him. He'd lay them out and then draw a big black X in pen when they were finished. At the moment, there were three Xs out of five on his desk. "Sooo...what'd she say in the first five pages?"

Cubby chuckled. And he wondered what he would have said if the tables had been turned. "I'd forgotten that you used to be short, too," Cubby said. "Short and wiry and sullen."

"I wasn't sullen."

"Did I say sullen? I meant happy and fun-loving."

"I did have a growth spurt freshman year. I went from five-six to six-one in two weeks. Well, it felt like two weeks. I felt like that character in the movies... The Hulk. I remember splitting my pants in the locker room. I wasn't even doing anything. It was embarrassing." But then Charlie's mouth went into a frown. "So that's how she kicked off her book? With her thinking that I'm short?"

"I think it's pretty safe to say...that wasn't the point of the first chapter. I think she was contrasting you to the girls. Back then, in fifth grade, both of them...well, they didn't tower over you, but they were taller. Only...she said that you were like their little personal bodyguard. No one messed with either of them without running into you."

Charlie smiled at the observation. "I may have been compensating a little. You don't know what it's like being a little..." He stopped and just looked at Cubby. "Anyway...I was trying in my own dumbass way to be Sir Lancelot or Bat Man...whoever..."

"What was it like being little and then suddenly getting big and handsome and hairy...captain of the football team?"

Charlie chuckled. "Ya know, this really is rich. When I was in school, barely passing and I joined the football team just because the coach made me. And that was only because I was big...everybody remembers you for something you never were. I wasn't the captain and I wasn't the q-b. I was just a member of the football team. It wasn't anything at all. It was nothing."

"I would have sold my left nut to have been on the football team...at all," Cubby said.

"You say that. But it's not true. I still don't get her writing about us. It kinda creeps me out."

"Well, she talks about Becky in the first chapter as well."
"What'd she say?"

Cubby turned past the cover sheet to the first coffee-stained page. He put on his wire-rimmed granny glasses and cleared his throat.

"My first real recollection of Rebecca and Susan was during the yearly Halloween pageant.

Everyone was supposed to make their own costumes... Well, they were supposed to, though if I'd held to that standard it would have cleared the deck on the entire pageant. Becky and Susan were back stage waiting for their turn to go on.

Becky was a knitter ever since I can remember and she was good...really good, even as a child. Her costume was supposed to be the black swan from Swan Lake, but she looked more like a black-bat-hooker. That's what Mr. Swain called it. He thought she was vulgar. He kept asking people if it was too vulgar to let her go on stage. I don't think either one of them had the slightest idea what vulgar was. They were just having fun.

She'd gotten hold of some black fishnet stockings and... Oh, good Lord, I just realized she had to have knitted them from scratch. There weren't fishnet stockings for little children back then. And they were perfect...in fact too perfect. And everything was perfectly form-fitting. You could have seen little pimple or any little curve if she'd had any. And there were black sequins everywhere, and she'd made her own magic wand...and a tiara that glowed. It was...breath taking. But then, standing right next to her in stark contrast was Susan...the white swan. And Becky had made her costume as well. They were blood sisters. And as dark and ominous as Becky's costume was, Susan looked like the perfect little ballerina. She looked like she was made of glittering snowflakes...only it all came from out of Becky's hands and mind.

The thing that I remember most, was how they were cracking up over something, I couldn't tell what it was. Becky's two front teeth had come out, but she didn't care. She still had the widest smile you ever saw. When she smiled, she looked like a crazy-insane happy pumpkin. And they were both just keeling over with laughter. That was my first impression. Two completely different kids...and yet inseparable."

Cubby stopped reading. "Do you remember the pageant?"

Charlie rolled his eyes. "Unfortunately. I remember them. And I remember I tried to make myself into a robot. I had three cardboard boxes and I sprayed them silver and drew some dials and glued on some knobs. Only the silver was rubbing off on everything and I still remember it really stank inside. I could barely see out and I think I was just woozy from all the fumes. "

"It was you... You were the robot that fell off the stage."

"Yeah, that was me all right. I remember some grown-ups holding me down. They thought maybe I'd broken my back or something. I just wanted to get the friggin' box off my head. Then I remember Becky and Suze staring down at me from the stage. They looked...amazing, only they were laughing, too. I must have looked pretty stupid."

Charlie thumbed through his copy of the manuscript. "I'm not sure how much of this I want to remember," he said.

"You don't have to wade through any of it if you don't want to," said Cubby.

"Do Becky and Susan have copies, too?"

"Of course."

Going Home

Everything was exactly the same as it had been seven years earlier...only smaller. Each time she made the trek back to Mom and Dad's, it seemed like the stone house she'd grown up in had shrunk, as if it'd been left in the dryer too long. The medium-sized yard she'd run across to get to the school bus wasn't medium-sized anymore. It was tiny and she made a mental note to revise her opening statements at a book signing from, *I grew up in a big stone farmhouse to... I grew up in a small house made of stone.*

    The rose garden in the front was smaller, too and older, like something out of Masterpiece Theater. As she followed the path down the slate walk, she spied 'old friends' from her childhood, the first hunk of slate next to the gate that was shaped like Texas. Thank God that was the same, and there were still the last vestiges of gold spray paint from when she and Becky had made some kind of costumes for *something*. The gold wasn't gold anymore, it was tan, but the leaf-pattern of overspray was still there.

    At the door, she took a deep breath and resolved not to be shocked by anything. She expected that Mom had shrunk some more in seven years and was probably paler.

    She turned the antique brass handle in the middle of the door, something she'd never seriously done as a child and to her knowledge no visitor had ever used. It made a mechanical *clink, clink, clink, clink, clink,* rather than sounding like a door chime. And when the door opened, she wasn't disappointed. Her mother was a thin pale wisp and there were liver spots on her chest and on her hands. She fought the urge to burst into tears...to apologize, to say, *Oh God, Mom, I'm sorry. I left you here...and now look at you.* Instead she closed the door softly behind her and they hugged gently.

"I was wondering when you were coming over," Mrs. Sorato said, her voice thinner than it had ever been, though there was still spirit in her voice. Behind the now translucent folds of skin, the eyes were still cheerful, still proud, and in a strange way, still young. Young bright brown eyes trapped in a withering body. Susan wondered what her mother thought when she looked in the mirror. And then her mind took her into an indeterminate moment of her own future. One day she'd look in the mirror...and see the same thing.

Inside, almost nothing had changed. There was a big screen television where the corner cupboard use to be and that was about it. The place still had that smell of old books and old antiques and some kind of Tung oil. She had probably oiled everything up in anticipation of her arrival, which was just what she and Mom used to do when *Mother* was coming to visit...Mrs. Sorato's mother, that is. And that had always been a royal pain in the ass. The Ice Queen, she used to call grandma and wow, did she live up to it.

The one time as a child she'd gone to visit grandmother out in Ohio, she was apparently holding court in her parlor. She remembered being escorted as far as the door and beckoned to go on in. At the time, it seemed like everyone else was just too scared to go in. Why the hell should she?

The inside of Grandmother's parlor was dark and she was sitting on a purple velvet chair behind her desk. A lone Tiffany lamp beside her made her look like a fortune teller and it seemed like she was in a trance. That was all she remembered...that and sprinting toward the door, afraid to look back lest grandma's eyes started glowing.

"You know you really don't have to stay at a motel," Mrs. Sorato said. "Your room is...well, it's just about like you left it. Plenty of room..." They looked at each other for the first time in a long time. "Oh, I suppose I understand. I remember when I'd go to visit Mother, I couldn't wait to get the hell out of there either."

"No, it's not the same," Susan said. "It's not the same at all. You and I had...*have* a different relationship. We get along. It's just my habits are different and in the big scheme of things, I think it's better for everybody." Susan looked around the house. Well, there was one thing missing, their old dachshund. "Where's Jasper?"

Mrs. Sorato's eyes slid to the floor and she sighed. She looked around sheepishly as if she'd done something wrong.

"I'm sorry. When did it happen?"

"Oh, gosh. It was years ago... You were busy getting your masters. We didn't want to trouble you."

So far she was giving the trip home a D-minus just for being such a huge bummer, and yet the guilty feeling was beginning to over-ride even that. She wondered if she had been there every day for every year, how different would she look...would the place look. Maybe her mind had just remembered things better than they'd been. It was possible.

"Coffee?" Mrs. Sorato asked.

"Uhm..." Her mind flashed back to that as well. Even at Sarah Lawrence she had learned of the possibilities of making a perfectly brewed cup of coffee, with raw cane sugar from Hawaii, coconut milk, and black roasted beans that smelled like they'd just fallen off the wagon. Tepid instant Sanka with Sweet & Low and skim milk was worse than nothing.

Mrs. Sorato seemed to be reading her mind. "I do have a coffee machine now," she said. "I can even brew you up some espresso if you like. It even does that frothy-milk thing, though I'm always afraid it's going to blow up."

"Just a regular cup of coffee would be fine."

"Of course, I have Sanka, too."

"Now that I think of it, I have to cut back on the coffee drinking. Even the decaf rots my stomach."

It didn't take ten minutes for her to realize that her mom had finally bought into the myth that once you're published and have been on an honest-to-god network TV show, it didn't mean you were rich and famous. It really didn't mean anything at all. The rich part was a joke, of course. Well, the famous part was, too. If someone hadn't managed to tune in to that one five-minute stint on Jon Stuart, then you weren't famous at all. The money... The money came at unpredictable times and in unpredictable globs. A sizeable chunk here or there, followed by long periods of waiting and wondering. But in hometown, USA, every famous writer was...*famous, goddamit.*

Most of the time, everyone wanted to know what Jon Stuart was like. He was just exactly like what he was like on camera...nice guy, just really busy, like he should be on roller skates. And being on camera? That part went so fast, she was just beginning to settle in and then it was over. Stuart was nice though. He had a nice handshake and said that he had made it to chapter twelve and was enjoying the hell out of it. Then he was gone.

"How long are you here for?" Mrs. Sorato asked. They walked together like old friends to the little kitchen at the back of the house. Things she hadn't thought about in a decade popped to mind. The bird feeder outside the kitchen window. It was the same feeder, only it was falling apart...and the same birds, too. Well, they were probably the great-great grandchildren of the birds she'd seen though it was impossible to tell.

The small maple trees in the back yard were huge now and there were water spots on the ceiling that foretold of a radiator leaking or a hole in the roof. Same white Formica breakfast table though and she took her usual spot next to the baker's cupboard. It was like an old shoe. As she sat down, she became a teenager again. Well...not really. There was that big wrinkle of time.

"I don't know," Susan said honestly. She watched as her mother turned on the stove and filled up an old sauce pan. She retrieved two cups from the cupboard and she realized she was going to get the Sanka just by default. "It was just going to be a day or two."

"I guess you heard about the manuscript then," Mrs. Sorato said, hunting around for the Sanka jar.

She could tell by Mom's voice that it wasn't a prying question, just something to talk about. "Yes," she answered. "How'd you know?"

Mrs. Sorato turned around and caught her eye. "What? Oh...Yes, that's right. I keep forgetting. You're coming to this whole thing a bit late in the day. Strange...and a bit ironic, I suppose. She didn't want to interfere with any of you. She mentioned, the prime directive. Did Alicia ever tell you she was a Treky?"

"...Alicia..." Susan said.

Mrs. Sorato stared at her. "Yes, Alicia. ...Mrs. Davis."

"She was always Mrs. Davis to us. It never occurred to me that she had a first name. I take it you knew her. I never knew that."

The water had just begun to simmer. It hummed on the stove. Mrs. Sorato poured water into the two cups and then plopped a heaping spoonful of granules on top. They floated there like two tiny islands waiting for it to snow Sweet & Low. By the time the cup was placed before her it was only a few degrees past room temperature and the skim milk had turned the whole thing a muddy-grey.

"It wasn't collusion or anything. Except for seeing her at the A&P, I didn't actually meet her until years later, about five years ago when she was finally getting her novel together. *The Milk Stool*. I kind of like the title, don't you?"

Susan set about trying to sink the swirling island in the middle of her coffee cup. Everything was tan foam now and she weighed out having to take a sip versus making her mother feel bad. She took a quick sip. "Sooo... she contacted you?"

"Well, I didn't contact *her*. That wouldn't make any sense, would it? Oh, don't get all paranoid. It was all very positive. *I was perfect. Remember?*

"She did hint just a little teensy-weensy bit about you and Rebecca. I think she was wondering if...well...you know. Whether you might have gone to the other side...at least briefly."

Susan put the coffee cup down too hard. "What?"

"Oh, don't get up on your high horse. I told her I didn't think so. But the times...they have changed. It's not a big deal anymore. Nothing's a big deal anymore. She just wanted to know more about the three of you. As near as I can remember, she had nothing bad to say about any of you. I wouldn't get all hot-and-bothered."

"Well, I'm not a lesbian," Susan said.

"Well, of course you aren't, dear. No one said you were." Then she stared in her eyes.

It was at that inopportune moment that Susan's cell phone chimed in her pocketbook. By habit, she checked the number. It wasn't familiar. But even the 794 prefix was something from a distant memory. "Hello," she answered neutrally. "Oh, Becky. Hi." She looked up at her mother and gave her an exasperated look. It said, *No...I'm really not a lesbian!* She thought about saying, *Can I call you back in five minutes?* but that would have been just as damning. "Yes, it does seem like a million years," she said, making sure her mother understood everything Becky was saying. "Sure. I'm not busy. How could I be busy?" she said. "Seven o'clock sounds great! ...Yes, I still remember how to get there. Jesus Christ, Beck. I moved to a different state. I didn't get lobotomized."

When she got off the phone, her mother didn't play any guilt cards. She said, "I'm really glad you're here. And I think it's very appropriate that you catch up on old times." It sounded a little like she was pleading a court case.

The Wookey Hole

Stay Away From the Wookey Hole
(An 'Olde' Half-English Tavern Song by Henry Harvey)

When I was a lad, me dad took me aside
Said Son, there's some things you should know
Watch out for your friends,
Keep close to your foes,
And stay away from the Wookey Hole

Oh stay away from the Wookey Hole
Tis a very bad place to go
There's snarfin' and barfin' and fartin' and beer...
And there's things we don't talk about here.

When I was sixteen, me dad came home from work
His cheeks were as red as a rose
His breath smelled like beer... said,
What're you doin' here?
And I told him I really don't know

Oh stay away from the Wookey Hole
Tis a very bad place to go
There's snarfin' and barfin' and fartin' and beer
And there's things we don't talk about here.

When I was nineteen I knew it was time
To go to the place you don't go
I saw me dad there,
And he bought me a beer
And introduced me to Susie and Flo

Oh stay away from the Wookey Hole
Tis a very bad place to go
There's snarfin' and barfin' and fartin' and beer
And there's things we don't talk about here.

I'm now thirty-seven, my wife tells me it's heaven
Though I'm really not sure this is so
I do miss the beer, and the farts and the cheer
And the sweet charms of Susie and Flo.

Oh stay away from the Wookey Hole
Tis a very bad place to go
There's snarfin' and barfin' and fartin' and beer
And there's things we don't talk about here.

And now I'm eighty-three.   I barely can pee.
Though farting's an art I have mastered
I still can drink beer. My wife thinks that I'm queer
And I remember my father, the bastard

Oh stay away from the Wookey Hole
Tis a very bad place to go
There's snarfin' and barfin' and fartin' and beer
And there's things we don't talk about here.

Susan pulled up in front of The Wookey Hole and looked around. Someone way back when had named it *really* appropriately. It was a tiny little pub, tucked-down beneath what used to be the a paper mill in the olden days. One floor above, a much ritzier restaurant squatted on top, catering to a completely different clientele. At night, if you let your eyes glaze-over, it looked like a little glowing pumpkin tucked-in beneath a mound of big leaves. The windows glowed yellow-orange and it looked like it was a happening place.

Becky pulled in five seconds later and they waved at each other. Susan stared at the little old but extremely shiny truck she was driving. Where other girls had lusted for Jimmy Choo shoes and bejeweled Judith Leiber handbags, Becky had always wanted an old funky pick-up truck from the 50s. Her excuse had always been that, when you do a lot of projects, you need to be able to haul stuff. But her little truck was way, way, *way* more cool than that. It was a 1951 Chevy stake-side with shiny black fenders and running boards and a Chinese-red body. Even the stake-side boards were cool. They looked to be hickory or maybe black walnut.

Susan slid out of her rental and trotted around to the side. "You got it! You finally got it!" she yelled and jumped up and down.

Becky slammed the door and adopted a Bonnie and Clyde pose on the running board. "All I need is a Thompson."

"My God! I can't believe you actually got it!" Susan cried out again.

Becky was listening for some irony or patronizing behind all the jumping up and down. There wasn't any. For a moment, it was just like old times. They were the inseparables again, at least for the moment.

Becky opened the door to show off the interior. "It's all

basically stock," she explained. "I wasn't looking to do any drag racing. Puts out 105 horse power...or it's supposed to. And the only concession to modern times was...." she turned a little black knob on the dashboard and Bernadette Peters began belting out *Gee Whiz* at 8000 db.

"I love it!" Susan squealed. 'How long have you had it?"

"'Bout three years. But it's only been looking this cool for the past six months."

Susan ducked her head inside and inhaled. "I love the smell of old cars," she said. "It's so comforting. It's like olfactory history." She leaned back out and looked at the old haunt. For the most part it looked pretty much like it had a twelve years ago. "Do they still play those old tavern songs where you bang on the table with your beer mug?"

Becky looked at her oldest, *bestest* girlfriend and her eyes focused. She put her hands up like a conductor and began singing and slapping her thighs.

"And it's moose... (clap clap) moose (clap clap) I like a moose.

I've never had anything quite like a moose. I've had lots of women, my life has been loose. But I've never had anything quite like a moose".

By the time she finished, Susan was laughing so hard the tears were rolling down her face. "Oh God, I'd completely forgotten about that. We used to have fun here, didn't we?"

"C'mon in. It's not exactly the same as it was. It got a little lighter in the loafers if you know what I mean, but you can still get a good beer and play........*darts*!"

Susan's eyes got big again, "Oh, I'd forgotten about that too! Remember how horrible we were? I think I almost hit somebody one time."

"Well, your memory's playin' tricks on you, Suze," Becky

said. "You didn't *almost* hit someone. Don't you remember? The ambulance? The...*funeral*? And all those reporters asking whether you were making a political statement with your darts! *La Femme Suzanna*."

Susan took a big breath and let out a sigh. "Well... At least you didn't change."

Becky's eyes changed just a fraction. "Yeah...I wish. Anyway, I come in here enough that I have a whole new routine. C'mon, I'll show you."

As soon as they entered, a young bartender toward the far end of the bar began shaking his head slowly at Becky, a gesture that wasn't lost on Susan. "Cute," she whispered. "Who is he?"

Becky looked at him and countered with a slow nod up and down. For a moment they just had a shake-nod contest, but then he shook his head a different way...in disgust but surrender.

The room was about half-full and most of them strangers. That was what was happening in Carver's Mill. The overflow from the oh-so-gay New Hope had finally spread the six miles up the road. Half the bar consisted of pretty damned good-looking well-dressed guys...in couples. And most but not all of them matched each other in some subtle way. Matching sneakers, or the same black t-shirts, each wearing gold chains...

"Oh, look Thelma Lou!" Becky said in her broadcaster's voice. "A dartboard! I saw a special on that on PBS. The British Dartmasters, or something like that. You want to give it a try?" Becky gave a little wave to the bartender and walked up to the dartboard. She pulled them out one at a time and stuck her finger on the point. "Ouch! These things are sharp!"

She walked back and leaned in toward Susan's ear and whispered, "Ya practice enough, you get pretty good at this." Then she was right back to the histrionics. She examined the darts and played with the goose feather flights. Then she went to throw it feathers first.

Susan was tuned-in by then. "No, Bonnie Belle, I think ya got it pointed the wrong way."

Becky looked at her. "I don't think it makes a difference," she said and released it with a deft flick of her hand. The dart flew sideways and landed in the exact center of one of the tiny occupied tables. "Oops," she called out. "Sorry." She went over and retrieved it and came back. The next shot went way short. It went three feet and stuck in one of the rungs of a captain's chair. "Man... I really stink at this," she said. She looked at the guy who'd just been sitting in chair. He'd moved off toward the back of the room. "Maybe it'd be better if I threw 'em all at once," she declared. There was a loud scraping of chair legs as the whole front of the bar emptied toward the back of the bar.

A slender bald man in a black turtleneck brushed past her. "You know, you're a real menace don't you?" he simpered.

"Sorry," Becky called behind him. "My dad used to tell me, everyone has to start *somewhere*."

"Just not here," came a voice from behind.

"Sorry," she said again. "I'm gonna give it one more shot. And if I miss...I quit." Then she hammered three darts in a row into the bull's eye. She turned around, expecting laughter and applause.

"Fuck you!" somebody yelled at the bar.

"You'd like to," Becky called back.

"No, we wouldn't," came back instantly.

As they sauntered toward the only empty corner in the now back-biased bar, Becky said, "Gee, tough crowd."

They sat down and held menus up in front of their faces to hide from all the birds that were being flipped.

"I take it you've done this before," Susan said.

"About once a year. This was one of the nastier ones,

though."

"You've changed...a little," Susan said. Looking at Becky's eyes now, she looked hungry, like one of those female vampires just before it goes for the neck.

"Well," Becky said. "Maybe we all have."

"Do you think I've changed?" Susan said. This wasn't the first time she'd been through this conversation. There'd been her roommate from Sarah Lawrence, Ashley Beane Freehold, the southern belle from Kentucky. But that was just one semester, and she'd never bonded with her like she had with Becky.

"I don't know," Becky said, her voice dropping back toward sanity. "Other than now, the last time I saw you was on Jon Stuart and that was what...three and a half minutes?"

"Just about," Susan said. "I know. It looked like I had a broomstick up my butt, right?"

Becky leaned her chin on her hand and grinned from ear to ear. "Wow...I'm impressed. I didn't know you could mind-read, too."

"I had it surgically removed though..."

Becky made a token glance under the table. "You sure?"

"This is the most fun I've had since... Maybe since I saw you last."

"Oh, tell me more!" Becky said, but then calmed down. "You mean it's not like on TV? They aren't whisking you around in limos?"

Susan looked at her. "I'm thinking of going back and getting my teaching certificate. Unless you're in the top-five super stars, writing is best viewed as a second career...make that distant second."

The waiter who'd given her the slow head-shake coming in was standing before them now. "That was the last time," he said to Becky. "I'm getting complaints...serious complaints. Apparently with that first shot you almost grazed the guy."

"Almost grazed the guy," Becky repeated. Then she deflated. "Okay. Never again. I promise. It was getting boring anyway. Should I send drinks over to his table?"

"You already did." He looked at her. "I covered for you. What are you guys having?"

"I'd like a vodka martini, very dry, very cold," Susan said.

"Any special vodka?"

"Stoly'd be nice."

Becky peered across the table at her old girlfriend. She still looked the same...sort of. But there was this whole other persona behind the eyes that didn't jive.

"You want the usual?" Mark Banks asked.

"That'd be great. Sorry about the...almost grazing."

"No problem."

After he left, they looked at each other. "Don't say it," Becky said. "He's young enough to be my...younger something-or-other."

"I covered for you," Susan said, trying to sound like a guy. She looked around. "It's nice here. I didn't mean the bar... I meant..."

"Carver's Mill. I get it. It's very...*comfortable*. I know where everything is. I know every cop between here and New Hope. But...if you recall, both of us were gonna do great things. You got the Whiting Writers' Award and you got to shake hands with Jon Stuart."

"Trust me, those won't keep you warm and cozy at night. And I see your t-shirts everywhere...Manhattan, Chicago, LA. In the big scheme of things...and even in the tiny scheme of things, I bet your *They Have to Teach You*, t-shirts have done more good than fifty thousand of my books. You really put out an important message."

Even as Susan was speaking, Becky was doing her finger-down-the-throat maneuver. "I am so sick of that. I get e-mails and letters...with all these saccharin stories about how so and so finally saw the light...because of my t-shirt? C'mon."

"Would you like to trade?"

Becky's hand jutted out to shake. "Sure. In a country minute. You just teach me how to write and I'll teach you how to cash the royalty checks from the shirts. Deal?"

When the drinks arrived, Susan took a sip and then a much longer sip. "Oh, God, that's good."

"It's no big deal," Mark Banks said. "You just keep everything in the freezer. *Everything*, and then no ice." He looked at her. "You're the writer, right?"

Susan sighed and nodded.

"I read *I'm Younger Than I Was*. It was good, moved along. I thought the ending was a little..."

"Contrived?" Susan offered.

"Uhmm, that may be a little harsh but...yeah."

"It used to have a different ending, but then when it got batted around at the publisher, they made me an offer I couldn't refuse. It either got published...or it didn't."

"Oh. Sorry."

"Yeah, me too."

After he left, Becky reached across the table. "How often do go through that?"

"Too fucking often."

Mr. Nichols

The following morning was the hottest so far of the summer. But it was also Sunday and so Cubby traded his usual work clothes as the Carver's Mill Patriot's food/fashion critic, and roving reporter for something more to his liking. He sauntered out into his small, but otherwise perfect vest pocket backyard garden, dressed only in an intricately patterned red-and-gold silk kimono, and a pair of Birkenstock sandals.

  The focal point of the tiny enclosed garden was a ceramic fountain. A cherub stood on tip-toe upon a large fat frog and eternally peed into the basin. Sluggo, his bulldog had found a cool spot tucked in beneath the basin. As Cubby approached, Sluggo's eyes opened to the tiniest silver slit to see what was going on and then he promptly went back to sleep.

  Cubby set down his coffee mug and spread out the morning paper as well as Mrs. Davis's manuscript upon the rickety wrought-iron table. He readjusted the folded matchbook that kept the table from teetering and then set to the task of poring through the Sunday paper.

It was a good paper, but not a great one...primarily because not a whole lot happened in Carver's Mill. Sam and Delta Harper did their best to stir things up, but it's a fact that when you have a small town of basically honest, basically hard-working people, there's rarely any front page news. And aberrations began to bubble up over the years. If one of Dr. Bert Emmerling's heifers had a pattern on its side that vaguely resembled Abraham Lincoln or the state of New Hampshire, it got a good quarter-page, and most recently in color. What was worse, people in Carver's Mill were interested enough that they'd drive down to Bert's to see it for themselves. It was widely hoped that one of these days, Jesus Christ or the Virgin Mary would appear in the black-and-white fur. At the very least, it would bring the crazies up from New Hope and vicinity and there'd be a little action in the village...maybe a short clip on the nightly news.

He paged through to see his latest *Bon Appetite* column, in which he gently raped the newest and the crudest of the emerging restaurants. Trouble was, after a decade or so, even the rapes became more like...just mildly aggressive dates and truth be known, like most areas, there just weren't enough horrible restaurants or stellar four-napkin-rings ones either. He had made it his personal point of pride to find at least one typo in every edition so he could show it to Sam the next day. It had come to that...searching for typos. Today it was a piece of cake. Sam, in his infinite arrogance had edited the word, *brie*, from correct to incorrect. Now it read, "A spoonful of melted brie is a pleasant touch to the Cock & Bull's version of French onion soup." It was unconscionable.

Cubby put it off as long as he could. He had a second cup of coffee and trimmed his toenails, but finally there was only Mrs. Davis's manuscript sitting there on the table...weighted down with a rock so that the pages wouldn't blow away.

He sighed and pulled the pages over. He adjusted the second metal chair so that he had a lounge of sorts and then paged through the sheets. It was strange to see the innermost thoughts of anyone, much less Mrs. Davis. She had been so...Auntie Mame, so Betty Davis... He paused for a second, wondering if there was any distant relation. *Hmmm...something to check on.* That would have been a front page story, in itself. *Where Did Mrs. Davis Get All Her Piss and Vinegar? Mystery Solved!!!*

He flipped through, looking for something juicy to key-in on, a naughty word, a sex scene, though nothing was forthcoming. In the back, he spied a thin gap between the pages toward the very end of the manuscript. He flipped to it and found an old and yellowed front page of the Patriot folded up and delicate like an autumn leaf that had been pressed for too long. He gently unfolded it and glanced around to find why Mrs. Davis had kept it at all. It was from twenty years ago, just before he'd moved to Carver's Mill. The format of the paper was different back then. It was even more crude and homey than it was now and there were pictures of cows on either side of the header.

The paper was dated February 27th and there must have been an ice storm or something that day. The front page was devoted mostly to damage shots. A large chestnut tree had keeled over into the Episcopal Church roof and more or less impaled it. Cubby chuckled. It seemed like Mother Nature was finally fighting back. He peered below to the next article. A school bus had run off the road and tipped its nose down into the O'Hanley River along Rt. 413. Apparently, the whole county was without power for a week. And toward the bottom, an old couple, Carl and Ilsa Hildebrandt were celebrating their fiftieth wedding anniversary. They looked happy but a little stuffed. Not really huge news... He flipped the newspaper over and scanned for something a little juicier. There weren't even any photos to speak of, just a lot of copy...something Sam really frowned on now. Newspapers had to be light and airy.

He scanned down to the bottom of the page. There was a small familiar penciled check-mark next to the continuation from the front page. Apparently the school bus driver's name was Mr. Ronald Nichols. He was sixty-eight. When the bus slid into the O'Hanley, he'd gotten stuck behind the steering wheel and it had pinned him in. The three students who were still on the bus had tried to save him from drowning, and had apparently been unsuccessful.

At work the following day, Cubby brought it up to Sam Harper. He unfolded the clipping carefully and laid it out on his desk.

Sam scanned it and nodded. He gazed at the header and the format. "That was a long time ago. I can't remember why we had cows on the header. It seemed to make sense at the time."

"What about the bus driver?" Cubby asked.

Sam made his usual prune face as he tried to force his mind to remember things he wasn't interested in. "That was a while back," Sam said. "He was an old geezer as I remember. Kinda tall and lanky...missing a few teeth, not terribly friendly as I recall. He went off the road, got pinned...and that was that. As I remember, he drowned." He handed the paper back to Cubby. "Why? What's the spin? What's the angle?"

Cubby shook his head. "I don't know. I hadn't even moved here yet."

AKA

"AKA?"

They were standing in front of Becky's little studio adjacent to Peddler's Village in Lahaska, PA. Becky chuckled. It was a question she heard *really* often. "It's Lithuanian. It's the word for a special knife they use to plunge into someone's heart and then they twist it really hard. It's gory and it's supposed to be really painful...lethal, too."

Susan blinked at her.

"Just joking," Becky giggled. "It stands for: *Also Known As*. I considered *Alias*, but I figured Bucks County isn't quite progressive enough..."

"I don't get it," Susan said.

Becky nodded and by way of an explanation, she opened the door to her little red pick-up and dug around behind the driver's seat. Tucked in behind were six magnetic signs. She pulled them out and did a little flip show. "First and foremost I am," she said using her Barnum and Bailey voice, "**The Infamous...T-Shirt Lady!!!**"

She flipped to the next sign. "Or, I'm...**The Mad Yarn Bomber!!!** Or... **Miss Becky's Dance Academy!!!** *I'm all of the above!*"

"You seem to have a penchant for exclamation marks," Susan said.

"Yes! What if everyone in the world would inject about thirty percent more exclamation marks into their lives? Wouldn't it be more exciting?"

"I never thought of it that way." She peered at the armload of signs. " And the other three signs?"

Becky raised her eyebrows. "Work with me, Suze. How many doors on the truck?"

"You're like Upton Sinclair. You're using everything, the snout, the curly tail, the body...even the *oink*. How do you decide what hat to wear and when?"

"No problem. I have a studio in the back for teaching basic ballet, tap, ballroom. And there's no overlap with that. That's just for fun. The Infamous T-shirt Lady pays the bills for everything else...plus it's the easiest. Now, all I do is come up with cool logos which I e-mail to China. Two weeks later, I have a cubic yard of t-shirts."

"What's a yarn bomber?" Susan said.

"It's kinda like a cross between a ninja, a graffiti artist and those little old ladies who knit baby sweaters. Only...instead of baby sweaters, I strike in the dead of night and wear black...well, sometimes. Sometimes I strike in the dead of afternoon in a little tight skirt and that works, too. I've covered up parking meters and the mayor's car, or it might be something just cool, like I'll knit covers for all the park benches, that big ole cannon down in New Hope, and I knitted a whole purple jump suit for the Rocky Balboa sculpture down in Philly. That actually made the news."

"That was you?"

Becky batted her eyes. "You didn't realize you'd grown up with a *radical lady ninja knitter* didya?"

Susan looked at her old girlfriend. "What makes Becky run?"

She sighed and rolled her eyes. "I know I'm s'posed to know that. It's literary, right? *What Makes Sammy Run*?"

"It was a big deal back in the 40s. Sammy Glick worked

his way up from being a copy boy to being a big cheese in Hollywood."

"How'd he do that?"

"By stabbing his... Now that I think about it, it's a pretty lousy metaphor. I misspoke."

Becky went serious. "Hey... As far as I can remember, I never knifed you in the front or the back. Am I wrong?"

"No, you didn't. It was just a lousy choice of metaphors. I was thinking more of you running around doing everything you do. That's all."

Becky unlocked the front door and flipped on the lights. "Ta da!" she said, doing a little pirouette in the entryway.

Susan stepped in the doorway and looked around. Three rooms worth of stuff had been jammed or stacked or packed into every possible cubby. Two grey carved wooden doors on a sawhorse occupied the space in front of the window. And not a square inch of table space had been wasted. Two or three hundred cups and bowls squatted there, filled to overflowing with beads, glass baubles, charms, silver trinkets, polished stones, coins, sea shells, and an entire universe of little things that could be sewn or glued or woven into a garment. The walls were a sea of cubbies all stuffed with yarn and she'd shaded them all beginning with at least twenty shades of black.

The lighting was simple enough, a dozen or two clip-lights from the hardware store all pointing in different directions. The few empty spaces next to doors and close to corners were filled with newspaper clippings and photographs...mostly depicting various yarn-bombing incidents.

"My God," Susan whispered. She peered through the door that lead to the back. The entire wall had been mirrored and an elegant ballet barre erected at just the right height. "The only thing I don't see is t-shirts."

"Yeah, and you won't either. Anymore, it's just this," she said holding up a sketchbook. "I come up with the concept and some little mill in China cranks out twenty thousand of 'em."

Susan smiled. "It's not unlike what I do. I write down some words..."

"Oh, *BIG* difference, Suze. I scribble down little zippy words that you can read in the time it takes someone to walk past you. You...are a writer. You create a whole world and then you make your characters dance and sing and drive around in Ferraris and drink champagne."

Susan grinned. "You never read one of my books, did you?"

Becky made a guilty face. "Sorry. Maybe I have a mental block..."

Susan spied a particularly old and yellowed newspaper clipping behind the cash register. "I remember that."

Becky spun around to look. "Oh... Yeah... That was my finest hour, I think and I was only eighteen. I have it memorized. Becky Pierce saves half the animals at the Bronx Zoo!...with her outrageous and miraculously knitted...wool thingies."

Susan nodded. "That one bitchingly cold winter..."

"You got it," Becky grinned. "I saved snakes...great big ole anacondas and pythons...but they were easy, just really long tapered tubes of wool. But some of them were challenges. I remember an ant eater that was just plain pissy, the monkeys were okay, but then I didn't have to actually put them on, I made sweaters for two zebras, a kangaroo...a bit of a challenge. It was a little bit of everything." She looked at her Susan, her eyes going crazy again. "That was funnnnn...."

"It looks like you're having fun now..."

Becky looked around. "Really? Where? Why don't you teach me to write? We can be the sexy and elegant dynamic-duo writing team."

"Writing's lonely," Susan said. "You sit by yourself and do a lot of staring out the window."

"Yeah, only you get to go to book signings...and get interviewed and written-up in Time. C'mon..."

Charlie

Cubby put his hand on the front door of Charlie's lawnmower shop and considered trying a different strategy. He always *flung* open the door and bubbled his way in, effusing small talk and making Charlie's door chimes clank and bang against the window. He suspected that Charlie had made them himself, probably from tail pipe tubes. The technique never worked and always seemed to annoy him. Today, he would very quietly slip inside so the chimes made no sound at all, and he would muster up his *hetero* voice...and see what happens. But then... Charlie had a short fuse and not much of a sense of humor, so it was also possible that he could get his friggin' head blown off before he could explain.

      He opened the door normally, the way he thought a normal guy would, and decided to go with the hetero approach. It wasn't all that easy. It was like studying Spanish for two semesters and then getting plopped down in Barcelona. The chimes...chimed with just the right degree of normalcy and he went on in and examined some kind of dirt-digging machine. It had rows of crooked metal tines on the front and it looked ominous. And there was a small herd of green-and-yellow John Deere tractors in various sizes. *Mama bear, baby bear, papa bear...really big papa bear, huge papa bear. ...So many choices.* Same thing with all the orange chainsaws. Some were big and had long noses or whatever they were called. Some were teeny-weeny and he wondered idly if it wasn't some kind of guy thing...that guys bought chainsaws that matched the size of their dicks. Better yet, if they were a size or two *larger* than their dicks. That made a whole lot of sense. Otherwise, what's the point? They all have nasty little chains that chew everything up and make a horrible racket. If gays used chainsaws, there'd be some quiet ones out in one week...and in some better colors.

He peered around on the shelves to see if he didn't have some small vestigial ability to pick a saw like a hetero would. He kept peering at the cute little electric chainsaw...or was it a hedge trimmer? And it had a little canvas carrying case that almost looked spiffy.

"Hey-- Chuck," he called out in his best impression of a guy's voice. "Where are ya'?"

No one answered, but there was some clinking of tools in the main garage and so he walked back. As usual, Charlie was on a creeper, beneath a big Kubota tractor. *Orange, too*, Cubby noted. Maybe the equipment didn't symbolize penises so much as...toys! *That was it! They simply hadn't gotten enough Tonka toys for Christmas when they were little!*

"What's up, Chuck?" Cubby sang out despite himself and instantly wilted. He knew he was going to get shit for that.

Charlie rolled out from under the Kubota and glared at him for one long second. "How long have we known each other?"

Cubby smiled with his teeth, but his eyes remained a bit dazed. "Sorry. I keep trying to break this hetero secret handshake thing and it never works...I mean *never*."

"Then why don't you stop trying?" Charlie looked as if he was about to roll back under the tractor, but at the last moment, he chose to stand up and stretch. He washed his hands off in that same funny surgical style and toweled off.

"How far'd you get?" Cubby asked.

"Well, I got the crankcase oil changed. But it's got five-hundred hours so I gotta change out the gear oil, too. Expensive shit...like forty bucks a gallon."

Cubby looked at him like he was speaking Martian. "How far'd you get with the manuscript?"

"Oh...that. Yeah... Well... You have to remember that I'm a one-man band here. I keep the books, do the repairs, I'm the number one salesman, broom-pusher, and garbage collector. I actually have had..."

Cubby nodded and held his hand up. "That wasn't exactly what I meant."

"Oh..." Charlie said, "I didn't know there was another interpretation of, *How far'd you get?*"

Cubby nodded at this too. It was exactly what he was expecting. "Look, Charlie, I'm honestly not here to be a pain in the ass. Really. It's just that we just had the funeral for Mrs. Davis and...I'm not sure how long Susan is going to be here. Mrs. Davis's manuscript is good...and it's really interesting. I'm just trying to do right by her. I remember you liked her a *lot*."

Charlie nodded. He knew Cubby had found his weak spot. "Yeah, I did," he said with a sigh. "She was a class act. She should have been on Broadway doing musicals or writing best-sellers. She had something...a quality about her. She was gutsy, take no prisoners, but she was also a good person, a *really* good person."

"Well, then... She did write a manuscript and it's a good one, I think. ...And you and Susan...and Becky are in it. She deserves..."

"Okay, I get it. I'll read it." He looked at his old buddy. "I promise, okay?"

"In that same vein, do you have a few minutes to talk about those years back then?"

Charlie walked over to the workbench and poured a cup. He waggled the pot in Cubby's direction.

"Thanks, but no thanks." He carefully retrieved the article from Mrs. Davis's manuscript and laid it down on the work bench.

"What's this?" Charlie asked and began reading. The words came out slowly and softly and then a second later he stopped. When he looked at Cubby, his face had changed. He looked like a great big little kid in man's clothes. Then he sighed. "That was a long, long, long time ago, Cub."

"So it *was* you. You and Becky and Susan were those three kids trying to save the bus driver."

"Do we really have to do this?" he said.

"No, we don't," Cubby said. "But for some reason, Mrs. Davis thought it was important...really important. If you can't go there, I understand."

Charlie made a face as part of his mind drifted back in time. "It's not that I can't go there," he said. He gazed back down at the article. "But it says it right here, *'Tried unsuccessfully to save Mr. Nichols.'* But we didn't do it, Cub. I wasn't able to... Aw fuck. That's about the last thing on this planet I want to think about. Thanks a fucking lot, Cub."

"But... You tried..."

Charlie took his coffee and walked over to the back window and peered out. The window was so dusty, it looked like there was a perpetual sandstorm going on outside. "Yeah, I tried. And that sure as hell helped Mr. Nichols."

"Can you tell me what happened?"

"I'd rather not..."

"Okay... Case closed. I'm sorry I touched on something painful for you."

Charlie looked around at the room, the Kubota...his business. He was farther along than he'd expected...primarily because of Mrs. Davis. *Shit...*

He turned around to face Cubby. "Remember that big ice storm? It hadn't shown up on the weather reports and the superintendent made the announcement on the loudspeakers."

"I actually do," Cubby said. "I remember in geometry class everybody cheered and Mr. Ayers got all pissed-off."

"Everybody cheered in every room in the whole friggin' school. I remember the buses were already all lined up and they hadn't even had a chance to salt the sidewalks yet so everybody was slidin' around and falling down. It was fun. It was great! I even remember Mr. Nichols... You didn't take that bus, did you?"

"No. I took number five. Mr. Slocum."

Charlie nodded. "Yeah, well Mr. Nichols was a sour old guy and skinny as a rail. Salt and pepper, going bald and missing a couple of teeth. Not a pretty sight and his personality matched. Really crotchety and that day he seemed even more crotchety, only looking back on it, he was probably worried about all the back roads. I thought about that later... And I remember there were some guys who were on the basketball team in the back of the bus and they were singing one of those stupid songs. Ninety-nine bottles or something equally dumb. Mr. Nichols pulled over and told them to shut the hell up or they'd have to walk home."

"Sounds like a prince," Cubby said. "So what happened?"

"It was pretty friggin' bad. I think he had sanders on for the whole trip and we just barely made it up Holicong Mountain. The bus was just about empty by then and then when we turned back onto 413, we were going real slow and we were going on a straight section... and then the front end of the bus just started drifting. Mr. Nichols yelled at us to hold onto something and we just kind of slow-motioned into the O'Hanley. It wasn't even that bad, we just slid down the embankment and went in...at a pretty steep angle. I remember Mr. Nichols yelled, "Fuck!" real loud. And the rest is history. End of story."

Cubby looked over at Charlie. With the exception of Mrs. Davis's funeral, he'd never seen him with wet eyes before. "Only...it wasn't the end of the story, was it? C'mon."

"No, *you* c'mon," Charlie said a little too loud.

"The three of you tried to get him out."

Charlie nodded. He wasn't in the workshop anymore. He was back in the school bus. "There were some littler kids... The whole front end of the bus was underwater and it was coming in fast. Susan made her way to the back of the bus and opened the emergency door. She got the little kids out. The ass-end of the bus was still on land, but the nose was way the fuck down in the water."

"So...what did you do?"

"Nothing. There was nothing *to* do. It was just...fucking awful."

Cubby looked at him.

Charlie stared back, blankly. "He was stuck. The steering wheel had gotten pushed back and he was just...freakin' stuck, pinned by the steering wheel. The water kept trying to push that articulated door open and I managed to jam my book bag so that it couldn't open. But then the water was coming in anyway. I remember... I remember looking out at the level of the river and then at the level of the water on Mr. Nichols. The river was higher by about ten inches. It was close. And then he kept screamin' at us to get out and save ourselves. He was cursing up a storm. And...it was freakin' cold anyway and the water was like liquid ice.

"All three of us yanked off our jackets and tried to pack them in around him but he was already getting a little out of it. And the water... It just kept going higher. Up to his neck. Up to his chin. Becky and Susan had sweaters on. They took them off and started packing it in but.... It was pathetic. The sweaters just got soaked and then they'd drift.

"I remember I heard sirens...Midway Fire and thinking, *Okay, all we gotta do is keep him alive for a few minutes...* I looked around for some kinda tube he could breathe through. The water was already splashing up past his chin. I yanked on the chrome supports in the bus...*fuck*...they were like quarter-inch thick. Even if I'd had a hacksaw... And then Susan came to the rescue...well sorta. She used to play the flute. She yanked it out of her book bag. I remember it was in a blue velvet pouch. Mr. Nichols kept screamin' at us...which didn't help and we were trying to figure out how to make it work. It was one of those simple cheapie flutes with just the holes, but Becky said we could just put our fingers over them...like we were playing. I know it sounds fucked-up but it was the only thing that was tubular. Then there was that extra hole...the one that makes the sound. I had some gum and I real-quick chewed a hunk and we jammed it in. Getting Mr. Nichols to use it was another matter. He musta figured we were gonna die if we stayed....so finally Becky just yelled at him like she was an adult. She said, "Just shut up! We're trying to help you!" I held the flute straight-up in the air and put my fingers over the holes and Susan and Becky kept having to screw around with the gum. It got frozen and kept wanting to fall out. And..."

"And?"

"Well, it worked...at first...sort of. The flute made a little sound when he breathed in, but then water kept getting in anyway. I think around his mouth. And then the tube started to sputter, like it had phlegm in it. And then there were just...fuckin' bubbles. He was just right there in front of us...blowing bubbles and drowning. We were all balling like little kids. It was the worst fucking day of my life."

"Shit, I'm sorry. I'm really sorry."

Charlie looked at the floor. "Yeah. Me, too. That's why I

didn't want to go back there."

"When the fire department came..."

"Oh, they ran down and pulled us away. But it was pretty obvious. They didn't try resuscitation or anything."

"Did you tell them what you tried to do?"

Charlie shook his head. "Why bother? We failed... We were...*unsuccessful*. God I hate that word."

"So no one knew except you and Susan and Becky."

"That's right. Oh, we told the firemen we were trying to pull him out, but...there wasn't much point in going into it. He died."

"Yeah, but... Mrs. Davis knew."

Charlie stopped. "Yeah... She knew. She figured it out. This was before they had a school psychologist. We really didn't need one either with Mrs. Davis around. I even remember what she said to me when I went into her office."

"What'd she say?"

"She said... *Spill it*."

Chapter Two

When she got back to the motel room, the light was blinking on the telephone. It was an old-fashioned telephone, like something from the seventies, and for a second her arm reached reflexively for her cell phone. But then she stopped. She knew it had to be her mother who had called and it'd be appropriate somehow to talk to her on an old phone. She even knew what her mother was going to say. That was one of the advantages...or disadvantages of becoming a writer. A writer can hear things in the tone, timing and nuances that others are completely unaware of. It's not fair, but it balances out some of the disadvantages.

Her mind played the conversation inside her head. "Hello, dear. I don't want to bother you, but...if you're not planning anything for dinner..." There was only one answer to that unspoken question. "No plans at all. I'll be right over."

As she pulled in the driveway, she noticed the slight changes in her perception from just the day before. The old house was beginning to look like a home again, not a tiny stone birdhouse. She skipped the ringer and knocked on the door and called out, "Hey, Mom, it's me!" She tightened her stomach for the shock of seeing Mom's frail face again, though she knew it would be okay this time. She had been inoculated the day before.

When the door opened, their eyes touched and for a

fraction of a second, her mother seemed to be struggling to figure out who she was.

"Oh, I'm so happy to see you!" she said and guided her into the living room. The big screen TV was blaring away with Entertainment Tonight and it was surreal. It should have been playing *The Waltons* and it seemed awfully loud. Mrs. Sorato scurried around and found the clicker and silenced it with a fierce press on a large red button. "There," she said. "Now we can talk like civilized people. Would you like a cup of coffee?"

"Uhm. I have to cut back on the coffee. Do you have any diet soda?"

Mrs. Sorato squinted. "I think so. It might be a little flat, though. All those bubbles upset my stomach."

"Just water, then."

As Mrs. Sorato filled an aluminum pan with water and put it on the stove, Susan looked around the small kitchen. It hadn't changed much since she'd been a teenager. She gazed around some more. *It hadn't changed at all*. The broken sprayer handle on the sink, the chips in the white porcelain, the fridge. Same cupboards, same fireplace in the corner, only it was clean and swept-out and looked like it hadn't been used in a decade.

"So, where did you go today?" Mrs. Sorato bubbled. "Did you drop by the high school?"

Susan gazed at her. "Actually, no. The thought didn't even occur to me."

Mrs. Sorato turned around. She looked like a veil of confusion had been swept away from her eyes. "Oh, you *should*. You really should. Everyone is so proud of you and your writing. I bet if you went over there, they'd probably devote a special day to you. Susan Sorato Day! Think of the young students you could inspire!"

"You may be just a little prejudiced."

"Oh. I plead guilty to that one. Only...it's warranted my dear. It's truly warranted."

"I stopped by Becky's studio."

"Oh, that's wonderful. How is she?"

"Great."

"The two of you used to be so inseparable. Do you remember?"

Susan nodded. It was depressing to see her mom finally succumbing to old age. *Sad.* She used to be razor-sharp and up on everything. She'd gotten her love of books from Mom, her feeling that she could do anything...accomplish anything. And yet...here she was. "She's doing the work of three people," Susan said, "T-shirts, the knitting, and she has a small dance studio in the back room."

Mrs. Sorato's expression darkened slightly. "Yes, that's true," she said. "But, jack of all trades... I always thought she should have focused in on just one thing the way you did. Dancing, t-shirts, knitting. Those are hobbies, not careers. You chose the right path, dear."

An hour later, Susan feigned an upset stomach. She gave her mom a quick hug, and walked quickly out to the car. A decade ago her mother would have gotten it and maybe they could have cut through the crap once more and had one of their old kitchen-table discussions. As it was, she threw the rental into reverse and when she looked up, Mrs. Sorato was at the door, like an old but skinny sheep dog, only grinning and waving. The way she was waving, it didn't seem like she even saw the car...and it broke her heart. She wanted to run back up the walk and give her a huge hug...and look in her eyes and say... *And say...* She backed out of the driveway and tooted *shave-and-a-haircut* to her like Dad had done in the old days when he was going off on a trip.

She stopped by a brand new strip center along 202. Twelve years ago it'd been a farm pasture. Now, it was jammed with cars and shops she'd never seen or heard of.

She got a slice of pizza with everything, a *cannoli*, a bottle of diet Pepsi and headed back to her motel room. And then the claustrophobia began to set in. It was happening more often now. She'd go to a book signing. Her smile muscles would barely make it through the line of people and then she'd go back and crash in her motel room. Twenty minutes later, a profound loneliness would set in. If she had some paperwork to do or a manuscript to work on, it was okay. She could disappear into the imaginary world. For some reason, the TV sets in the rooms were never the same as being at home. Even the TV series she watched seemed different in a motel, as if they were subtitled and in a different language.

She pulled Mrs. Davis's manuscript out of her attaché and flipped to where she'd left off. *Chapter Two*. It was oddly intimate seeing Mrs. Davis's editing marks and comments on her own manuscript. It was like seeing a split-personality on paper, Mrs. Davis the writer vs. Mrs. Davis the editor. She was quickly getting to like the writer more. The editing hat seemed to breed God-like pontifications. She skipped the red-circled typos and went to the first paragraph.

Manuscript of Alicia R. Davis

Chapter Two

After the accident with the school bus, I began seeing changes in all three of them. I wasn't sure whether it was temporary, which would have been understandable, or whether they were like saplings that had been bent too far over by heavy snow. Would they remain bent or would they slowly return to the way they were?

The first red flag was that time they were sent to my office. All three of them...at the same time, and they were a most unlikely trio. They came into my office, Susan dressed in a little eyelet summer dress, all blonde and scrubbed, a matching ribbon in her hair. That was something I always noticed...everything was perfect and color-coordinated with her...always. In the middle was Charlie, looking like something out of an Our Gang cartoon, scruffy, jeans with holes in them and dirty sneakers. And he hadn't had his growth-spurt yet. Susan must have been a foot taller.

And Rebecca...Becky, with those crazy curls and crazy eyes. She looked like a cartoon, too, but from another comic strip. She wasn't as tall as Susan, but still a good nine inches over Charlie. I couldn't have found a more unlikely trio if I'd sat down and planned it. And why were they there? They'd gotten into a fight out on the playground...though not with themselves, that's what was interesting. One of the bigger students had started picking on Susan, apparently making fun of her...her height mostly but also the way she dressed so...perfectly. Then Charlie showed up a foot shorter than the boy who was picking on her, but he took him right out, and Becky was in there slugging away as well.

I had to punish them. I couldn't very well say, Way to go, Charlie! though that's what I was thinking. They had to stay after school and I had each of them write five hundred times, I will not fight in school.

I remember peering in the window, watching them write. They were three totally different creatures, Charlie the little tough guy, Susan the willowy unapproachable blonde, and Becky, the Tasmanian Devil. And yet there was something about them. They were a unit now and I suspected it had something to do with the accident.

Her cell phone twittered and she rolled over to the night table to get it. It was disorienting. In just a page or so she had traveled back in time. She was a tall five foot-seven and perpetually worried whether the ribbons in her hair were supposed to match her socks or her blouse, or both. It took a moment to think. She looked at the glowing numbers and recognized them. It was Maia, her literary agent. "How are we doing?" she said.

"The question is, how are *you* doing, Susan?" Maia said. "Are you having a *Big Chill* visit?"

Susan looked around the room. "Not really. Not unless eating pizza in your motel room is suddenly...*groovy*."

"Mmmm. Sorry to hear. If you like, I can give you an excuse. I can schedule a book signing in...let's see... you're in Pennsylvania? I could schedule something in Philly or maybe one of the malls. It'd have to be impromptu though. It's kind of short notice."

"No, that's all right."

"How are we coming with the manuscript?"

She listened to the words. Even though she was one of the winners in what Maia liked to call her *stable of writers*, it was probably a sentence she used five or ten times a day. She'd come to realize it wasn't criticism so much as just keeping all her writers' plates up in the air.

"No writer's block," Susan said. "But, I think my muse is off on vacation. I'm having to actually grind through, paragraph by paragraph."

"Well, you're in good company my dear. That's how most writers do it. Ultimately it's a war of stamina, not scintillation."

"Strange to hear you say that."

"Well, eventually a little truth dribbles out here and there. And you've been around the track long enough to know that."

Leaf Blower

Charlie watched as Becky's red-and-black pickup truck pulled in front of the shop. Oh, he'd seen the truck a hundred different places, in front of Wawa's, at the gas station, the post office, just tooling down 202.   But it had never driven up and parked in front of his shop. *Never...*

He glanced down at his hands. They weren't *too* bad. He'd replaced the carburetor on an old Briggs and Stratton rotary that morning, but the parts were right out of the box, not stinking of grease and gasoline. Still, his heart was beating faster as he watched her hop out and slam the truck door. It wasn't that she was decked-out or anything. She was dressed pretty much the way she always dressed, tight jeans and whatever was her *t-shirt du jour*. He didn't recognize this one. It wasn't famous yet. There were what looked like a lot of old photographs on it.

She flung the front door open the way Cubby usually did and the metal pipes clanked and jangled. Then they chose to fly completely off the door and landed in a jangling heap. For a moment they just looked at each other. She looked down at the pile of exhaust tube cut-offs. "Oops."

"Not to worry. You've always had a way of making a grand entrance."

Becky grinned. "Oh, that's nothing. You should see my

exit!" They looked at each other again. "That came out a little weird."

"Maybe a little," Charlie agreed. He tried to look at her t-shirt in such a manner that it didn't appear that he was staring at her breasts...a difficult task. "I see you've got a new t-shirt line."

Becky grinned and turned this way and that to model it. "You like it? I'm doing a field test. You're my first victim. What do you think?"

Charlie read the words on top slowly out loud, *I Used to Be...Cool*. He looked below at the old photographs printed on the shirt. It was a collage of twelve images of Becky during various stages of her life... A couple of them he even remembered. The last few were a bit too far away to see what was going on.

"What are those bottom ones?"

Becky peered down. "Oh... They're a couple of my yarn-bombing exploits. I was gonna put in a shot of me in handcuffs being shoved in the back of a police cruiser but...I thought it might send the wrong message."

Charlie looked at her. "But, I don't get it."

Becky nodded. She was expecting the question. "Okay... Everybody...well, *almost* everybody looked pretty good or sorta cool when they're in high school or college. But then later on as time goes by, everyone starts to get fat or old, or creaky or dumpy. With a t-shirt like this, you can put it on and show everybody that..."

"I used to be cool."

"Exactly. What do you think?"

Charlie's eyebrows rose on top of his forehead. His mind whispered, *I'm thinking you look better right now than I've ever seen you. You look friggin' gorgeous.* He said, "I don't know."

"C'mon. You gotta say *something*. Do you hate the idea? Do you like it?"

Charlie tried to keep it professional. "I don't know. I guess the question is: can you make a profit out of it? You're gonna have to set up a whole bunch of shots for every shirt and that takes time. What if you get like fifty thousand orders?"

"China," Becky enunciated. "It's doable. There'd just be a lead time and...you'd work the price accordingly."

Charlie grinned. There wasn't a lot to not-like about Becky. She was just so damned cheerful all the time. And there was that killer body that she liked to taunt people with. "Well, you just might have a winner there," he said. "But...I really doubt you drove all the way over here to show me a t-shirt."

Becky squinted at him, sizing him up. "Yeah, it's been a while since I've been in."

Charlie looked at her. "Yeah... Like never."

"I'm looking for one of those leaf blower thingies. Do you sell leaf blower thingies?"

Charlie gazed up on his pegboard wall. There were six to choose from. "How big's your yard?"

Becky blinked at the question. "I don't know. It's big enough to throw a Frisbee, but not big enough to play football...well, maybe touch football, if it's just a couple people."

"Do you know how long it is?"

Becky looked at him slyly as if he'd asked something dirty. "Noooo..."

This was really frustrating. Becky seemed to vacillate between being ultra-coy and ultra-invisible. If she could just settle in to one persona, there'd be something he could focus in on. She was a moving target. As it was, he was approximately eighty-seven percent too old-fashioned to keep up with her.

"Okay. Let's try it this way. Do you have a budget you want to stay within?"

"Yeah. Cheap. What's the cheapest one ya got?"

"I got an electric, but you don't want that."

"Why not?"

"Well, for one thing, electrics are weaker than shit. And then there's the cord you have to drag around which is a royal pain in the ass."

"Then why do you sell them?"

He was beginning to remember now. Becky was beautiful to look at and smart as a whip. But her mouth... Her brain seemed specifically designed to give you a headache. "There are some little old ladies and corporate executives who can't start a gas engine and...that's what they come in for."

"Sooo..." Becky cooed, "you don't think of me as a little old lady."

Charlie ignored the comment and pulled a small gas blower off the wall and put it on the counter. "This one's good. It's powerful enough and the price isn't bad."

"I'll take it," Becky said. She looked around the shop. "I like your place. It's..."

Charlie looked around as well, trying to see his shop through her eyes. It looked extremely ordinary to him. "Well... It's a shop. Other than that..." The last thing he wanted to talk about was leaf blowers or the décor of his lawnmower shop. "Sooo... Didya start reading the manuscript yet?"

Becky's face changed. "No. Well I started to but..."

Charlie looked up, suddenly interested. "Boring?"

"No. I wouldn't say it's boring."

"Crappy writing?

"No, not that either. She's actually pretty good. Makes me wish I'd paid more attention in class than going to cheerleader practice. I guess Susan did. Maybe that's why she's writing today. I'd never put two and two together. I take it you haven't started it either."

Charlie shook his head. "I've been busy."

Becky stared out the window. "Yeah, I hear ya. It might be better if you don't read it."

Charlie's ears perked-up. "Really? Why? Did she make me look bad?"

Becky stared in his eyes, grinning but also looking slightly crazy. "No. You could never look bad...least not in Mrs. Davis's eyes. She liked you. I think she liked all of us. But I think she liked you the most."

"You really think so?"

"Yeah... Remember that last line in The Wizard of Oz? Dorothy says, *I think I'll miss you most of all, scarecrow*. I think it was like that, though I don't think of you as a scarecrow. You're more like the Tin Man, only with a heart...*hopefully*."

"I have no idea whatsoever what you just said."

"Good! Then I accomplished my mission. *Obfuscations Are Us!* Wrap that sucker up, Mr. Blair. You just made a sale!"

At the cash register, Charlie attempted the delicate balance between trying not to look at Becky's breasts and trying to figure out the twelve photos on her shirt. He'd glance, then look away, then look back, then look away again. He could only get the images in dribs and drabs, and half the shots were impossible to read because they curved around her breasts.

"It's okay," she said. "I know you're just looking at the pictures." And then one second later, "Oh my God, I've never seen you blush before! I didn't know you could do that. It's so cute!"

Charlie began glowering. "I was *truly* just trying to sort out the photos that you've chosen to display on your... It's kind of like your own little scrapbook...right there on your chest."

"My boobs," she corrected. "So...you like the idea?"

He knew there was nothing he could say that wouldn't get him in trouble. "I think there's merit in it. I see ya got the one where we all went Trick or Treating."

"Yes, I was the evil, sexy, black witch. Remember?"

He wanted to say, *Yeah, things haven't changed a whole helluva lot*, but it wasn't really true. Becky was more like a force of nature than an evil witch. But forces of nature could tear out oak trees and burn your house down, break your heart. "Yes, I remember." He tried to change the subject. "So... How do you like your little truck? It's running okay?"

"I *LOVE* my little truck. I'll take it over a big ole fat Mercedes or a pompous BMW any day."

"Do you have it tricked-out? You know, like a bigger engine or headers?"

"Nope. It's just stock."

Charlie nodded. "Good call. They have enough old cars and trucks that have been butchered so you can't even tell what they were. Stock is good." *God I sound like a moron*, whispered inside his mind. "Have you gotten together with Susan?"

Becky looked at him. "Just briefly. Have you?"

"Nah, why would I get together with Susan? She's..."

"Yeah, I hear ya."

Charlie waited while Becky retrieved her checkbook from her handbag. It was one of her knitted creations, in the shape of a skull and crossbones, only she'd made the eyes sexy with long eyelashes and wooly mascara. He stared at it as she fumbled around looking for her pen, trying to fathom what kind of mind could come up with such a thing. The funny thing was, it was just right for her.

She scribbled out the check and Charlie slid it in his cash drawer.

"*You need to see an ID?*" she whispered, managing to make even that sound salacious.

"No, I think I know who you are."

"Oh, yeah?" she said milking the moment for all it was worth.

"Sooo...if you have any trouble with your blower *thingie*, give me a call."

"I will," she grinned.

She was heading out the door and he allowed himself a long stare to try to memorize what her fanny looked like. It was good. It was aces, just like every other part of her. "Oh, Cubby stopped in," he said, just as she got to the door.

She stopped and pivoted. "Oh? How's ole Cubby?"

Charlie waggled his hand, the universal limp-wrist maneuver.

"Did he make a play for you?"

"Not this time."

"Good. I don't want to have to come back and defend your honor."

Charlie chuckled at the thought. "He was talking about the manuscript though."

"Oh? What part?"

"...Mr. Nichols."

"Oh... Yeah... That..."

The Patriot

The geographical nerve center of *The Carver's Mill Patriot* was, coincidentally, the second floor of Samuel Harper's old barn, complete with barn swallows, spiders, and the occasional field mouse. It was a nice barn, not quite old or rustic enough to be an Eric Sloane barn, not enough woodpecker holes or tattered shingles. However, what it lacked in holes, it made up for in other things.

 Oddly enough, Cuthbert Miles had been hired to this very small-town newspaper, not in spite of his somewhat loose-in-the-loafers demeanor, or his fastidiousness with regard to restaurant food, but because of it. As much as Sam Harper was a small-town old fart of an editor, he was also smart and highly aware that small towns tended to get dumber over the years and set in their ways. His wife, Delta, quietly helped him along toward that conviction. Sam could often be quoted down at *The Country Gent* with his favorite slogan, "We may be small...but we're not stupid!" To which Lou Terkel, the proprietor, would reply, "Hear, hear! That's high praise if I ever heard it!" It was a concept with which Cubby grudgingly agreed.

 In the far corner pocket of the top floor of the barn, Sam peered at the computer screen, savoring the destruction of any e-mail that popped up that wasn't absolutely necessary. Though at James, his son's urging, Sam had finally gotten a powerful work computer, he was still of a mind that anything that was extra slowed down the machinery.

 "Oh, here's a new one of Crazy Becky's t-shirts," he called out to no one in particular. "We've been handling this like it's news. But...isn't it really just a thinly veiled form of free advertising? At best it's a puff piece."

Delta drifted across the room and peered over Sam's shoulder. Delta was more or less the decision maker on ethical conundrums. "It's a good idea," she said in her slightly thinning southern drawl. It had been a good twenty years since she'd been back in anything deep South for any length of time. She was finally beginning to get northernized. "Is it news? If it catches on and takes the world by storm, we will have been the first ones to cover it? Otherwise...it's a puff piece."

Sam swiveled around in his chair and looked at her. For heading deep toward 50s territory, she could still slice and dice women twenty years her junior. She often joked with Sam that the babies had been switched at birth. Becky Pierce should have been their daughter, not James, their awfully stuffy son. That was the in-road that Becky always had with the paper. Delta related to her. "That's fine," Sam said. "But do you realize you essentially just said nothing?"

"Let's run it like a story. Only when you e-mail her back, tell her we want two *I Used to be Cool* t-shirts...gratis."

"Three!" Cubby called out from his cubicle.

"You're not old enough," Delta called back.

"Thanks...I guess," Cubby called. A moment later, however, he padded over from his pint-size cubicle. "Okay, hold on a sec.. If Becky gets an order from some kid who's twenty-five and he sends in a bunch of shots from when he's like a one through twenty, do you think she's gonna send the money back?"

Sam's fingers wiggled impatiently on the keyboard and he began humming softly.

"Okay. Three then," Delta said. "But if you're going to run any shots that have to do with your working here, I want you to run 'em by me first."

"Are you infringing on my First Amendment rights?"

Delta glared at him. "Yes, as a matter of fact."

"That's fine. Just checking..."

"Oh, by the way," Sam said. He blinked innocently at Cubby but none of Sam's *oh, by the ways* were innocent. If they'd had swords, it would have been the equivalent of *en guarde*.

"You've been working on Mrs. Davis's funeral story... Do you think we could get something timely written up before she starts to decompose? It's supposed to be a *news* paper, emphasis on the *news*."

Cubby had already retreated to the twenty square-feet of his cubicle. He leaned back on his chair and looked at Sam. "The funeral story's a piece of cake. It's just boilerplate. But there's a back-story and it's getting bigger and bigger. I'd really like to pursue it."

"That's fine," Sam said. "I'm assuming you're talking about her manuscript."

"Yes, there's that, but there's more. It could be pretty interesting."

Sam listened and squinted. "Yeah, okay. But get the boilerplate out of the way and make them two separate articles." He nodded over at Cubby. "What's the back-story?"

"I've been reading her manuscript. She kept a chronicle of three of her students. One of them's Becky, one's Susan Sorato, and the other is..."

"Charley Blair down at the lawnmower place."

Cubby took a moment to think. "Yeah... You already had a meeting with Mrs. Davis."

"Her name is Alicia... Yes, Delta and I have had many meetings with her if you want to call them meetings. We were what I'd call *sometimes* friends. We could go on for a year or two and then suddenly she'd want to bounce something around and we'd all go out and it'd be fast and furious for a month. She was an original, a real pistol."

"Maybe you should be writing this story," Cubby said.

Sam thought for a moment. He nodded his head slowly. "I suppose I could," he agreed, his voice now terribly agreeable, which was a bad sign for Sam. "I could probably go around to the restaurants and write up their cheese soufflés and give them two or three napkin rings, too. Or I could..."

"Okay...okay... I'm on it."

"Actually, I'm just curious to see your take on it. But if you need some help...I can give you a couple of pointers."

"Can you give me a hint...just so I don't waste The Patriot's valuable time? Can you tell me how you would have written it?"

Sam shook his head. "No, that'd be cheating, but nice try. I think we were too close to the story... Tell ya what. I'll give you this. The original title of the book wasn't *The Milk Stool*."

"Oh?"

"It was going to be, *Three Oysters*. I talked her out of it. It would have been misconstrued... Her book would have ended up in the cooking section."

Back in his cubicle, Cubby pushed the computer keyboard off to the side to make room for Mrs. Davis's manuscript. In a world of zip drives and memory sticks the size of a Chiclet, it felt odd to sort through hundreds of dog-eared, coffee-stained, marked-to-hell pages. He felt like a gumshoe, dusting for fingerprints and looking for splatters of blood on the bed and leaving no stone unturned. *Oysters*... He did a quick search on the computer, just to see what they were all about. They only things that came to mind were Oysters Rockefeller and pearls...not terribly exciting stuff.

Oysters are bivalve mollusks and live in brackish or marine habitats. His mind wandered over the possibility of Carver's Mill being a symbolically brackish habitat. Someone from Manhattan might probably agree.

He scrolled down. *They are also considered to be aphrodisiacs.* If you really pushed the envelope, Becky could possibly pass as a walking aphrodisiac, but it was really hard connecting that image to Mrs. Davis sitting in homeroom correcting papers.

And there was that pearl aspect. You could make a good case for Susan, a lesser one for Becky. T-shirts and knitting weren't exactly pearls. But Charlie...repairing lawn mowers? No way in hell. There was also something about oysters making pearls because some sand got inside the shell and irritated it, but that didn't help much.

Oysters are filter feeders and can filter over a gallon of water in an hour. Their reproductive organs have both eggs and sperm so it is technically possible for an oyster to fertilize its own eggs. During the first year they spawn as males, the second year...females.

Cubby imagined himself walking into Charlie's shop and saying, "Did you know Charlie? You can go fuck yourself." It was funny but he'd have to wear sneakers and run like hell if he tried it. And then there were the recipes of which there were *thousands*.

It was tempting to call across the room to Sam. *Okay, I give up. What's the deal with oysters?* but he knew what the answer would be. He'd just give him one of those supercilious old-fart grins and he'd be right back to square one.

Just on a whim, he scrolled down to Oysters Rockefeller and began reading down the ingredients. *Two slices of bacon, crumbs, green onions, hot pepper sauce, extra virgin olive oil, one teaspoon anise-flavored liqueur... spinach, bread.* At the far end of the room, Sam's old police radio crackled with men's voices one and a half seconds before Midway Fire's big sirens began blaring.

Cubby started to yell across the room to turn up the volume, but was instantly shushed as Sam turned the volume to loud and leaned in toward the speaker. The fire chiefs from Carver's Mill, Midway and Doylestown were in a three-way conversation. At the moment, Bert Emmerling, Midway's fire chief was dominating the conversation. "It's the Carver's Mill Lumberyard and it's a sitting nightmare...a death trap...the worst of the worst. I'm sending everything I got and I suggest everyone do likewise. And if it's taken hold in the main building, you might as well stand back cuz nothing's gonna stop it. I don't want *ANY* dead heroes today, ya hear?"

"We're already on our way," Mitch McCormick's voice came over thick static. "What kinda scenario we talkin' about?"

"Two-story main building and I'm bettin' fifty bucks that's where it's at. It's wood, wood, and more wood, and it's crammed beyond belief. You gotta walk sideways to even get up to the counter and it's older than shit and dry as a bone. I'm outta here. God save our sorry asses."

Cubby looked at Sam.

"You go ahead, I'll be right behind you," Sam said. "And for God's sake, stay the hell out of everybody's way. In five minutes there's gonna be wall-to-wall fire trucks over there. They don't need anything else to worry about."

Sam walked up to the four-light window on the North side of the barn. It was blue sky but already there were billows of black behind the trees. When he opened the door, all three fire departments were howling in harmony.

Speeding down Mechanicsville Road, it sounded like the sirens were all around him, wailing, shrieking, moaning, and with every curve in the road the billowing black smoke got more ominous. It looked like a stationary tornado now and the instinct was to stop and turn around. Up ahead, he saw Midway's big tanker, a half-second later a yellow fire truck turned a corner and was closing fast, its air horns blatting behind him. He pulled over into the grass as it roared by. He began to pull back on and a red fire truck appeared, followed closely by Charlie in his big Dodge Ram. By the time he got back on the road, they had already disappeared around the next corner.

He already had a mental image of what he was going to see. Huge billowing smoke, gargantuan orange flames dwarfing every and any building. By the looks of it, the whole lumberyard was already shot-to-shit. He was surprised when he pulled down the small gravel road that the main building looked normal...in fact perfect. But behind it, as if it was a scene from a different movie, huge grey-and-black plumes boiled eighty, a hundred feet into the sky, just beginning to lick fire. There were men scurrying everywhere, dragging hoses and they were just beginning to wet down the main building.

Cubby pulled way off to the side of the road and into the forest. He slammed the door and trotted around toward the back of the building.

There, of all things, it looked like a fight was going on...five guys from three departments gesturing, pointing and screaming at each other. Cubby worked his way a little closer.

"Look, it's a sucker bet!" Bert Emmerling screamed at the group. "No matter how much water you put on this building, it's a goner. And when it blows, there are like fifty gallons of gas in that truck and whoever's within fifty feet is toast!"

"We do nothing...the whole fuckin' place is toast!" came right back to him.

"Tough shit," Emmerling hollered back. "It's just fuckin' wood!"

Charlie was already suited-up and listening. But then he trotted over to the back building and got so close that Emmerling yelled, "What the fuck are you doing?"

"I got a solution," Charlie called back.

"I don't want to hear it! Get your ass back here!"

Charlie started walking back just as Doylestown's pumper began spraying water onto the roof. But then he just kept walking, past the gaggle of men and back around to the front.

A moment later, Charlie's big Dodge Ram came backing slowly from around the front of the main building. He came right up as if he was going to run over the men, and as they ran off to the side, the truck slowed and then lined up with the big truck inside.

The whole first floor was orange now. All you could see was the outline of the truck. The paint was already gone. There was a second of grinding of gears as Charlie jammed the truck into Low-Low and then as easy as if he were backing into a parking lot, he backed into the flames, tapped the front bumper of the truck and then hit the gas. There was an awful moment of spinning of all four wheels and then a huge crunch as the back of the barn gave way. The Dodge disappeared entirely and for a moment, Cubby thought, *That's it... I just saw Charlie die.* But then the tanker that had been spraying water on the building changed its aim and began spraying water behind the building. Ten seconds later, Charlie appeared, utterly drenched and sprinting beneath the water like he used to sprint down the football field. He ran up to the group of men, dripping and coughing.

"I got it backed-up...fifty feet more. I didn't know it was swamp back there. That old truck's dug-in pretty deep. But...I guess it beats the alternative."

Bert Emmerling glared at him. "You're fuckin' fired."

Free Fall

Charlie didn't argue with Bert Emmerling, didn't raise his voice, didn't cuss under his breath or roll his eyes or spit. He just looked at him and said, "...really?" At which point Emmerling read him the *fucking* riot act. He'd gotten lectures before about not being a team player, trying to do everything himself, not giving any consideration as to whether he might get burned to a crisp or crushed to death, or any one of a hundred things.

It was when Emmerling used the word, *grand-standing* that Charlie stopped and began looking at the ground. He was still pumped with four-hundred percent adrenalin from having rammed the old fuming truck right through the back wall. In truth, he hadn't really thought about it, weighed-out the pros and cons. It had just seemed like everyone was standing around having a conference...and while they were conferencing, he might as well try doing *something*. It hadn't been grand-standing. There wasn't even the fleetest of thoughts that he was doing anything special or heroic. It just seemed like the only option at that moment. It was the way his brain was wired.

He stood there, like a soldier and let Emmerling rip him up and down and backwards and forwards. And when Emmerling was finished, Charlie just stood there a final second, at which point he said, "...okay."

He walked back down into the swamp behind barn and climbed up into his truck. The pumpers had beaten down whatever was smoking in the barn. Without fifty gallons of gasoline to contend with, the job had suddenly gone to textbook mode. As he drove out from under the jets of water, a few of his buddies cheered and saluted. They didn't know what else had just happened. Charlie nodded grimly at them and drove slowly away. He knew Bert Emmerling would be watching and he didn't want to give him the satisfaction of showing any emotion at all. There would be...*nothing*. He made a point of putting his turn signal on at the end of the driveway. He looked left, then right, and then slowly and conservatively pulled out onto Mechanicsville Road. No burning of rubber, no hitting the gas...*nothing*.

    With his brain on auto-pilot, he drove back to the shop. There was no one in the parking lot and the little cardboard sign he'd used fifty times for when he had to go on a call hung crookedly in the window. It said simply, *At a fire. Be back as soon as possible.* Looking at it now, something tightened in the back of his throat and he looked down at his gear, his pants, his jacket. He stank of smoke, but it was always that way. He backed up again and pulled back on the highway. He drove over to the firehouse. There was no one there. The threat of a lumberyard fire had drawn all of the oxygen out of three firehouses. He scrubbed off the soot, rinsed off his boots, and ripped his name tag off the Velcro patch on his jacket. He folded it all neatly, slipped back into his jeans and left his name tag on top so there wouldn't be any confusion.

    He was alone and he took one long moment to stare around at the firehouse. It had been a home of sorts, a place to come, to do stuff, and try to do some good. It had been that simple. He fought the little-kid urge to cry. That was stupid. Only little kids cry...not firemen. As he drove out of the parking lot, he bit down hard on his lip to have the pain give him something else to concentrate on. But then the blood pouring into his mouth did about the same thing and he reached into the glove compartment for something to blot it up. There wasn't much, just a few old receipts from buying gas.

He drove down to New Hope, vaguely aware that he was vulnerable now, that he might do something stupid, miss a stop sign, clip some tourist stepping out into the street and so he concentrated just on his driving. Just that. Just make no *fucking* mistakes...

He drove down 32 out of town toward Washington's Crossing. A little sports car came up fast behind, beeped at him and then roared around. The speed limit was 35 and normally, he would have blared back at him with his air horns and maybe given him the finger. As it was...he just drove on down, doing the speed limit and trying not to think about anything.

On the way back, he retraced his path exactly. Nothing had changed. He didn't feel any better at all. It was all just burning inside him. He hadn't even realized how important being a fireman had been. It had just been...something to do...to try and help out somehow.

As he got closer to his shop, it began to get worse again. He turned off of 202 so he wouldn't have to drive by the fire station. He took the back road behind Peddler's Village. He came to a stop and looked into the little strip center where Becky's shop was. He just sat there for a moment. A car came up behind and gave him a little toot. Without knowing why, he pulled in and pulled up in front of her shop.

From the driver's seat, he peered in the window. She was in jeans with a black V-neck sweater and she was bubbling and effusing with some tiny grey-haired woman who kept holding up one skein of yarn and then the other. It looked like she couldn't make up her mind between purple and blue. Becky was animated as always. She looked like a Muppet, nodding and grinning and agreeing.

The tiny woman finally chose purple. Becky rang up the

sale and put the skein into a brown paper bag. The woman came to the door and then trundled off in the direction of Peddler's Village.

His mind had toyed with the idea of going in, but he wasn't sure whether he could keep it all glued together. No, that wasn't true. He was pretty sure he *couldn't* keep it glued together. He turned the key in the ignition. Two red idiot lights came on as always and just as he was getting ready to turn the key the rest of the way, Becky appeared in the doorway.

He found the shredded part of his inside lip, the part that was aching now and he bit down on it again. For a moment she just stared at him. She gave him one of her little waves and then stepped out into parking lot.

"No, don't," he whispered inside the cab.

"Hey stranger!" she bubbled outside the driver's side door. "If I'd known when I bought my little leaf thingie that I got free instruction I would have bought it three years..." She stopped and looked at him. "Hey... What happened? You okay?"

The blood was trickling out of his mouth now. He stared at the dashboard.

"Good Lord, you're bleeding... Should I call the ambulance?"

"No. It's okay," Charlie said softly. "I just bit my lip."

"I heard the sirens." She leaned in on the doorsill and smelled the smoke inside the cab. "You were over there, right?"

Charlie nodded. "Yeah, I was over there."

"What happened? You okay? Anybody get killed? Hurt?"

Charlie listened to the words. "No. Nobody got killed. Nobody got hurt. Everything's fine." And then he couldn't handle it any longer and he looked in her eyes.

"Okay. Turn the truck off. You're coming inside."

"No... I'm okay. Really."

Becky grabbed the keys and yanked them out of the

ignition. She opened the truck door and held it for him.

She held the front door open for him as well and when he went inside, she looked around the parking lot. There were a few women strolling in her general direction. She flipped the sign on her door backwards to *CLOSED*, and locked the door behind her.

She had made a tiny office for herself from a cubby in the corner. It wasn't big, and she had knitted a room divider out of some loopy acrylic with big #15 needles. The effect was that she could see someone coming in the store but they couldn't see her. She took her seat behind her desk and Charlie sat down hard and looked around.

"This is nice," he said. "You made a really nice life for yourself." He looked around at the walls, the knitted sculpture, the newspaper clippings. "It's all you...not a lotta B.S."

Becky didn't say anything. She peered in the bottom drawer of her desk. "I got scotch and I've got bourbon. Take your pick."

Charlie chuckled though his eyes hadn't changed. They remained on the floor. "No. Seriously, Becky, I'm okay."

She just sat there for the longest time. And then she said, "Okay...let's cut the crap. We go back to kindergarten for god sakes. What the fuck happened?"

Charlie frowned and took to examining fingernails. They needed a trim. "Like I said, nothing happened. There was a fire at the lumberyard. Everyone was scared shitless that the whole place would go, but...everybody got it out okay. Like I said, nothing happened."

Another long moment went by. "What happened?" she asked again. She grabbed his hand and pulled it toward her and he yanked it away. Then his eyes began to contort and squeeze down tight. A drop of fluid escaped and ran down the side of his nose.

It was horrible watching a man trying not to cry. It was painful. It was gut-wrenching.

"Charlie," she said in a whisper.

He was glaring now, his eyes wet and running. His teeth were clenched and she watched the muscles in his jaws rippling and contorting. "Okay. You wanna know what happened? I fucked up. That's what happened. Emmerling fired me...right on the spot, in front of God and everyone. I don't work there anymore. Are you satisfied?"

"Oh, my God, Charlie." She pulled back to look at him. "Did people get hurt? Did...somebody?"

Charlie shook his head and made a strange face. "No. It wasn't like that. In fact, you're missing the whole point."

"...what? I don't understand."

"The fact of the matter is, no one was hurt at all. And the place didn't even burn down. We nipped it in the bud...or to be more accurate, I nipped it in the bud. But, the thing is, I also didn't follow orders and that's everything when you're a fireman. You have to work as a team...and I didn't do that."

Becky began to reach for his arm again, but stopped.

Charlie finally looked her in the eyes, but only for a moment. "You don't get it. I had an idea. There was this truck sitting in the barn. And it was on fire. It was getting ready to blow, and then the whole place would have gone up, maybe killed some of the firemen. So...I hopped in the truck...this truck and backed it into the barn, only real fast. I connected with the truck and just...rammed it through the back of the barn. Nothing happened. The barn didn't even burn down. Half the guys were cheering, dancing around."

Becky began nodding her head. "I get it. But you risked your life."

Charlie looked at her differently now. "You got it. I risked my life, so now I'm fired."

Suze?

She found the little scrap of paper Susan had given her with her cell phone number and pressed the buttons. She was anticipating having to say who she was. It had been a long time since they talked on a telephone together. Maybe a decade. But when the phone clicked to life Susan said, "Thank God, I thought maybe I was in radio-free Carver's Mill."

"Hey..." was all she said, hoping their relationship hadn't rusted over completely over the years. Only a heartbeat went by.

"What's up? What's the matter?"

"Can we meet? Can I come over?"

"If I don't get out of this motel room, I'm going to go down to Tanner's and buy an AK-47."

"You can borrow mine," Becky said.

"No. We'll need two."

"Yeah, good thinking. How 'bout *The Gent*? It's quiet."

"Quiet's fine. When do you want to meet?" Susan asked.

"How 'bout now?"

"I'm on my way. Anything I should know?"

"No. Oh, yeah. Remember when you and I and Charlie drove down to Georgetown senior year?"

"It's burned into my subconscious," Susan said.

"Yeah. Good. Think about that."

On the way over, Becky put on an oldies disc from a

decade ago. It might even have been the one they played going down to Georgetown. It had been their first big getaway trip together...freedom, being adults, no one to answer to...except Charlie, it turned out who made them buckle their seatbelts and *not* hang out the windows and make faces at the cars going by.

Susan had chided him. She even remembered what she said. "You're such a *man*, sometimes," was what she'd said only Charlie had failed to take it as an insult.

He just grinned at the windshield. "When we're in D.C. I'm responsible for you...*both* of you. That's the deal."

And they made outrageous fun of him, making their voices deep and growling rules back and forth to each other. Because Georgetown was three-speeds faster than Carver's Mill, the cars drove faster. They all seemed to have attitudes down there, and everyone was a LOT more hip.

Walking down the main drag, Charlie insisted that they hold his hand, crossing at the light. She remembered squirming out of his hand and feeling claustrophobic. It had almost gotten nasty, but Charlie said, "I've got the wheels. Hold my hand or ya ...walk the fuck home."

"When you put it like that," Becky cooed and gave his ass the tiniest tweak. It was the first time she'd ever done that.

The Cavern seemed to be the coolest place to be at the time and the three of them clumped down the black wrought-iron spiral stairs to...The Cellar, which was dark and ninety-percent smoke.

They'd had two pints apiece of the darkest beer she'd ever tasted and then three guys came clomping down the spiral stairs all dressed in the same navy-blue windbreakers. There were some kind of Greek letters stenciled in white on the front and Charlie seemed to sense before anything even happened that they were in trouble.

The three frat guys flanked the three of them at the bar, two of them cozying up to Becky and Susan, the third one apparently designated to keep Charlie occupied.

"Hey, what frat you guys in?" Charlie asked, trying to keep it light.

"Hay...seed," the one right in front of him said, then laughed at his own joke.

Charlie laughed at the joke. "Well, you got that one right," he agreed. His eyes darted over to Becky and Susan. They flared to over-wide for one second and he mouthed, "Get out...now." It was a maneuver that was not lost on the frat guy directly in front of him.

"Ya know, you don't look old enough to be their *father*," he explained.

"I'm not," Charlie agreed. "Look...can't we just keep this nice and easy? Nobody needs to get hurt. C'mon."

"Look Dufus, why don't you just take a hike while you still can. You're in our country now and in case you don't know how to count...we're three and you're one. Do you understand the gravity of that math?"

Charlie nodded. He smiled, and then he propelled his glass beer mug into the nose of the frat boy in front of him. He got the guy on his right as well, the one who was grabbing Susan's ass, but then everything went black. After that, there was the Georgetown police station followed by a quick three-hour drive back to Pennsylvania and Bucks County. No one said very much on the trip back.

Susan arrived first. She stood next to her rental, looking out-of-place. She looked like she was waiting for a train. It was odd how being away could do that to you. She was a stranger to Carver's Mill even though she'd spent two-thirds of her life there.

They waved and Susan started walking over toward what had been the old entrance to The Gent in the *olden* days. Now, almost everyone went in the new entrance and sat in the new and improved section. She was going to correct her, but then thought the better of it.

"How long's it been?" Becky asked, holding the old front door for her.

Susan looked at her and then at the entrance. "Forever."

Inside, they went to the old corner where they used to sit. The same dinky, rusty lampshade hung down crookedly over the table. Looking around, nothing had changed at all, same Spanish matador print, same still life of a clown bank. Just the people had changed. They were all new and looked like kids compared to way-back-when.

The waitress looked like a little country girl and Becky began seeing everything through her old girlfriend's eyes. They ordered pints, like they used to, only now they were Sam Adams Summerfest in a frosted mug...a long cry from the Genny Cream Ales in brown bottles.

"This must be really weird for you," Becky offered.

"Mixed review," Susan said and then realized it was a term Becky might not get. "So far it's just strange. I feel like I'm walking around in an old dream. Everything's different and everything's the same."

"*You're* different," Becky said. She looked down at the table and then up at her.

Susan nodded. "Yes, I know. But so are you."

"I didn't mean it as a cut."

"Neither did I." And then she relaxed a little. "Now that we got that out of the way, what's up with Charlie?"

Becky frowned, something she didn't do often. "There was a fire this morning at the lumber yard and...Charlie's a fireman. He drove up in front of my shop and he was looking like he was going through seven-worlds-of-hurt. I never saw that before. I took his keys. I dragged him inside and kept pecking away at him like I always do and he finally lost it."

"What'd he say? Did he tell you what happened at the fire?"

"Eventually. I wormed-it out of him. I don't understand the nuances but it sounded like there was a truck full of gas inside the warehouse and Charlie backed his truck up and rammed it right through the back wall and into the swamp...essentially saving the mill from blowing up or burning down...and no one was hurt."

"So, what's the problem?"

"The problem is, Charlie just *did it*. He didn't coordinate or check it out with the fire chief. He just...did it...the result of which he was fired right on the spot. It sounds like one of those *guy-ego* things to me."

" Can't they just...hire him back?"

"I don't know." Becky's eyes went distant and serious. "He also said that he couldn't save Mr. Nichols. That part just kinda bubbled out."

"...wow. That was a long, *long* time ago."

"Yeah..."

"I'm a psychologist, not a psychiatrist. I'm really not qualified..."

"I know. But we were all friends before we were what we are today. And there was Georgetown. Charlie didn't stop at the bar and say, 'I don't want to get involved.'"

"It sounds like PTSD. That's what soldiers get when they've been through more than a human being should have to go through. I think Charlie's brain couldn't handle trying to save Mr. Nichols and then not succeeding and having to stand there and watch him drown." Susan became preoccupied, wiping the condensation off every other facet of the beer mug. It looked like it was half-clear, half-frosted glass.

"Suze?" Becky said.

Susan didn't answer. She began making a delicate scalloped ring around the lip of the mug.

"Suze?" Becky repeated.

"...yeah?" she said softly. She began making a matching scallop at the bottom of the mug.

A long moment went by, but then Becky said, "Did you ever get over it?"

Susan didn't look up. She didn't say anything. She just wrinkled her nose. "How 'bout you?"

A car pulled into the lot, just in front of their window. The driver revved his engine and then killed it. Two doors opened at the same time and then a man walked around the front of the car and held the door for a woman. Becky watched the whole thing as if she were mesmerized. She almost seemed to be smiling. "Nope. And I'm thinking Mrs. Davis shoulda come up with a better title for her book...something philosophical like....*three broken toys*."

Manuscript of Alicia R. Davis

Chapter Three

Becky Pierce...The Second Leg
(NOTES)

Becky Pierce will either become the first female president of the United States, or she will become the first woman to land on the moon...or...perhaps she'll be the first woman to legalize both marijuana and prostitution at the same time, and the whole country will crumble to dust...or thrive. Becky has seeds of greatness. It's just that no one has any idea what she's going to do or where she's going to land. She should have been my daughter!

Right now I've just reprimanded her for making the sexiest little Black Swan costume in the history of the planet. I think I can say with authority that no costume for a ten-year-old has ever come close. It's a miracle of inspiration how she was able to make the costume flare out into perfect tiny little boobs, and décolleté no less. And she has somehow managed to find stretchy black yarn and has knitted herself fishnet stockings with black sequins, of course to go with the whole thing. I almost have to bite my tongue because part of me wants to say, "My

God! Where did you learn to do all that? How did you come up with the ideas?" And I have to tell her that it's not appropriate for little girls to be knitting boobs and sexy stockings. It's all I can do to keep from yelling, Yay, Becky! Keep it up!!!

And it's not as if she has a fixation or anything. She also knitted and sewed Susan Sorato's costume, the "good" white swan and it's as if God came down and blessed Becky's little fingers. Susan looks like a little fairy all glowing in iridescent white...and with white feathers and sequins sewn all around the tutu!

What if Becky decided to design a house or an eggbeater...a new kind of car...maybe one that consumes water and shoots peppermint gas out its tailpipe? And yet I dare not try to steer her. She's already her own force of nature. It's not for me to decide which future she chooses. She wouldn't listen anyway.

Fourth Grade: Notes

(September): Charlie & Becky sittin' in a tree...K, I, S, S, I, N, G. For the foreseeable future it looks like Buckingham Elementary has a roving puppet show thanks to Charlie Blair and Becky Pierce. Charlie has made a clever little stage and theater out of liquor cartons he's stapled and glued together. Becky made the curtains from burgundy velvet and gold lace and Charlie rigged it so they open up and close. Becky has made her own puppets as well. I'm in

amazement.

(October) Charlie brought his guinea pig in. It's going to be one of the characters in one of Becky's plays. The pig, which Charlie had named after himself is now...ZORRO! Guess who came up with that? Becky made a tiny black cape, a black mask, and a hat. I didn't know you could knit something that small. Unfortunately Zorro ate the mask.

You Forgot Something?

Charlie was sweeping out the work area in the back of the shop when Becky pulled in. He didn't hear her drive up, kill the engine and come in the front door, even though he'd rehung the chimes wrong so that they banged against the glass at even the slightest provocation now. He was in his own world, replaying Bert Emmerling's words over and over and over. "You're fuckin' fired. You're fuckin' fired." He mouthed the words to himself as he swept and he swept with such rage that tire irons, lug nuts and large clumps of dried mud rocketed out the back door as if shot from a gun.

  He swept everything out the door that was large enough to sweep: parts of carburetors, welding rods, cardboard boxes. He hit the pan of oil that he'd just drained from a Snapper mower's oil change. The pan flipped and he just swore at it and swept everything as viciously as he could. Dirty oil went everywhere and then he finally just kicked the pan out the door along with everything else.

  When he finally looked up, Becky was standing in the doorway with the leaf blower she'd bought in hand. When their eyes touched, she said, "Maybe this isn't the best time... I can come back."

  He looked at the blower, absolutely positive that it was a bullshit visit. "Lemme guess, it won't start."

  A long moment went by. "Well... Yeah. Sort of. In a way... I know you gotta mix some oil in with the gas. But it doesn't say what ratio. Actually, that's not accurate. It gives like a whole bunch of ratios. I just don't know which one. I don't want to ruin it."

Charlie walked over to a low cabinet and pulled out an orange gallon jug of something. "Here," he said. "It's premixed. It's on-the-house." He made a point of avoiding her eyes. "Anything else?" he asked in such a hostile voice that it precluded her saying anything at all.

"No," she said finally. "Thanks..." She walked out and shut the door very gently behind her. He watched the truck back-up and do a K-turn and then drive up the gravel to the highway. Then he watched her do a big circle and drive back to the front of the store.

"You forgot something?" he snapped when she came back in. He glared in her direction but couldn't look her in the eyes.

"No, I didn't," Becky said. "But you have to remember who your friends are. I didn't do anything to you. I'm on your side. In fact...I've got half-a-mind to drive down to ole Bert Emmerling's farm and rip him a new ass."

Charlie's eyes went from angry to scary. "Don't you dare," he said. "You don't talk to Emmerling about *nothin*'." He finally looked in her eyes, but he was all battle armor and battle axes now. "I'm serious. You say one word to Emmerling and we're through. We're finished. Do you hear me?"

"I hear you," Becky said back. "Only... Why?"

"Because Chief Emmerling was right, that's why. I deserved to get fired. I was a fuckin' loser twenty some years ago and I'm a loser now. And I'll always be a loser. You shouldn't come around here anymore. It might rub off on you." Charlie picked up an old hunk of rubber fuel line and tried to toss it six feet into the garbage can. It hit the rim and bounced out, at which point Charlie walked over and put it in, then kicked the hell out of the can. It fell over and rolled around.

"You're not being yourself right now," Becky said.

Charlie jerked the can back up and jammed it back in the

corner. "Yeah, like you really know me."

"I'd like to think I do," Becky said.

Charlie looked at her. "Listen...would you please just go? I'm not up for this shit."

"Well, that's just too damned bad, Charlie, cuz I'm staying."

Charlie looked around. "You're staying? That's great! You stay. You can have the whole fucking place for all I care." He tromped out the back bay of the shop and climbed up into the Dodge. He burned rubber backing up. Then he burned rubber going forward. A cloud of smelly grey smoke drifted inside. Out on 413...same thing.

(two hours later)

Charlie's temper was like a lot of guys'. It flared hot and fast but was rarely acted upon. When he did act on it, it was mostly small stuff: breaking pencils in half, throwing magazines against the wall, kicking things, rocks...hopefully small ones. He'd learned his lesson kicking large ones in the eighth grade when he'd broken two of his toes kicking a tree stump. And it was all usually over in five minutes, at which point he'd go collect the magazines off the floor or put the pieces of pencil and pen into the waste basket. But tonight had been different. There'd been the same flare-up with Becky provoking him, provoking him until he popped. Even as he was doing it, he knew he'd probably burned twenty bucks worth of rubber off his Goodyear All Terrains, but he couldn't stop himself. Screeching rubber all the way down 413, he knew that Becky would be able to hear. It was his own way of crying out and swearing at God or the heavens or...whatever. It was the closest he could come to crying at all. Girls...women don't understand that.

Driving back to the shop, the practical side of his mind began to take over. It was nearly dark now and he wondered how many people had wandered in, found no one around and maybe helped themselves to a chainsaw or a Weed-Whacker. Hell, someone could easily have backed a truck up and emptied the place out. He decided ahead of time that whatever was gone would be his punishment and he would take it like a man...quietly and without griping or complaining.

He began to imagine what he might run into upon turning into his driveway. A big U-Haul backed-up and guys tossing stuff in the back? He took a big breath and determined ahead of time that he'd already popped-his-cork once that day. If there were guys and a U-Haul, he'd just back on out and call the Buckingham cops. They'd be cooler anyway and better prepared.

From a quarter-mile away, he saw that the lights were now on in his shop. When he'd left, it had been afternoon, and he didn't have any automatic light sensors. "Aw fuck..." he whispered out loud. He slowed down quietly, killed his headlights and coasted into the entrance to the shop.

Yes, indeed, two cars were there. Make that one car and one truck...Becky's little cutey-pie Chevy and some car he'd never seen before. He coasted down the driveway and pulled over to the side of the garage. He got out quietly and closed the door to his truck like a cat burglar.

He listened to the conversation going on inside. It was Becky, bubbling away as always. "Oh, you wouldn't believe how great they are!" Becky chimed away. "I just bought mine a couple of weeks ago and I swear I'm going to throw my rake away. These things are like twenty times faster! ...Yup, this is the one Charlie recommended. The electric ones are crap...too weak and who wants to drag a cord around? This one's the best bang-for-the-buck. Oh, and I highly recommend you get a can of premix gas.

You don't have to get all oily and sweaty and it only costs a few cents more per gallon. It's the way to go."

Two minutes later, an older couple walked out to their car and popped the trunk. Charlie listened to the man's words to his wife. "Very personable young woman. It's nice to see enthusiasm."

Charlie waited till they drove off before he came in.

Becky looked up, her eyes still bright and twinkly from being in sales-mode. Before he could say anything she said, "I had to wing it with the credit card machine. I swiped the card and I know it's in there somewhere. You may have to press some buttons or something. With my machine you have to have an access..."

Charlie just looked at her. "...thanks."

"Hey... No problem. Friends gotta stick together." She looked around on the counter. " Oh, there was something else... A guy came in and needed a new belt for his something or other. He had the number and I found the thing. You just don't have any prices marked. I charged him thirty bucks and took his number in case it costs more. I figured...better to make the sale."

"You did great," Charlie said.

"Well... Oh, I did do one thing. I was starving so I called out for a pizza. It should be coming any minute. I told them to charge it to Blair Lawnmowers."

Charlie was too wrung-out to get teary-eyed and too tired to fight. "What kinda pie didya order?" he asked.

Becky squinted, trying to think. "Well...I didn't know where you were so I ordered what *I* like, pepperoni, sausage and mushroom. Is that okay?"

"Yeah. It's just fine. In fact...it's perfect. And, for the record, I feel like a total asshole."

"You are *waaaay* too hard on yourself. You'll never be an

asshole in my book."

Charlie looked at her closer. "Really?"

"Yes. Really. Well, okay...once in a while you can be...a bit difficult, more like a dipstick, or maybe a douche bag. No, that's not right. You aren't ethnic enough to be a douche bag."

Despite himself, Charlie began seriously suppressing a grin. "You really got this stuff nailed down, don'tcha?"

"One semester in a girls' dormitory and you learn *everything* you need to know."

"Okay, I'd like to kinda get this thing nailed down once and for all. It's sounding like I'm a dipstick, and I have no frickin' idea in the world what that would mean...when applied to people, of course. I'm not seeing the symbolism."

"Okay," Becky said more softly. She looked at him now like she was a cat about to eat a large mouse. "Once and for all... Let's see. I would have to say...that you are a hunk, clear and simple. A smart, sophisticated, while at the same time, slightly blue collar...*hunk*."

"I guess I can live with that." His eyes were smiling, but then they began to track a vehicle coming in fast off the highway. "...*fuck*."

Becky turned around and saw the white Silverado of the Buckingham Fire Chief pulling in fast. "That's Bert Emmerling, right?"

"Right," Charlie answered, still tracking the truck as it pulled in, exactly in front of the door. "You need to get out of here," he said, not looking over.

"Or maybe..."

Charlie's eyes darted over to her. "No. This isn't a debate. You need to get the hell outta here...*now*."

"Okay. I understand. Good luck." She reached over to squeeze his hand, but he was already heading toward the door. He looked back for one second and looked at her. "And thanks. Seriously. Thanks."

Emmerling and Becky passed each other at the exact midpoint of the front door. His face was grave, but he managed to say, "Hey Becky," as they passed each other. Charlie had stationed himself in front of the counter. It wasn't going to be pretty.

As Bert Emmerling approached, both men had identical faces, both grim. Finally, Emmerling stopped. He put his hands in his pants and looked around the shop. There wasn't much to say...but he finally said, "I wanted to talk to you."

The sentence just floated there in the air between them and then slowly drifted away. "Yeah. Well... I think you pretty much said it all the other day. I fucked up, and you fired me. I accept it, though I'm not going to apologize for what I did. I did what I did, and that is that. I don't see much more that we have to talk about."

Bert stood there, listening to the words and looking at the floor. "Yeah, well... The fact is, everything worked out all right. Nobody died, nobody got hurt. And for the life of me, I can't figure out how the barn didn't even burn down. You were lucky as hell."

"Yeah... Nobody got hurt." His eyes flashed to Bert's and for a moment they just glared at each other.

"Well, okay. You make a good point. You got hurt. I'm sorry about that. But when you're in charge of a bunch of men, the first thing you have to do is take care of your men. You put their safety first. That's the deal. I'm not looking for a bunch of dead heroes, or having to go to someone's house and explain why their husband or their father isn't around anymore."

Charlie looked at him. "Tell me this, how many times have you had to do that?"

Bert laughed a small humorless laugh. "Never. And that's

my point. I try to take care of my men."

"Yeah. Well, bravo for you."

Bert took in a long breath and let it out slowly. "Yeah, well... I can see why you're pissed."

This actually seemed to piss-off Charlie even more. "Look, you fired me. I deserved it. I took it. I didn't back-talk you. What the fuck are you doing here?"

"Well... The fact of the matter is, things are grey. You made a judgment call. We all have to make them when lives are at stake. You chose... You chose to put your life on the line, when you didn't have to. And that's what this is all about. You made a bad call. In my opinion, you made a bad call."

"And you've never made a bad call?"

Bert Emmerling chuckled. "Oh, I've made a hundred bad calls, maybe a thousand. But the difference is..." He stopped.

This time it was Charlie's turn to cop an attitude. "What? The difference is...what? Finish your goddamn sentence."

"Look, if you're expecting me to apologize to you, forget it. I said what I said, and at the time, I meant it. But the stuff we put our lives on the line for is a grey area. It's *always* a grey area. That goes with the job."

"Sooo.... What the fuck are you saying?"

"I'm saying, that if you want to come back to work, I'd like to have you."

"Really?"

"Yeah. By the way, nice job."

A Strange Request

Becky had just finished teaching the intermediate-level ballroom dancing class, though classifying any of the eleven adult students in her class as *intermediate* was really stretching the point.

Three couples had already taken the beginners' class four times and they were reluctant to move on to more challenging than the box step. The problem was essentially 100% the men's fault and it was a constant source of amazement that they could dance so horribly and yet, still manage to walk through a door, down five concrete steps and out to their cars where presumably they could start their cars and actually steer down a highway without bumping into something.

On the dance floor...she'd seriously considered getting bicycle helmets and leg pads...not for the women but for the men banging *into* the women. The only exception to this was a young couple in their thirties. The guy was okay...better than okay, he could keep a beat and had rhythm, even a bit of smoothness to his transitions. But his wife had been a professional ballet dancer for twenty years and it was she who was the problem.

"Ballet dancers," she would explain in her *happy-camper voice,* "are professionals at the highest level of expertise. Unfortunately, they are trained to dance *solo*...which makes it a little tough on anyone trying to lead them... pretty much *anywhere."* Becky'd give a little conspiratory wink to the former ballerina, but then she'd say, "I didn't write the rules, but when you're doing ballroom, the *GUY* is supposed to lead, or at the very least, appear like he's leading."

And there was one dirty old man in his sixties who kept

taking the class alone, which left him with no partner. *Sooo... guess who fielded that one.*

On that particular night, she was breaking-in a new couple. The guy was in his sixties, the gal in her late forties. He was ostensibly some kind of well-respected eye doctor, but he seemed unable to follow more than two steps at a time. Stringing along a little routine was impossible and it had become an in-joke. Becky finally said, "Whatever you think the next step should be...do the other one," hoping that by the law of averages he had to do better than what he was doing. But no, it remained eighty percent mistakes no matter what. Then he'd just cackle like it was the funniest thing in the world.

When the last car had pulled out of the parking lot, Becky found her cell phone and dialed Cubby at the paper.

"Cuthbert Miles," he answered with his professional voice. It sounded like something he'd practiced a hundred times in front of a mirror to get just the right tone. On the phone, he was a rich dapper English businessman.

"Hey, Cubby, it's Becky..." A moment passed. "Becky Pierce, you know... The weird gal who did the yarn bombing. I have the little shop..."

"Oh, good heavens, I *know* who you are, dear. I was just curious to see how you define yourself. It's a little thing I do sometimes."

Becky deciphered the words. "Okay... Did I pass?"

"Oh, with flying colors. I had no doubts whatsoever. You see yourself as...*that weird gal*. Interesting as well as accurate!"

"Well, the reason I called. I have something of a strange request. If you don't want to do it, that's fine, but... I was wondering if I could borrow Sluggo for an hour or so."

The line went silent for about five seconds. "And for exactly what purpose would that be?"

"You're not gonna believe this," Becky said in her usual upbeat *patois*.

"I haven't heard it yet and I already believe you. What do we want to do with poor ole Sluggo?"

"Well, it's kind of hard to explain. In fact, I'd really rather not. But I'd like to take Sluggo for a physical...over at Dr. Emmerling's, if you don't mind. Of course I'll pay for the visit and I'll have him back to you, good-as-new, maybe even better if he needs his toenails clipped or his teeth brushed. What do you say?"

"Well, Sluggo's breath hasn't been exactly Cover Girl sweet, and...I'm guessing you really don't want to explain why."

Becky nodded in the receiver and then realized he probably couldn't see the subtlety in her nodding. "I'd really rather not," she agreed. "Is it okay?"

"It's fine, dear."

On the way over to Dr. Emmerling's veterinary clinic, Becky had to roll down the windows. Sluggo was friendly enough, but he had a very pronounced odor that was hard to ignore. And then, turning onto Carver's Mill Road he let off a noisy one that was bad enough that she had to pull over and hop out. She waved the truck door back and forth a few times and for a second, she considered putting him in the bed of the truck...but if anything happened. He didn't look like a jumper, but it wasn't worth the gamble.

It hadn't occurred to her exactly how she was going to explain taking Cubby's dog in for a vet visit. There was about a ninety-five percent chance...make that a hundred percent chance that he'd recognize Sluggo, so she couldn't pass him off as her dog. Better to stick as close to the truth as possible.

Bert Emmerling's clinic was essentially the downstairs of an old rambling farmhouse. The barn was of the same period and a good dozen cows were wandering about in the field next to him. He was an old-fashioned kind of vet with an old-fashioned kind of reputation. It was common knowledge that he liked animals one helluva lot more than he liked people... and he probably wasn't going to be too pleased once he knew why'd she'd shown up. It was just too transparent for her to really get away with it. But then, there weren't a whole lot of options either.

There wasn't any receptionist when she opened up the screen door. Just a handful of old captains' chairs and straight-backs, a black-and-white linoleum floor that had seen better days and a yellow pine coffee table with some fishing magazines.

She went in and took a seat. Sluggo seemed at home with the whole idea and hunkered down next to the magazine rack. There were voices in the next room, one a deep heavy baritone, the other a woman who sounded like she had her hands full trying to control something.

A moment later, Dr. Emmerling peeked out into the waiting room and looked around. He looked at her and then at Sluggo. "Hey, Sluggo, old buddy!" Dr. Emmerling called, "What's up?"

For a second, Becky just sat there, as if Sluggo might be able to answer for himself. When she opened her mouth to speak, Dr. Emmerling said, "Be with you in a minute," and went back inside. She was determined not to get any more nervous than she already was. She picked up a tattered *Field & Stream* that looked decades old, put it back on the table and looked around. This was definitely not the place to catch up on *What's New?* She contented herself with staring out the side window at the cows. The ones with the most black on them seemed like the prettiest. She wondered whether blondes would come to the opposite conclusion.

There was a sudden waft of Lysol spray from the next room and then Dr. Emmerling burst through the door with the energy of linebacker. He peered down at her as if she just might have stolen

Sluggo. As always, he got right to the point. "Well... I recognize Sluggo. But you don't look a whole lot like Cubby."

She'd had a rough plan sketched out in her mind. She'd go in, make small talk and somewhere along the line, she'd mention Cubby and how they used to go to high school together...and that would segue into Charlie and she could take it from there.

Instead she stood up, looked him in the eye and said, "I'm afraid I'm here on false pretenses. I really, really need to talk to you and this was the only way I could think of."

Bert appraised her carefully, looking like Charlton Heston coming down from the mountain with two stone tablets in hand. "Did you maybe consider just giving me a call?"

Becky's eyes squinted in thought as she listened to his words. "Briefly," she said, "but if you give me five minutes of your time you'll see why."

"So...this has nothing to do with Sluggo."

Becky looked down at the big bulldog. His eyes were open but he was snoring loudly, and drooling. "Well, unless you have some kind of magic dog food that prevents farting. I had to pull over on the way over here."

"Okay, Miss..."

"Pierce. Rebecca Pierce. My friends call my Becky."

"You look familiar. I remember now. You're the gal that was yarn-bombing everything. Right?"

"Uhmm... Yes. I also make t-shirts and I teach dance in a little studio next to Peddler's Village. Does the yarn bombing go against me?"

Bert shook his head. "Naah. I couldn't see much point in it but it didn't seem like you did any harm." He resumed squinting at her as if she were some kind of lab animal. "There was something else though..."

"I also model my own t-shirts in the Patriot."

Bert shook his head. "No, I saw that." Then his eyes brightened. "The zoo. You're the one who was saving all kinds of animals with your knitting. Didn't you knit a sweater for an anaconda or something?"

This wasn't exactly the way she'd figured the conversation was going to go. "Yes. But that was a long, long time ago."

Bert nodded and smiled. "Yeah... But I'm a vet. Those kind of stories interest me. I always wondered how you got it on him. What can I do for you Miss Pierce?"

Becky took in a huge breath to collect her thoughts and let it out. "Okay. I have a couple of things to say...and as soon as I say one of them, you're gonna get all huffy. If you can just hear me out for thirty or forty seconds without chopping my head off. The truth is you're a little scary."

Bert Emmerling pulled up a chair and relaxed down onto it like a jock. He was a tall guy, a cross between a cowboy and a farmer, only his face was more fine-boned and there was an extra intelligence behind the eyes. Except for his lab coat, nothing would have indicated that he had any knowledge of animals. "I'll give you two minutes. How's that?"

Becky nodded. She looked around, trying to collect her thoughts. "Okay... Here goes. Charlie Blair told me that if I came over here, we'd be finished and he'd never talk to me again. And I think he means it. But... I care enough about him that even if that is the case, you need to know a couple of things. First off, Charlie's a really, really, *really* good man. I've known him since kindergarten. He's saved my bacon more times than I can remember. Susan Sorato, too. She's..."

"I know who Susan Sorato is. Go on."

"Oh... Okay. Well, I know you fired him the other day and I'm pretty sure I know *why* you fired him. You think he's a loose cannon, a grandstander, like he just wants to be a quick hero or something. And he isn't like that...*at all!* In fact, he's the most unloose person I think I've ever met. He's not looking for glory. I promise you that. In fact, he told me that you were right and that he deserved to get fired. And we both know that's not true. He's a good man. He has the utmost respect for life. He'd put his life on the line for anyone. A long time ago, something happened. He was just a little kid, and even then he was trying to save someone...a school bus driver."

Bert finally put his hand up like a traffic cop. "Okay... I think I see where you're coming from."

"You do?"

"Yeah. Only, it's all taken care of. The other day, when I passed you going into Charlie's, we had a talk. Charlie's back on the team."

"Oh, that's wonderful! You just made my day! Thank you sooo much!"

"Please don't repeat this, but Charlie's the best guy in the department, next to me, of course. He's smart, he's quick. He's got good instincts, but he's got a syndrome. I don't even know if it's got a name, but, he's maybe a little too willing to put his life on the line. And that's what it was all about."

"Damn. I wish I'd known. I hate wasting people's time. I feel a little like a doofus."

"I didn't know Charlie had a girlfriend."

"What? Oh, no, we're just friends. We don't... Well, you know what I mean."

"Sorry. It just seemed like something you'd do for someone you're...close to."

Comparing Notes

One of the last things that Mrs. Sorato's husband had done before he died was to install a glider between the two maple trees in the backyard. Mrs. Sorato had seen it in a catalogue. It was cast aluminum and painted black to look like cast iron. It was all filigree with leaves and buds twisting and turning everywhere. It looked opulent and very Old South. It looked like if you owned one, life probably couldn't be that bad.

It was pretty all right, but not terribly comfortable and over the years, Mrs. Sorato had bought all kinds of cushions and pillows and padding to solve the problem. Now, Mrs. Sorato spread out an old pillow from the bedroom on top and sank down into it. "It's a pity," Mrs. Sorato said. "Even now, when I look at it, it snookers me. It whispers, *Give me one more try. I'm more comfortable than you remember.* And of course it isn't. The older I get the more uncomfortable it becomes. I don't think I have quite as much padding as I used to." She reached down and grabbed an inch of her backside as if to prove it to her daughter.

"I finished the manuscript," Susan said.

"Oh, that's wonderful, darling. I'm sorry...which manuscript are you working on now?"

Susan looked in her mother's eyes. The look, the twinkle was still there. It was still her mother, but the finest invisible veil had been pulled down between them. They were almost in the same world, only they were out-of-phase. She'd read articles and essays in the *New York Times* and *The New Yorker*. She'd seen specials on *60 Minutes* about when your parents start becoming children again. This was the first tiny step.

"No, I'm sorry. I was talking about Mrs. Davis's manuscript. Remember? We were discussing it?"

"Oh, that old thing," Mrs. Sorato said. "I don't think there's much chance of it getting published now that she's gone. I imagine publishers are looking for writers with a future. Alicia doesn't have much of a future now, unless you count decomposing and becoming worm food."

It was strange to hear her mother talk this way. She had always prided herself on her elegance. "I'm not sure I agree with the conclusions she came to. She made it sound like the three of us were little happy-go-lucky kids until that day, and then we were all different, as if we'd been scarred somehow. I don't remember it that way."

Mrs. Sorato smiled at her. It was hard to tell if it was a searching thoughtful smile, or just the simulacrum of one. "How do you remember it, dear?"

"What I remember most was that it just came from out of nowhere. I remember that we were all psyched-up because we were getting out of school early. Everybody on the bus was kind of rowdy. And then I remember Mr. Nichols swearing as we started to skid. I remember thinking that it wasn't very professional for him to be swearing in front of little kids. And then... Oh God, Mom, it was horrible. He was sitting there, trapped behind the steering wheel and he was worrying about us and telling us to get out. We tried everything we could. Charlie tried to make my flute into a snorkel so he could breathe...and nothing worked. It was horrible. I could see the moment when he couldn't breathe anymore. And then for a second or two, he could. He was coughing, but then the water got higher and it was just bubbles coming out. And then nothing. His eyes were still open and he was looking straight ahead. Afterwards, I think Charlie took it the hardest. Maybe because he was trying the hardest to save him."

"Do you remember, right afterwards you gave up playing the flute?"

Susan looked at her mother. "Oh, I see where you're going. You think it was because of the accident."

"You don't think it was?"

"I don't know. I never thought about it that way...till now. I think the water and the storm killed Mr. Nichols. I don't think my flute did."

Her mother was looking at her with great love and patience now as if she were visiting her in a hospital. "Do you remember the essay you wrote about Mr. Nichols?"

"I hadn't. Not till I went through the manuscript. To be honest, it still seems a little creepy that Mrs. Davis kept such a close watch on us."

"That was your first literary attempt...and a damned good one. I doubt that you could improve on it very much today. You had an ability to write, even back then." Mrs. Sorato shifted her position slightly on the glider. She smoothed out the wrinkles in her cotton sundress and glanced at her watch. It was an antique, gold and exquisitely delicate. She squinted at the tiny face of the watch and slipped her glasses on. "Oh dear, your father will be coming home for lunch soon. He doesn't like it if there's nothing waiting on the table."

Susan tried to catch her mother's eyes and hold them. She

tried to, but it seemed like her mother was now a wind-up toy determined to go through some motions. "Mom..." she said.

Mrs. Sorato glanced at her. "Yes, dear, what is it?"

"Do you remember what a *beautiful* funeral Dad had? Remember the speech that Father Shandley gave about what a wonderful man he was?"

Mrs. Sorato's eyes brightened. "Oh, I'll never forget *that*. He said that our family was like three peas in a pod, living in perfect harmony. Father Shandley can really spread the bullshit around thick and deep. And I love him for it."

"Maybe we could go out for lunch," Susan said.

"Oh, that would be *wonderful*!"

Headlines

Sam Harper peered up at the glowing computer monitor and grinned with satisfaction. "Well, you really hammered this shot, Cub," he said. Compliments were a rare thing from Sam and were highly coveted. The shot of the fire was so good, in fact, that Sam called everybody over to look, and then proceeded to explain to Cubby exactly *why* his shot was good. ...That part was a little harder to take.

"We're goin' a full half-page color on this one," Sam began. "For Carver's Mill, this is like the shot of the century." Delta and James winked at each other and then at Cubby. It was nice seeing Sam overtly happy about anything. "Ya see, that old horseshit about a picture being worth a thousand words..."

"It's not true," Delta said deadpan. "A picture's worth *more* than a thousand words."

Sam glared at his wife. "...cute. Do you want to see a blow-by-blow of what makes a shot great...or not?" For reasons of self-preservation no one said anything. "Okay, first off, you got it cropped just right. There's not a single square inch of blue sky. It's all either orange flames or billows of black clouds. It looks like the newspaper itself is on fire. Then ya got the key players all in the foreground like football players in a huddle. See Bert with his finger jutting over toward the barn? It's like he's a prosecuting attorney. *You are GUILTY and we're gonna kick your ASS!* But the best part of all, you managed to get, not only that big truck blowin' through the back of the barn, but you got actual boards in mid-air. Then look down here. The whole back end of Charlie's truck is off the ground. Everything's in mid-air! One second later or one second earlier and it would have been a B-shot. As it is, I give it an A-plus, plus, plus. Now, all we need is a headline that's as good as the shot. By all rights, the lumberyard should have burned to the ground. There shouldn't be anything left at all...and that would have been a bang-up, too. But this one, amazingly enough, is even *better*! We're gonna need a little history. It's older than shit. Maybe George Washington slept there or something."

"Eighteen twenty-eight," Cubby said. "Probably not Washington."

Sam wrinkled his nose. "Okay, okay, but you got the concept. Right?"

"Yes, boss," Cubby said, pretending he was suddenly working for the Daily Planet instead of the Carver's Mill Patriot.

"How about, *Mother Nature: Zero Midway Fire: Ten*?" Delta said.

"It's good," Sam said, "but right now, I'm looking for GREAT."

"How 'bout, *Just Another Day at Midway Fire*?" James said. "It'd be a good juxtaposition of understatement against that shot?"

"That's actually pretty good," Sam said. "It's just..."

"It's a little too effete," Delta said. "Half of Carver's Mill won't get it."

"Are we supposed to be playing to the *lowest* common denominator?" James said.

Sam looked at his son. "No. But this isn't The New Yorker

Magazine either. Let's whack 'em on the side of the head with something meaty...satisfying."

"How 'bout...*Midway Fire kicks ASS!*" Cubby said.

"There's our headline. I want hundred-point font. How 'bout an interview with Charlie...find out if his truck's okay. Or maybe a two-man interview, Charlie and Bert Emmerling."

This time it was Cubby who was wrinkling his nose. "Before we go down that bunny trail, maybe I should fill you in on the rest of the story."

The First Decadeinal: *In Martini Veritas* Reunion

Becky scribbled some sentences on a crib sheet, tried reading them out loud and then decided to just wing-it. She flipped her cell phone open and mouthed the first line one more time before pressing Susan's cell phone number. It rang twice and then Susan answered.

"Hellooo, Susan!" Becky sang out, "This is a *recording* sooo...no point in talking. This is more like an easy-listening kind of message. Okay...ya ready? The first Decadeinal In Martini Veritas Reunion is taking place in one hour. If you will recall, twelve years ago at graduation the three of us had a little party...and you know where. Decadeinal was as close as I could come...they don't seem to have a word for every twelve years *sooo*...I'm making do."

"Becky?" Susan said. "You don't sound like a recording."

"I know," Becky agreed. "Isn't it cool? This is the new interactive computer technology. But rest assured...I am a recording. How ya doin' by the way?"

"I'm fine. I'm..."

"See? That's all part of the technology. We could go on for probably half an hour and you'd never even know but I know you want to talk to the real Becky soooo...be there or be square. You remember the place, don'tcha?"

"Of course. The Falls. What can I bring?"

"Good question. I anticipated your asking that. Well for starters, you know you *don't* have to bring a bathing suit. Second, I've got a quart of Stoly chilling at exactly zero degrees, some Martini and Rossi at twenty-six degrees and some frozen chili peppers. These babies are gonna freeze your esophagus. If you want to bring some crackers and cheese or something to soak up the acid..."

"What kind of cheese are you eating these days?"

"Nothing special. Same ole shit. Brie, cheddar, Monterey Jack."

"I think I can do better than that."

"Atta girl. I figured you would."

Susan chuckled at the other end. "This is really an impressive software program. I'd swear I'm talking to the real Becky."

"Yes, it's pretty impressive all right...all right...all right... Oops, gotta go. See ya."

Becky pressed *END,* and mentally congratulated herself. "One down." Then she looked up the number for Blair Lawnmowers.

"Hello Charlie!" she began.

"Hey. Is this Becky?"

"Actually this is a *recording* of Becky's voice so not much point in talking, Charlie. This is more like an easy-listening kind of message. Okay...ya ready?"

"You don't sound like a recording," Charlie said.

"Well...I am. May I continue?"

"Yeah, sure. I guess..."

"The first Decadeinal *In Martini Veritas* Reunion is taking place in one hour. If you will recall, twelve years ago at graduation the three of us had a little party...and you know where."

"What does Decadeinal mean?"

"It means every ten years but Decadeinal was as close as I could come...they don't have a word for every twelve years *sooo*...I'm making do."

"You *really* don't sound like a recording."

"Well... Tough shit. You just haven't kept up with the sophisticated software programs. I could probably talk to you for half an hour and you wouldn't even know. I could tell you the capital of Rio de Janero."

"Isn't that a city?"

"Yup. Trick question."

"I can also tell you the best restaurants in your area."

"That's easy. There aren't any."

"Work with me, Charlie."

Charlie looked at the telephone receiver and then sighed. "Okay. I guess I get it. Is Susan coming, too?"

"Of course. It's gonna be just like the old days...only better. Remember how we all drank Stoly and got all plastered and told the truth about everything? Remember Susan came up with, *In Martini...Veritas*?"

"I remember we all got sick."

"Yeah. Well, we're older now. Soooo...ya coming?"

"Are you gonna pull this shit every ten years?"

"We'll just have to see... Isn't this computer technology amazing?"

"What do you want me to bring?"

"Just yourself."

"Pizza?"

"Yeah okay. See ya."

"Goodbye software program."

"Bye..."

It was the best-unkept secret in Bucks County. At the

bottom of the hill, just as Fleecydale Road flattened-out and made its final run toward the Delaware River, there was a sharp turn in the road. The sign said, *slow to fifteen miles per hour*, and it was sharp enough that you had to pay attention so that you didn't hit anyone coming the other way. And because of that, almost no one ever noticed the tiny gravel trail that dropped-off sharply to the right. The secret was sloppily passed down from one generation to another, with each one thinking they'd discovered it.

Upon graduating from high school, it was promptly forgotten by the then grown-ups who had better things to do than trespass down an overgrown trail to go skinny-dipping at The Falls. The whole pool was less than a hundred feet across with a tiny gravel beach and crayfish. The falls were only twenty or thirty feet across but had great sound, and the boulders were green with slippery algae so you could drink a beer, do a slippy-slide, make-out, take a dip, with or without, and be pretty sure no one would bother you.

Becky went over early and set everything up. She parked the truck right on the beach and dragged off some old comforters that had been in the attic. Way back when, they had come to the conclusion that unlike beer or wine, there was something about super-cold vodka martinis that forced you to tell the truth, plus it gave a nice friendly high, unlike wine that could be depressing sometimes. She checked the cooler. The Stoly had spent the afternoon at sub-zero temperatures between two half-gallons of ice cream. The vermouth, which had less alcohol, could only go down to about twenty-eight degrees. Any more it was a giant Martini- and-Rossi popsicle. The martini glasses were caked in frost and by all rights, when they poured the first drink, the little Peppadew red peppers would freeze solid by the time you got to the bottom of the glass.

Charlie arrived next and then right behind him, Susan

pulled in. The trail was so steep that from the beach it looked like the two of them might topple over and hit the beach. Susan's car made a loud crunch as it bottomed out and finally they parked off to the side. As they walked over, it looked for a second like it was Charlie and Susan out on a date. For a second, Becky's mind short-circuited and she made a point of over-correcting.

"Hey strangers!" she called when they were ten feet away. "Welcome to the first..." She couldn't remember the word she'd used, "twelve-year reunion of the *Veritas Club*. C'mon down. Take a load off."

Just as she'd imagined, Charlie was in jeans and a black t-shirt. Except for his expression, he could have been a textbook illustration of what a hunk should look like. Tight jeans, nice ass...*really* nice arms and shoulders and a nice straight nose, not cutesy and turned up, and not a mountain...just a nice ski slope. His eyes... He was a troubled hunk.

Susan looked like she'd shown up for a photo-shoot for Elle Magazine...stylish threads for a weekend in the country. They were so perfect, Becky glanced around to see if there were any tags still hanging.

Charlie looked down at everything. "Is it just me or is this all a little weird? Oh, by the way, I talked with your software program. I'd send it back if I were you. There's something wrong. It didn't know that Rio is a city."

Becky grinned at him. "No, it's fine. I just set it to *Dumb Broad*. It works better with men." She poured three martinis and handed them out.

"Oh, we're gettin' right to it, are we?" Charlie said.

"Cheers," Susan said and took a long sip. "You know, it never occurred to me where I got my attraction to frozen vodka martinis. It was here. I never realized it. I thought it was at some meeting with a publisher in New York. Strange..."

"Is it strange being here now?" Charlie asked.

Susan looked at him and then looked away nervously. "Yes. Really strange. I feel like I'm in the here and now, but part of my brain is still in the...*way-back-when*. It's...disconcerting."

Becky chuckled and took her own long drink. "Potato... *Potahto*... You say, disconcerting, I say fucked-up." She tasted the vodka and looked at it. "See? It's already beginning to work. *Veritas*. I think the thing with cold vodka is you can't even taste the alcohol. It feels like I'm drinking water." She poured another one and took a sip. "Ya know, ever since you came back, I keep trying to see everything from your eyes. I bet everything looks...really basic now, like we all have hayseed in our hair, and say 'shucks y'all.'"

The first martini was just beginning to do its work. Susan looked at Charlie and realized she'd always been a little frightened of him. Frightened that she might just lose herself if she ever let the guard down. There'd always been that wonderfully impenetrable wall that no one could see...or ever get through. It was very safe inside its borders. "It's not like that," she said. "It's more like, you guys are real and I've somehow lucked-into this little world...and I'm a complete fraud. At book signings, people come up to me and tell me how talented I am and how insightful. And I want to throw-up."

Charlie looked at her for possibly the first time in his life. "Wanna trade?" he asked. "Wanna c'mon down and learn how to sharpen lawnmower blades?"

"At least you're not a fraud," Susan said. "At least you can actually sharpen a lawnmower blade...look at it and know that it's sharp."

"Okay, time-out," Becky said. "This is s'posed to be fun. Maybe we need some cheese or pizza or something to slow down the truth serum. You said you were gonna bring some really cool *up-town* cheese for us to try."

"The more up-town it gets, the more it smells like baby shit or tastes like moldy hay."

"Given a choice, I'd prefer the moldy hay," Charlie offered.

Susan laughed. She laughed like the old Susan. The one with no tits, no ass, and Catholic-school clothes from J.C. Penney. "I picked up some brie and cheddar...and some Triscuits. I haven't had a Triscuit in..."

"Twelve years?"

Charlie actually grinned a little. He downed his martini in one gulp and chewed on the frozen pepper. He opened the pizza box and held it out. "It's an up-town pizza," he said. "It's white and has broccoli and arugula."

"Mmmm..." Becky giggled. "I hate arugula."

Charlie looked at her. "Really?"

"Yeah. I really do. It makes me want to go out and let the air out of people's tires."

"Wow... I didn't think that..." And then he caught her eyes and realized she was pulling his leg

"I'm afraid I don't like it either," Susan giggled. "It tasted like old newspapers. Do *you* like it?"

Charlie smiled beneficently and began picking it off his slice. "Not really. I just figured... It sounded up-town. I figured people with good taste would like arugula." He topped-off everyone's drink and held up his glass. "In honor of the twelve years, I'd like to propose a toast. To the writer...The artist slash certifiable whacko, and...the lawnmower guy. No one would have figured we'd be back here twelve years later, drinking Veritas."

"I'd like to propose a counter-toast," Becky said, "To the successful novelist...you got the whacko part right, and to the only person sitting here who's a certifiable hero...someone who's saved people from dying."

"Stop," Charlie snapped. "I'm not a hero. And, I don't want to go there...okay?"

"Sure!" Becky said too quickly.

Susan looked at the two of them. "I don't want to belabor the point, but every hero I've ever seen interviewed...and these were all true heroes. Every single one of them instantly said what you just said. *I am NOT a hero*!"

"And the ones who say they are...aren't." Becky said, "Okay. How 'bout, to the famous novelist, the certifiable whacko, and to the still reigning super stud of Carver's Mill."

Out of character, Susan downed her second martini in two rather long gulps. "My turn. To...myself, the fraud, to the only one who's always had the cajones to say whatever she needed to say, and...to Charlie, who has, indeed, saved both our asses and probably many more."

"I can see this martini thing could get out-of-hand real quick," Charlie said. "Toss me over a hunk of cheddar so I can get the rest of this stupid arugula taste out of my mouth."

Susan handed him the whole package. "I never heard anything about your stint in the Navy. Was it exciting? Eventful?"

Charlie made a face. "There's an old diddy they used to sing. 'I joined the Navy to see the world...and what did I see? I saw the sea'. As it turns out, mechanical skill can translate into all kinds of things, particularly landing gear and hydraulics on aircraft carriers. It's like its own little...make that *big* little world. I guess we went all over, Sea of Japan, Persian Gulf, North Atlantic, but when you're three decks down in the bowels of the ship...it all looks the same."

Susan nodded and sliced off a hunk of brie. "I remember when Becky knitted you that infamous Morse Code scarf. You were probably in the South Seas at the time...and you get a wool scarf."

Becky's eyes went from normal to huge and she shook her head slowly from side to side at Susan.

"No, that was a really nice scarf," Charlie countered, "and the fact of the matter was, we were in the North Atlantic when I got it. It was really warm. I've still got it, by the way. But...Morse Code. Why is it a Morse Code scarf? I don't get it."

"Oh, shit," Susan said to Becky. "I'm sorry."

Becky put her head down in her hands and just started shaking it slowly back and forth. "Nothing. Nothing at all. Next topic."

"No. You can't do that," Charlie said. "You can't just say something and then cut it off."

"In this case, I really can," Becky said. "Just drop it, okay?"

Charlie nodded. "Okay. That's cool. But I've still got it at home. I always kept it cuz you made it."

Becky threw the rest of her martini on the beach and groaned. "Look, I've never asked you for a favor...*ever*," she said.

"That's not true," Charlie said. "You've asked me for plenty of favors."

"Okay. Fine. You're right. Only this is a really, really big one. When this is over, I'm gonna follow you back and you're going to tell me where you have the scarf stashed...and then I'm going to take it back...and make you a new and even better one. Okay? Deal?"

Charlie looked at her. She looked to be about four sheets to the wind at the moment. "What's on the scarf?"

"She thought since you were in the Navy, you'd understand Morse Code," Susan said.

"You wove something into the scarf," Charlie said, "and me, being a complete dumb-shit, missed it. Now, I really need to know what you knitted."

"No ya don't. Look, I'll make you a deal. You give me back that scarf and Suze and I will both dance the hoochey kooch *naked* for you under the falls."

"*Hey*..." Susan said.

"*No!* I'm calling in ALL my cookies. We're gonna dance the hoochey kooch in the water and I'm gonna get my scarf back. This's a done deal."

Charlie looked at the two young women he'd tried to protect from the entire rest of the world. Now it looked as if the whole thing was falling apart and it was somehow because of him. "Okay, this whole thing has gotten way outta hand," he said. "We've all had a little too much to drink...and nobody has to dance the hoochey kooch. ...I don't even know what the hell a hoochey kooch is. And...I don't need to know. Okay? We're done. *Finito*. We're all still friends."

It was Susan who stood up and walked to the edge of the gravel beach. She kicked-off her sandals and put her foot in the water. She waved it slowly back and forth and then she turned back to face both Becky and Charlie. "I'm drunk," she said, "but that's not why I'm doing this." She unbuttoned her blouse and slid it off her shoulders with an economy of emotion. She looked like she was alone and getting ready for bed. She undid the thin silver Coco Channel buckle from her white linen pants and slid them down with equal economy. She was as she had always been, a long-legged little girl, all pale and smooth, like a slender cookie that hadn't been in the oven yet.

"What are you doing?" Becky said softly. "You don't have to..."

Susan smiled back at her. "You're the unpredictable one. You're the spontaneous one. Tonight...it's *my* turn." She reached behind her and undid her brassiere. It was pale blue silk and like her underpants, nearly transparent. She tossed the tiny garment toward them and it landed between them. "And last, but not least," she said, pulling her underpants down over her knees and to her ankles. She kicked them away with a splash of water. And then she did a very slow turn-around so they could both see exactly what she looked like. "What do you think?" she whispered, and then she started crying.

"Aw shit," Charlie said under his breath. His eyes darted to Becky. They said, *what the hell do we do?*

Becky looked back, wide-eyed and for once speechless. She shook her head in the twilight. It was getting darker by the moment now and Susan seemed to be doomed like an alabaster statue to remain standing in the shallow water. "You're beautiful," Charlie said. "You look like a goddess. But when you go skinny dipping you're all supposed to strip at the same time." He looked at Becky and pulled his t-shirt over his head. He kicked off his shoes and hopped around trying to pull his jeans over his legs. "What do you think? Socks on or off?" he said to Susan.

"Uhmmm. I don't know."

"Take 'em off," Becky called, stripping out of her tube top and cut-offs.

Charlie stripped as fast as he could. He pretended he was getting into his fire gear...only backwards and then he did a shallow dive out into the water. He shook the water out of his eyes and turned around. Becky was just stepping out of her underwear. Though they were both beautiful women, they were complete opposites. Becky was all curves punctuated by a tiny black triangle below her waist. But before he could see anything clearly, she was racing toward the water. She did a cannon ball at point-blank range. It knocked Susan over and a second later, they were all standing in waist-deep water looking at each other.

Becky grinned at Susan. "Well...ya got us this far. If we can make up something and do the hoochey kooch...I get my scarf back. Ya game?"

Susan looked at her old girlfriend. It was hard to tell what were tears and what was water. She glided over toward the falls and stood up again. Becky swam over next to her. They both stood up in what was knee-deep water. Becky leaned over and whispered in Susan's ear. Then she sang out, " A one...and a two and a..." It was a two-girl Rockettes performance...and as pretty simple one at that. Left-kick, right-kick, left-kick right-kick...

Charlie watched. He had no idea what to make of it or what he was supposed to do...or how the hell they were going to all go back and put their clothes back on and...*what they hell were they all supposed to say?* It was just...weird.

Thirty minutes later, they were all dressed, damp, and drunk, and getting back in their cars. Becky held the door of the truck half-way open and looked at them. "We all still friends?" she called.

"I'm in," Susan called. "I'm freezing...but I'm in. This night never happened...right?"

"Never happened," Charlie agreed. "It's a shame though. You're really beautiful."

"I'm following you back to your place," Becky called to Charlie.

He looked at her. "What? ...Why?"

"The scarf... We had a deal."

"Are you serious?"

"Oh, yes...deadly."

Charlie drove ultra slow back to the house, partly because he'd had too much to drink and partly to protect Becky in case they got pulled over. In the darkness it was a tight, slow two-truck caravan. On the way, Becky kept getting glimpses of the back of his head at the stop signs. At one, he turned around in the seat and gave her a little nod. It said, *you okay?* and she gave a tiny toot with on her antique truck horn.

She followed him past the turn-off for his shop and suddenly realized he didn't just live in the shop. That was always how she imagined him...in the shop or fighting a fire. They drove down 413 and then made a turn down a little gravel lane. It crossed over the railroad tracks for the New Hope-Ivyland Express, somewhat of a misnomer considering the train was a tiny black choo choo that escorted tourists seven miles up the tracks, then seven miles back, through scenic Bucks County. He put his turn signal on way in advance and she followed suit, though in truth they were out in the middle of nowhere and there was only the two of them.

The house was a small nondescript Cape Cod. In the headlights she saw the reflectors on a big orange tractor that looked strong enough to uproot entire trees. A big muddy blade hung off the front.

He hopped out of the cab and waited for her. "You might want to wait," he said. "I wasn't exactly expecting company."

"Let me guess. There are pizza boxes everywhere and little boxes of half-eaten Chinese food."

Charlie looked at her in the darkness. She was just a shivery shadow, her hair still damp and dripping, her tube top half-soaked. "No, it's not like that. Not all guys turn into complete pigs just cuz..."

"Because they're alone."

"It might be better if you wait."

"Yeah but... If you get the scarf, I know you're gonna look at it. You're gonna see dots and dashes. Then you're gonna look it up on the internet."

Charlie looked at her hard, his face dead-straight serious.

"Yeah... But it's a scarf that you knitted for *me*. I was *s'posed* to read it. That's why you knitted it."

"Yeah, but that was way back when..."

"Okay. I get it now." Charlie smiled at her but only with his mouth. "So...whatever the message *was,* it's...not that way anymore."

"No..." Becky said too fast. "It's just that... Shit. You're screwin' this up."

Charlie was standing one foot from her in the darkness and all he could see was the tiny reflection of the porch light in her eyes. Right then she looked like a vampire in all the shadows. All shadows and those crazy eyes. "Ya know what's weird?"

"Yeah. Us standing here."

"No, it's not that. I've known you since you were five. I've seen you without your two front teeth. I've seen you arrested for whatever that yarn thing is you do. I've seen you in various stages of being naked...at least four or five times."

"Bullshit. Except for tonight..."

"No, you're wrong. I saw you when you were getting into your Halloween costume...not much but I saw *something*. I saw you when you were cheerleading and your bra strap...snapped. I saw you one time when you were getting gas and the wind blew your skirt..."

"Man you sound like a real perv..."

"No, c'mon. I'm trying to make a point. If you've been around someone for like...*forever*, you see stuff. But for all that, I never even gave you a peck on the cheek...nothing. Absolutely nothing."

"Is that it? You want to give me a peck on the cheek?"

"Yeah. I think that's fair. If you're gonna be an Indian-giver and take my scarf back."

"Well... You don't deserve it. I can't believe you joined the

Navy and don't know any Morse Code."

"Hey-- They've had a couple of technological improvements since then. I just wasn't expecting I'd need a code book to go with my scarf."

"That's it," Becky said. "I want that freakin' scarf right now. It's *toast*. Five minutes from now it's gonna be a little pile of ashes...and *you're* history. Do you understand?"

"Okay. So be it. Only I want that peck on the cheek...to remember you by. That's the deal."

"Fine."

"Fine."

"Which cheek do you want to *peck*?"

"Oh, good. I have a choice?"

"Yeah, big spender. Knock yourself out."

Charlie came closer to her and became part of the shadows. He could only see her eyes because of the reflections. She could see his dimly in the same reflections.

"Well... Can't make up your mind?"

Charlie chuckled. "It's a big decision for me." Two pairs of eyes staring at each other in otherwise darkness. "Hey wait a minute, I've got an idea. I'll do it like in those foreign films...one cheek...then the other. That way it's balanced." Charlie kissed her softly on her left cheek. He noticed her eyes still twinkling back at him in the darkness. Then he gently kissed her on her right cheek. Her eyes fluttered closed for a moment.

They were nose-to-nose now, but still there were only the two tiny reflections in her eyes. He saw two tiny replicas of his porch light. *How was it possible for porch lights to twinkle at him?*

"I had a thought," he whispered. "...it's just a thought..."

"...what?" She leaned imperceptibly into him. The zipper on her cut-offs barely touched the zipper on his jeans.

"I've...got *another* scarf," he whispered. "It's grey-and-black or something and...I hardly ever wear it."

"Yeah?"

"If I throw that one into the deal... You know..." He looked down at her lips. It was a vision he'd imagined a thousand times before.

"Yeah... I guess..." she whispered back.

At that moment, every touch was a first touch. It was as if he had never seen a breast before, never gently caressed a backside. And finally...no words were spoken.

Becky finally looked around them. There was a low hedge, gravel, and some lawn. "Where are we gonna..."

Charlie looked around. The lawn was soaked with dew and...well...not much else. "Yeah, right. Dummy that I am..." He gazed past her. She had left the lights on in her old pick-up. They already looked a shade dimmer. "I'll get your lights," he said and walked quickly back to her truck. He leaned in the window and fumbled for a moment and they went out. A half-second later the beeper went off in his truck. It seemed like they were tied together somehow. But then four seconds after that, the big sirens on top of the Midway Fire House began spooling slowly up to their dull frightening moan. It sounded like a monstrous wolf, howling at the moon.

Becky was standing on the porch now, under the porch light. She looked like a model from the movies, just standing there, staring at him. She shook her head and shrugged in an odd way. It wasn't hard to read. It said, *what do we do now?*

"It must be some kinda mistake!" Charlie called. He ran to his truck and climbed up on the aluminum floorboard. His beeper was pulsing like a blue firefly inside the cab. He looked at the message window. It was Chief Emmerling.

Charlie pressed the comm. button. "What's up?"

"Charlie. I need ya over here."

"Where ya at?"

"The fire's at the Furlong Getty station. The big tanks haven't blown...*yet*. I'm on 202 across from Bountiful Acres. Buckingham's got everything blocked-off half a mile in every direction."

"Okay... I got it. I'm on my way."

"Oh...I already got your gear with me. You can just come straight here. Ya got it?"

"Yeah."

Charlie trotted back to the porch. His head was spinning. So were his emotions. "Look, this is really awful timing."

"What's on fire?"

Charlie caught her eyes. She was smiling at him. "It's the Getty station. It could be bad." She was still grinning at him. "What's so funny?"

"Nothing," Becky said, still smiling. "Only... I know you made me promise not to talk to Dr. Emmerling but..."

"You *WHAT*? *You talked to him*?"

Becky made a weird little face. "Kinda."

Charlie climbed up into the Dodge and slammed the door so hard the interior lights popped on. He gunned the engine and sprayed gravel all the way up the driveway. At the road, she saw him fiddle with his lights and then a jammed a long blue flashing light up on the roof.

Furlong Getty

He looked over at the orange glow behind the trees from a mile away. The Buckingham police had commandeered the traffic light at 413 and 202 and were turning cars back, but it was a mess. People intent on heading toward Philly and points South were threatening the cops and shaking their fists. The cops were local and doing the best they could.

    Charlie came up from behind, passed fifteen cars and nosed around a white Lexus with Jersey plates. He got a whole string of fingers and sharp blares of the horn. He was used to it. He did the same with the next car and the next until he was up to the intersection. Dale Stephens, one of the older cops, was manning the black-and-white wooden barriers. When Charlie got up to the front, Stephens dragged the long sawhorse back ten feet and gave him a nod. Charlie nodded back and accelerated up 202. A handful of cars that had squeaked-by were doing K-turns now and returning back down the hill. It was bad. Even from half a mile away the flames were huge and billowing as if small atomic bombs were going off. He flipped his visor down so he wouldn't get blinded. For a second, he thought the gas storage tanks had already blown, but they couldn't have. He would have heard that from the other side of the county.

The second set of saw horses were already opened by the time he got to them. "What's the status?" he called to a young sergeant he didn't recognize. He got a shake of the head. He was a kid and looked petrified. "Am I safe enough back here?" he yelled at Charlie.

Charlie looked at him. "Yeah, you're good. If the main tank goes...you're gonna have a half a second where you see a huge flash. If you see that, put your hands tight over your ears and open your mouth. It'll keep you from blowin' out your eardrums." Even as he said the words, the kid went through the motion to try it out. "Yeah, that's it," Charlie said. "But ya gotta do it like instantly."

As Charlie crested the hill he realized Midway was the only company that had gotten there so far and they had everything out. The tanker and the trucks were all backed-up a hundred feet farther away than was usual. That was good. And four big jets of water shooting high and coming down right on top of the station. The row of parked cars and vans over at side were all charred and flaming.

He spotted Chief Emmerling's white Silverado parked next to the pumper and he drove down next to it. His gear was on the hood of the truck and he climbed into it as fast as he could. The heat was bad. It felt like a bad sunburn just in the seconds it took him to suit up. Emmerling was standing on the floorboard of the tanker conferring with someone. He trotted up, not knowing what the hell to expect.

Emmerling looked at him a half a second longer than he usually did. "Good," he said. "Dabrowski's in the front of the shop trying to find the shut-off valves. Once he gets that accomplished..."

Charlie did a quick calculation. "Look... Chief... I don't want to fuck with ya. But there's shut-off valves at the pumps. If you don't get them, it'll feed right down..."

Emmerling glared at him.

"Look, Chief, I used to *work* at a station," Charlie said. "I used to work at *this* fuckin' station for god sakes!"

"Where are they located?" Emmerling asked.

Charlie stopped and looked at him hard. "I'm not lookin' to be dead. I'm really not looking to be burned-to-death. I just know where the fuck they are. Who's best qualified? C'mon chief, this is a gimmie."

"Okay. I'll have number three put down a suppressive for you. It goes first. Then only when it's clear, you follow it in. Second set...suppressive...you follow it in. Anything...*anything* goes wrong. You get the *FUCK* outta there. You hear me?"

There were four sets of pumps on two islands. Two for full-serve, two for self-serve, a total of eight pumps. He'd spent many an hour hunched over some fender doing fill-ups. Charlie trotted toward the closest island like a quarterback returning to the huddle.

Just as he was at a point where he'd have to stop, an ocean of water raced right over his head and landed twenty feet in front of him. He knew who was running interference for him. Only one guy in the group could cut it that close. He slowed, but just a little. The whole world in front of him was water with a wavery halo of flames everywhere else. It felt like he was underwater when he got there and his feet just slid out from under him, but the grey metal valve was right in front of him. He screwed it clockwise, then jammed his yellow-gloved hand up in the air. The rocket of water moved fractionally forward and he crawled the twelve feet over to the second valve.

The second island went like clock-work. He was half done already.

He turned toward the full-serve island now. It was thirty feet closer to the station. His plastic visor was all steam now and it felt like he was breathing hot sooty water. The two bays were ablaze. Two vehicles were still up on lifts. One of them had been a van. The other was just a skeleton.

With his right arm, he pointed at the full-serve islands. The torrent of water moved like a psychotic rain cloud over to the first island. Behind the spray, he saw something bubbling flames inside. It looked like soup...flaming soup. It didn't look right and then something flared inside. He hit the deck just as the whole side of the garage blew out. Everything was orange and searing. He was on fire but there was nowhere to run. Everywhere was fire. Then everything went black.

A Light in the Sky

After Charlie had roared away up the driveway and disappeared into the darkness, Becky just stood there in the gravel, listening to the Dodge's big V-8 getting farther and farther away. For a good thirty seconds, she knew exactly where he was by the sound of the exhaust...coming to a stop sign at Hansel Road, then roaring away again. As he crested and went down the hill into the trees, the sound faded abruptly and was gone.

      She turned around in a semi-state of shock. Five minutes ago, she'd been angry. Four minutes ago, she was ascending to something approximating heaven. A minute and a half ago, it had all gone to hell in the space of one ill-conceived sentence. Although she'd never allowed herself to think about it head-on, she realized now that Charlie was a huge part of her life...and always had been. *Funny that that could be the case and you didn't even know it.*

      She took three steps toward her truck and stopped. This was the one and only chance she'd have to peer into Charlie's life... see what he was like, what kind of life he lived day-to-day, where he slept, where he kicked-back, where he made breakfast.

      She turned to look at the little Cape Cod in the darkness. It was tidy, white clapboards with barn-red shutters and trim. The chimney and bottom half of the house were field stone. Whatever image she'd had of him before...and she wasn't even sure what it had been, she hadn't imaged him as tidy. And yet it wasn't frilly either. She imagined him saying something like, "Well, I like things clean. I'm just not into a lot of bullshit."

She knew it wasn't right to snoop. She never liked people who did. It was tacky and it was low class. But these were extenuating circumstances. There had been *some* reason why he hadn't wanted to bring her in...and she needed to know what it was. She walked up to the porch and turned around and then looked up at the sky as if she belonged there...as if it were okay. She imagined some neighbor peering out the window at her and wondering who the hell she was. It was wrong. But then she sauntered back just as casually and peered in the living room window.

There was a hall light on and a light in the next room, but the living room was in shadow. A huge brown fuzzy sofa dominated the far wall with a long coffee table in front. The walls were all knotty pine. It was a guy's house, all right. From the set-up she assumed there'd be a TV somewhere close to her, maybe next to the window. She peered down to the left and...sure enough. It was tidy and no mess anywhere, but it was a guy's house, pure-and-simple. No eyelet curtains in the windows, no soft coordinating throw pillows, not even a painting on the wall. Nothing, just a little picture frame next to the sofa. Even in the darkness it looked vaguely familiar. *What the hell was it?*

She opened the screen door and tried the front door knob, half-hoping it'd be locked. If it was locked, she could do the right thing and just go home. If she went in, Charlie would know about it for sure. He'd deduce something or she'd leave a footprint or maybe he'd catch the scent of her perfume. She more than hoped it was locked, but it wasn't. The brass doorknob twisted in her hand

and she quietly opened the door. "Hello," she called out, just in case. "Hello," she called louder. "Anybody home?"

She walked toward the light in the next room. It was a small kitchen, also knotty pine. There were pans and dishes in the sink and she noticed that they both used the same dishwashing liquid. Even with the pans in the sink, his kitchen was about eighty percent tidier than hers, and that was without him even knowing she was coming over...breaking-in.

The dining room was just off the kitchen. It was small with a little built-in breakfront. Everything nice and tidy, but it looked like it had never been used. The dining room table was set with plates and silverware for four, but it looked like it had sat that way for years.

At the far end of the house was what was probably the master bedroom. Finally...finally she found the pig sty that she'd been hoping for, the one that matched her own bedroom. Sheets, pillow cases, dirty laundry, clean laundry, bath towels lay strewn everywhere. She went over to the bed and sat down and touched the place where he slept. She imagined him lying there, probably in his skivvies, if anything, racked out and snoring. He looked like a snorer. The nightstand was stacked with car magazines, Popular Science magazines and a handful of John le Carré novels. She looked around for some girly magazines. There weren't any.

Her conscience finally began to get the best of her and she backed out of the kitchen and turned toward the front door. Then she remembered. There was some little picture he'd framed. She turned around and bent over to look at it. It was a newspaper clipping of her yarn-bombing the Rocky Balboa sculpture in Philadelphia. *Why in the name of God had he framed that?*

She stepped back out onto the porch where the air was cooler and closed the door behind her. She stopped and considered pushing the little brass button and locking the door for him. No...

That's how he would have caught her...locking the door for him. He'd know. He'd remember. She pulled the door tightly shut and then let go quickly as if it might jump or buzz or blow up or something. Then she breathed a sigh of relief. No harm done. The light was still on in the kitchen...front door still unlocked. She turned and began walking back to her truck. Because of the fire, everything was bathed in a pale orange-pink glow. It was almost pretty, like the light of a brilliant orange harvest moon, but then the pink suddenly flared to brilliant orange. It lasted for five seconds and then there was a deafening *BOOM!!!* as the whole sky lit up. She turned to look down the mountain. *Oh, my God. Charlie just died.*

For a long moment, she watched the glowing orange in the sky flare more and more brilliantly, then slowly ebb and fade. By reflex, she pulled out her cell phone and flipped it open. She stared at the glowing dial. There was no one she could call.

In a daze, she drove down the main road and followed the path Charlie had probably taken, down the mountain, down into the trees where she finally came out at the intersection with 202. It was jammed like 5pm on Labor Day Weekend. She waved and nosed-out and immediately hit a line of stopped traffic, all of it being turned back. Maybe...just maybe, Charlie had gotten stuck too. Maybe he was ahead up there, stuck like everybody else and swearing up a storm. *No...not a fireman with those little blue lights.*

She punched-in Cubby's number.

He answered after two rings with, "*Really* not a good time." In the cell phone, one of the tank trucks hit its air horns and people were screaming. She heard the same horn a half-second later through the window.

"I know. I know," Becky said. "Just... Everybody okay?"

"Who the fuck knows?" Cubby said. "It's like a war zone."

Then he hung up.

She did a quick U-turn at the first chance and took off North toward New Hope. The traffic was already backed-up half a mile and people going South were getting out of their cars to see what was going on. She drove down past her little shop, past Lahaska. She put the turn signal on to go back to her house, but then she flipped it off. Two miles down on the right was the motel Susan was staying at. In the parking lot, she hit Susan's number. She said, "What room are you in?"

Susan sounded horrible on the other end. She said, "You don't want to come over."

"I'm in the parking lot. What room are you in?"

It took a moment. A toilet flushed close-by and the sound was echoy. She was in the bathroom. "One-seventeen. I warned you..."

There was a space right in front of her room. When she pulled in, the door to 117 was already open an inch. Inside, it smelled like Listerine and vomit. Susan stood stooped-over in the threshold to the bathroom. She looked like the girls in the movies who'd been sold kidnapped as sex slaves and been drugged-up. "So much for frozen martinis," she mumbled and wiped the side of her mouth with a wash rag.

"Sorry," Becky said.

Susan groaned and sat down at the desk. "Well, it's not like you held a gun to my head. What's up?"

"After you left..."

"Yeah?"

"Things went south really fast," Becky said. She proceeded to give a blow-by-blow of following Charlie back to his house to retrieve the scarf. She didn't mention that she'd also broken-in to his house and gone in every room. "Then we had a quick bad fight. I had promised him I wouldn't go to Chief Emmerling and plead for his job back...and then I did just that. Then we're standing there in his yard fighting and he gets a call from Emmerling. He's the Midway fire chief. There's a bad fire at Furlong Getty. You can see the glow from here. Charlie roared off and... and... from the looks of it...the station just blew up. I think Charlie might be dead."

ICU

It was one-thirty in the morning and the main lobby of Doylestown Memorial was empty except for a gaggle of men whose only thing in common was their expression and that they all smelled of smoke. Becky and Susan came in, sharing nothing with the men other than their expressions.

Chief Emmerling was at the counter, still in his fireman's boots. He was talking to a silver-haired woman with wire-rimmed glasses. From the looks of it, the old woman was Doylestown Memorial's main line of defense, keeping the men from just walking upstairs and finding Charlie for themselves. Emmerling stood there red-faced, partly from the fire and partly from the frustration of it all. "Look, Mrs...*Peterson*," he said in his big voice and looking at her name tag. "It's not like we're here to storm the Bastille or plant bombs. I just want to know his status and what floor he's on."

"Are you a member of Mr. Blair's *immediate* family?" Mrs. Peterson repeated for the third time in as many minutes. She said it word, by word as if English was his second language

Emmerling was beginning to lose it. "Look... I just answered that question. But ya know what? Yes, I damn well am a member of his immediate family, if you want to call putting your life on the line for your family. Every guy here is part of Charlie's *immediate* family."

"I'm sorry Mr. Emmerling."

"Chief Emmerling."

"I'm sorry, Chief Emmerling but, I don't make the rules."

"Yeah. And they don't pay you to have any common sense either," Emmerling muttered.

Becky broke away from Susan and walked to the counter. Emmerling turned around, looking like Charlton Heston peering down at the heathens from Mt. Olympus. At the moment, he was an angry, red-faced, pissed-off god. He caught Becky's eyes and his own eyes flared wider.

"S'cuse me," Becky said, pushing past him to the counter. "I can vouch for Chief Emmerling. I'm...Charlie's sister. Becky Blair. Is that *immediate* enough?"

The old woman eyed Becky. "Do you have some identification?"

"Sure. It's probably soggy. I was just over at the fire trying to find Charlie." She reached in her jeans pocket. "Shit... My wallet fell out."

The woman eyed her skeptically.

"Look, Ma'am, it's not like we're trying to break into a bank or something. My brother's up there. His name is Charlie Blair. He's got the little lawnmower repair shop over on 413. Chances are you bought something from him. He sells chain saws, lawnmowers, weed eaters. He lives in a little Cape Cod on Stony Hill and he's got a Kubota tractor with the snowplow blade still on. He's fixing up his '64 Vette in garage. You want me to tell you how many molars he's got in his mouth, cuz I can you know." Becky stared at the old woman. "Okay...look at me. Big brown eyes? Brown hair? Kinda cute? You must have seen him. He's practically my twin!"

"All right," the woman said, "I'll need you to sign in and...I'd appreciate it if you come back when you find your wallet. It's nothing personal but the rules are strict here."

"I understand." She turned the plastic clipboard around on the counter and began scribbling. She scribbled Becky and then had to think a second before scribbling Blair the same way. She looked at the overhead clock and scribbled in one forty-five. She stared at the woman, "Okay, as his sister am I allowed to vouch for Chief Emmerling? He's right you know. He's like Charlie's Dad...better...he's alive."

"Yes, Miss Blair, he's in the burn section, the third floor, section C."

As she turned around, she saw Susan walking fast toward the restrooms. She looked green and gave her a look that told her the whole story.

As the doors slid shut in the elevator, everything went muffled. Far below an electric motor hummed and there was a slight hum as cables propelled the carpeted and paneled tiny room upward. Chief Emmerling seemed intent on pretending she wasn't there. He stared at the wall and then he stared at the ceiling.

"How badly was he burned?" Becky said in such a soft voice that she had to repeat it. "I mean..."

"I don't know," Emmerling replied in a voice that surprised her. Then he said, "This had nothing to do with you."

Becky looked up at him. His eyes were no longer hard. They vaguely resembled her own eyes. They were dark and locked-down tight. "...what?" she whispered.

"When you came over to the clinic with Sluggo. When you were trying to get his job back... You should know... That didn't carry any weight. I didn't call Charlie because you came over. I called because... We were four men short and it was a big dangerous fire." Becky looked in Emmerling's eyes and saw an emotion she recognized.

Just as the elevator came to a halt, Emmerling looked down at her. "Before we go in... I don't know how bad he is, but you should tighten-up. Whatever it is you do to keep everything together, get that up-and-running. If he's badly burned..." Emmerling looked away. When he looked back his eyes were darker. "If he's badly burned...you may not want to go in."

Janet Smalley, the head nurse in the ICU, peered into a computer monitor and typed in the latest data on Charley Blair. He was suffering from smoke inhalation, and had first-degree burns over twenty percent of his body and second-degree burns over ten percent of his face. There were no third degree burns, thanks to whoever was working the water cannon. He had apparently decided he'd rather drown Charlie than watch him burn to death. It had been a good call.

The first degree burns were common and not a problem. A week or two and they would disappear with a little ointment and salve. The second degree burns were the most painful...worse than third degree burns primarily because third degree burns destroyed so much tissue, even the nerve endings were gone. The second degree was *where the action was*. Watched carefully, treated quickly, they would heal, possibly not needing skin grafts or artificial skin. If infection set in, however, the whole thing could go south in a handful of hours.

Nurse Smalley looked up at the sound of Chief Emmerling's size-twelve boots clomping down the hall. Next to him, was a young woman in scrubs. She was pretty but looked like she'd been through the mill. It was a common sight.

At the desk, she couldn't help but talk mostly to Chief Emmerling. He had that presence about him...and he'd be easier to talk to. Every time she looked over, the young woman looked like she was about to lose it.

"It could have been worse," she began. "For the most part, his gear protected him. He has second degree burns on his right hand. He must have taken his glove off."

"Yeah. He was trying to turn off the valve to the gas pumps," Emmerling said.

"Also on the side of his face, the back of his neck and his right arm. He's going to live, but..." She couldn't help but look over at the young woman now. "There may be some disfigurement... Of course we're going to do the very best we can."

"What room?" Emmerling asked.

Janet Smalley looked past them. Blair was just being wheeled back from a clean room. He was on a gurney and his right arm was encased in what looked like a clear plastic balloon and there was an odd, similar looking balloon encompassing the right side of his face and neck. He looked like a cross between the *Phantom of the Opera* and one of the Borg cyber-creatures from Star Trek. "Second degree burns are one of the most painful things a human being can endure. We have him sedated, but short of knocking him out entirely, which isn't an option right now.... It's likely to get worse before it gets better. And, he may not be all that coherent." A male nurse wheeled him into a room half-way down the hall.

"Maybe you should wait out here," Emmerling said to Becky.

"No. No, I'm going in, too."

"Okay, just remember. Whatever it is you use to keep your mind together, tighten it down right now. Box it up. Put it away."

There wasn't a door to knock on, just pale green translucent curtains that slid upon curved chrome tubes up above. "Knock, knock," Emmerling said, opening the curtain slowly,

Charlie's eyes had been closed. They opened slowly and peered at Emmerling and Becky. "What's the status on the fire? Did it go up?"

"No," Emmerling said. "The station's toast, but the big

tanks didn't blow." He was going to add, 'thanks to you,' but he didn't.

"I'm sorry, Chief," Charlie whispered. "You were right. I fucked up." He looked over at Becky. "I fucked everything up." Then he winced in pain. "Shit... Can somebody either knock me out or give me a friggin' 357? I can't put up with this shit. I feel like I'm being fried."

"You're doing great," Becky whispered. "You're a hero."

Charlie tried to make his face laugh, but it hurt too much. "Yeah, I'm a real hero all right. Look at me. And then go have another little chat with the chief. Yeah, I'm a real hero, all right."

Little Becky Doolittle

It was snowing outside and the snowflakes were so large that they brought to mind the folded-paper ones that Mrs. Davis had taught them to make barely the week before. The first three steps were easy. Make a square of paper. Fold it on the diagonal. Then fold it *again* on the diagonal. After that it got a little tricky and Mrs. Davis had to go around to each desk to avert any potential disasters. Half the boys in the class had gotten off on the wrong track and were making snowflake paper jets, which didn't fly very well. The girls, however, seemed to have an instinctive superiority when it came to using scissors.

    Becky and Susan were already a team by then. It seemed like they'd always been that way, brunette and blonde, salt and pepper, quiet and saucy, they sat together on the bus, and they'd pick out some boy and point and whisper and giggle until he slunk away. And then Susan would get all red-faced and they'd start on something else. They had developed their own secret language as well. Didn't even need to pass notes. Becky would look over at Susan, wrinkle her nose, give a little jerk with her chin or a half-nod and Susan would burst out laughing. Mrs. Davis saw it but didn't see anything wrong with it.

Roll-call began as usual thirty seconds after the bell. It went alphabetically though Mrs. Davis was a wily one and every once in a while she'd start with the Zs instead of the As and work backward. Every time she did it, the whole class thought it was the biggest joke. It was their own little secret. No one else at Buckingham Elementary called roll starting with the Zs. And there were, of course, two factions, the "*Heres*" and the "*Presents*". The boys for the most part, were all "Heres" with the exception of Jonathan Macomber, who was the tallest boy in the class, pimply but aristocratic, he seemed to be stuck as some minor character in a Shakespearean play. He would pronounce, "present" or "I am present" with such forcefulness that everyone else went into hysterics. Jonathan never seemed to notice though.

Strangely, Susan and Becky were not in lock-step on this one. Becky said, "Heeerrre" making it sound like she was declaring war on the Mongolians, while Susan pronounced "*present*" with such perfect diction that she sounded like a tiny Masterpiece Theater announcer...*vetty* English. Then Becky would crack up and so would Susan.

This morning, however, when Mrs. Davis came to Becky's name, she hesitated then said, "Becky *Doolittle* Pierce." The whole class went bananas. Becky collapsed on the top of her desk as if she couldn't stand the shame of it all, though no one was buying it for a second. Her one eye remained open and dreamy behind her elbow and she was grinning from ear to ear.

Mrs. Davis held up the front page of the *Carver's Mill Patriot* for the class to see. At the bottom of the page were three photographs, one of a cat with no left front leg, though it was sporting a red wool sweater that Becky had made to accommodate her handicap. The second shot was of a shaved raccoon. It'd been hit by a car and someone had brought it into the vet. Dr. Margenau operated on it, but to do it, they had to shave the fur off its back...and it was winter. For this emergency, Becky made a different type of sweater and Mrs. Davis asked Becky to come up to the front of the class to describe what she'd done and how she'd done it.

"See, it's like this," she began, fidgeting and squinting at the ceiling as she tried to recall exactly how she'd started the project. "I figured a raccoon is wild, so it's gotta have a sweater that's really warm and gonna last. A regular sweater, well, it'd just rip that to shreds and it wouldn't be warm enough anyway. Soooo...I made a thing called a *felted* sweater for it."

"Could you tell us what that means?" Mrs. Davis said, giving her a little cue.

"What? Oh yeah...sure. Felting... Well, it's no big deal. If you're really, really, really good...which I'm not *yet*, you can just make a sweater a special way and then wash it in hot water and then put it in the dryer. You'd better put it in a stocking or a garment bag or something though, because it'll really mess up anything you put in with it. The hot water shrinks everything up so it's like puppet size so you have to account for that. And...the wool doesn't shrink the same way in both directions so... It's really complicated. What I did was easier. I knitted like a whole little wool blanket and felted *that*. Then when it came out of the dryer I just used it like a hunk of material. The cool part, though, was that I figured...it being a wild animal and all, it'd have to get along with the other raccoons and possums and stuff, so I used brown wool and then I wove in black stripes...like the tail."

A boy in the back of the room yelled out, "Yeah, but raccoons aren't striped all over!"

Becky squinted at him. "Well... They *sorta* are...aren't they? Anyway, I had to go over to Dr. Margenau's to take

157

measurements. Dr. Margenau had to knock him out with some gas so that we could get it on him. But I guess it worked okay."

Mrs. Davis held up the paper again. The third photograph was the largest. It was a close-up of the raccoon, sitting in the crook of a tree with the sweater on. It had a walnut in its little grey claws and seemed to be content with the world.

After school, Becky tried to show Susan how to knit.

"It's easy," Becky kept saying. "Once you get the hang of it, you could do it in your sleep."

"What about all that fancy stuff?" Susan asked.

"It's just counting," Becky said. "...*basically*. And you know how to count."

Susan watched the blur of motion in Becky's lap and knew she'd never be able to do it. She went home early that day and wrote her first short story. It was entitled, *The Raccoon with the Striped Sweater*. Becky was the child heroine. She lived in an enchanted forest in a little wooden cabin and worked her magic for all the forest creatures. The next day she showed it to Becky who not only loved it, she *LOVED* it, and a partnership had begun.

Mrs. Davis referred to it as "getting hit over the head with the lucky stick." In Becky's case, four days after the Carver's Mill Patriot was on the newsstands, Becky's mother got a call at home while she was making dinner in the kitchen. The caller was from the Bronx Zoo in New York and he didn't actually want to talk to Mister or Mrs. Pierce, he wanted to talk to Becky.

The Pierces still had the old black telephones then, one in the living room and one in the master bedroom. When Becky talked to Susan, she'd use the upstairs phone and drag the whole thing into her room and then close the door. The phones were heavy, but smooth and comfortable and when you were talking into one, it felt special and important. It was like getting a handwritten letter in the mail and there was always the chance it was a love letter. Only this time, Becky took the phone, looked at her mother, pale and wide-eyed and questioning. She said, "Hello?"

"Miss Pierce? Rebecca Pierce?"

"...yeaaasss?" she said, drawing it out and making it into a question.

"I'm Norman Samuels with the Bronx Zoo in New York. I wonder if I might have a moment of your time?"

"Sure," Becky said, crossing her eyes at her mother and then shrugging. It said, *I don't know what the heck is going on either*.

"Miss Pierce, a friend of a friend sent me an article from...The Carver's Mill Patriot. The subject of the article was your sweater making and first of all I have to congratulate you on your efforts. Your parents must be very proud, and I can see a wonderful future for you in zoology...or perhaps knitting for that matter." He allowed himself a small chuckle. "At any rate, the reason I called...we have a young giraffe that seems to be having difficulty acclimating to the temperatures in the Northeast."

Becky's eyes drifted slightly at the words. "You mean she gets cold."

There was a moment. "Why, yes. How did you know it was a *she*?"

"I don't know," Becky said. "What's her name?"

"Her name is Daisy. We have some other animals you might want to look at as well, but for the moment, Daisy is our main concern."

...Limbo

The front door of the *Blair's Lawnmower and Repair* had two locks, an old antique deadbolt on the bottom and a new shiny key lock that Charlie had bought at Lowes on top. Both were locked up tight. Her little trick with the credit card worked on the new lock but not on the old one.

Around at the back, the slide-down bay door was locked, too. It had a big sliding bolt that locked it down. You could see it in the bottom right corner of the window but unless you smashed the glass, there wasn't much you could do about it.

Becky thought for a moment, her brain humming. There had to be a way to get in without messing everything up. She tried to think like Charlie and on a hunch, she walked around to the side of the garage and found a little concrete extension on the back of the building. A sign on the door said, *Ask Manager for a Key!* She wiggled the doorknob. It was open. Better yet, inside the restroom there was another door which said, *Employees Only*. Her Texaco card fished around for barely half a second before she found the brass pin that held the door shut. No bells started ringing. No sirens went off. She thought, *I'm in!*

She found the circuit breaker box behind the door to his

little office and flipped the switches on one-at-a-time. A bank of fluorescents flickered on in the show room. The air compressor in the back bay rumbled to life, then the DVD that had been playing in the office went back to where it had left off. Ray Charles was crooning "Just a sad sweet song...keeps Georgia on my mind." It had never felt intimate listening to the song before. She thought, *you're a softie after all* and smiled at the revelation. With the music on, it felt as if a small essence of Charlie was residing in the shop, watching over things. Maybe she'd learn something about him from the songs he'd picked...

As it turned out, opening the front door from the inside was almost as hard as trying to break in from the outside. The little brass knob on the lock didn't work and she finally found a small brass key inside the cash register. It was in the penny drawer. The easy part was now officially over. Now...how to run a business about which you know absolutely nothing.

From eight am to eleven, no one stopped in, no one called. She kept walking outside and looking around to see if there was some extra sign she should be hanging up or dragging out to the road. At eleven-thirty she scribbled a *back in ten minutes* note and stuck it on the front door. She drove down to check mail and put a sign in her own window. It said, *Due to a family emergency, please call or stop by Blair Lawnmower if you need yarn, t-shirts, or want to take a dance class.*

Back at Charlie's place, she was just unlocking the front door when a truck pulled down into the lot. She recognized it. It was Bert Emmerling's. Today he looked neither like a fireman or a vet. He looked like a farmer, old jeans, old knock-about boots cowboy boots and a grey sweatshirt. His face was still that of some regal predatory bird, however. He was a hawk or an eagle. Just the way he looked around at things, taking them in at a glance. He looked at her standing in the front door and caught her eye for barely a tenth of a second. But in that tenth, a lot of communicating went on.

"How'd you get in?" he asked, following her in the door. His voice wasn't accusatory, just curious.

"Oh, it was locked-up tight," Becky said. "Except there's a little door inside the bathroom that says, *Employees Only*."

Emmerling nodded, still looking around at the shop. It looked to be instinctive, perhaps from having made so many fire inspections in his time. He gazed into the back bay and then looked at her. "So. You opened up for him."

Becky looked up at his eyes. He seemed intent on *not* looking her in the eye for any length of time. "Yeah."

Emmerling glanced in her eyes again and then he looked up at the orange chainsaws on the pegboard. "That's good," he said.

"Why are you here?" Becky asked.

"Same reason." Despite himself, he looked in her eye for maybe a whole second before looking away. "I figured..."

"I get it," Becky said softly.

Emmerling's eyes darted to hers. "No, you don't. You *really* don't."

"Sorry. I don't."

Emmerling winced at the words. "It's not that. It's just that...you've never gone through this sort of thing before."

And you have... her mind whispered. *Now I get it.* "He left half of a sticky bun in his office. And I made some coffee," she said instead.

Emmerling put his hand up like a cop. "Nah, that's all right. Charlie doesn't need two of us here."

Becky nodded. "It's pecan praline. It's not stale yet, but by the end of the day... I'll just have to chuck it."

Emmerling looked at her. "Yeah, okay."

She poured two coffees. He took his black. It figured. She

poured in about a half cup with cream and stirred two sugars in while Emmerling watched.

"Ya know, that's no longer coffee," he said. "It's like that Starbuck's crap. Frappa-mocha-chino-something or other."

Becky grinned at him. "I know. I *love* Starbucks. Whenever I go there, I order frappa-mocha-chino-something-or-other. It's great."

Emmerling looked at Becky. "And you love Charlie?"

Becky's eyes got huge. "Wow, we're really getting right to it, aren't we? Are you his father or something?" She saw Emmerling wince at the words. "Sorry. You've got some back-story I don't know about and I'm accidentally pronging you. I don't mean to. But asking me whether I love Charlie or not. Well, it's none of your damned business."

Emmerling nodded. But then he grinned. "You already answered my question."

Pain

This time, when Charlie awoke, he could feel every square inch of the burns on his body, right down to a few square inches on the side of his stomach where his shirt must have ridden up. At that exact moment, the pain wasn't that great, though he could tell it was artificial. They had put something, maybe some kind of Novocain, covering everything, plus he had that dreamy, ethereal feeling that he'd been drugged to the hilt, probably oxycodone. It felt good not to be in hideous, excruciating pain for the moment and he hoped he could just drift back off to sleep and oblivion.

    A nurse was changing the bandages on his right shoulder and it felt freezing cold the moment she removed them. It wasn't bad, it didn't hurt so much as he could tell. It would be off-the-scale, if he wasn't all drugged up. He looked past the nurse to see an elegant blonde woman sitting in the only other chair in the room. It was Susan.

    "Hi," he whispered as alertly as he could.

    "Hi," Susan whispered back.

    "How long have you been here?"

    "Oh, not long. Maybe a few hours."

    "That's a pretty long time," Charlie said.

"How ya feeling?"

"Oh. Well... Not too bad, I guess. As long as nothing wears off that they're treating me with. But as soon as anything starts to wear off... It's a good thing I don't believe in Hell. I'm getting sort of an idea what it'd be like, roasting in Hell for eternity. It seems kind of extreme for not picking the right religion." They looked at each other and laughed, quietly. "Remember those deep searching discussions we used to have?"

Susan allowed herself another chuckle. "Remember what Becky used to say? She said, if she was dying and a priest was there, asking her to renounce the Devil..."

"Yeah. She said that probably wouldn't be a good time to be making enemies..."

"Yeah, just in case." And they both laughed.

"You okay?" Susan asked.

"I have no idea." He looked at the nurse, who was now rewrapping his bandages. "Am I okay? Am I going to live?"

"You are definitely going to live," she said, tucking in his sheets and fluffing the pillows. "You'll be back, saving the world before you know it."

Charlie looked at the nurse and then at Susan. "S'cuse me, did I piss you off somehow?"

"Oh, not at all. The truth is, my house is less than a quarter of a mile from Furlong Getty. They're saying if the main tank had gone up, it could have destroyed... Well, there's a good chance I wouldn't have a house now."

"Oh... So that's a *good* thing."

"That's a very good thing. Only, it's never good to joke about the Devil, particularly when you're...in a hospital."

"Sorry," Charlie said.

"Oh, that's quite alright. Thank you very much for saving my house...and maybe my family. Bless you."

165

After she left, Susan dragged the chair over next to his bed. "That was weird," Charlie said, looking at the doorway the nurse had just gone through.

"Do you get that a lot?"

"What, that? No, almost never. Usually, it's something like, thanks for saving my bass boat, or my workshop or something. Once in awhile, people will get a little weird. But you learn to slough off that sort of thing. We go out. We're a team. That's the main thing. We take turns. We spray a whole shitload of water, and...sometimes we get lucky."

"You ran into a wall of fire. I saw the footage, Charlie."

"That sort of thing is deceptive. It looks worse than it is. They lay down a suppressing wall of water. You've got as much chance of drowning as getting burned."

"Oh... Well, that explains everything," Susan said in a strange sarcastic way. "Do you think, in some weird kind of way, this is a result of Mr. Nichols?"

"That's not fair," Charlie said, glaring at her now. "And it's a low blow. It's beneath you."

"Oh, God, I'm sorry. It wasn't meant to be a cut. You were there. I was there."

"And Becky was there," Charlie said. "So, what does that prove? You're famous. You do something special. You create a whole world and people pay money to enter your little world."

"You got suckered," Susan replied. "It's a lot different than it looks. It's lonely. When I'm writing, I'm completely alone."

"Maybe. But, you're special. You do something *special*."

"Charlie, look at what just unfolded in the last five minutes. You saved that nurse's house, and possibly her family as well. That's real. You did that. Nobody can take it away from you. I'd trade all my..."

"Stop," Charlie said, "before you say something stupid and

full of bullshit. You could train a monkey to run into a wall of flames."

Susan looked at him.

"Okay, maybe not a monkey. A monkey would be too smart to do that. But, you get what I'm saying."

"Do you think it's possible that Mr. Nichols affected both of us?"

Charlie laughed harshly. "Gee, ya think?"

Out in the parking lot, Susan ran right into Becky, as she climbed out of her little truck. They peered at each other.

"How is he?" Becky asked.

"They've got him pretty well drugged-up."

"Good. That's exactly what he needs right now. How does he look?"

"He looks just like Charlie."

What Is Heroism?

Up on the second floor of the barn, that was the hub and nerve center for The Carver's Mill Patriot, Cubby sat at his little nook, looking out at what was the wrong side of the barn. Buckingham Mountain rose steeply on the backside and at that angle, the only view was a point-blank view of some rocks, dead leaves and the trunks of some trees. Occasionally, a deer would wander into view and it was so close, if the window was open he could have thrown his popcorn and hit it on the head.

    Right now, he was musing, thinking about the essay he wanted to write. To the untrained observer, he might have looked like someone just blowing off time. But there was something about the way his swivel chair swung back and forth that told Sam he needed to be left alone.

    After about forty minutes, Sam drifted by to see what the topic was. "How's it going?" he asked neutrally.

    "It's going," Cubby replied, though it was unconvincing.

    Sam pulled up the chair that they used for stacking things to be copied. He sat down hard and yawned, which was pure bullshit. "It's a difficult topic," he offered, off-handedly. "It's not what you think."

"Yeah. No shit. I Googled it and it was no help at all. The definitions are just what you'd expect from Google. But then when you go to You Tube, not one single guy wants to be called a hero. Not one. In fact, it seems to seriously piss them off. Why would it piss them off?"

"I don't know," Sam said. "I don't think anyone knows, not for sure, but there was a time when I was TDY in Osan, Korea. There was a fighter pilot that was having hydraulic trouble and, I guess, one way or the other, his plane was going to land real soon."

Sam looked over at Cubby, but then resumed peering out the window. "He could have taken the easy way and just punched-out and he would have been safe. But then, *after* you punch-out, you have no idea where your plane is going to crash. It might just go into the trees, or, it could be something horrible."

"What'd he do?"

"He brought it in, dead-stick and no hydraulic pressure at all. I understand it's nearly impossible to steer a plane without hydraulics. But he managed to do it.

"When he got out, there were about twenty or thirty people crowded around, clapping and cheering. He started to climb out and then he didn't want to. Nobody knew what was happening. Turns out, in the process of dead-sticking it, he'd pissed his flight suit, big time. He was embarrassed about the wet spot on the front of his flight suit.

"They finally pulled up a ladder on wheels to the cockpit so he could be a little more discreet. His buddy went up to get him and they whispered back and forth for a minute and then his buddy turned to the group. He yelled, *'Pete just pissed his pants...in the process of saving a 12-million-dollar fighter and maybe half of Osan. And he's embarrassed. Can I hear a big Fuck that shit?'* Well, the group started into a chant of, *Fuck that shit.* I think what it boils down to is, the people who do these weird acts of bravery don't do it because they're brave in the comic book or superhero sense. They do what they do, in spite of being scared shitless, or in this case, pissless. I think, maybe it's so serious to them, they don't want a pat on the head. They don't want to be thought of as a superhero...or a hero, or anything. These people do what they've programmed themselves to do, usually in advance."

Cubby nodded and began pulling himself in closer to the keyboard. "Yeah. If you think about it, all the super heroes have super powers. Bullets bounce off them and they can leap tall buildings. Most guys I know don't have that stuff going for them. And maybe they piss their pants afterward or they start bawling, or they just look out the window. But they do what they do...anyway, not because they were fearless, but because they weren't."

The Healing Process

Against doctors' orders, Charlie left the hospital after a mere nine days of what he called, *lying on his ass and doing absolutely nothing.* The only reason they allowed him to go home was he promised, on his love for his Corvette, that he would rest one half of every day and only do light work. The doctors and nurses over at Doylestown hospital had no idea what Charlie considered half a day (12 hours) or what he considered light work to be, (anything where he wasn't going into a burning building).

At his own insistence, he learned how to do his own PICC line so that nurses wouldn't have to come out every day. It was only 12 steps, but each one had to be perfect. When the nurses asked him if he could do perfect procedures every single day, he just peered at them from behind the bandages... and they understood.

The first week, he resembled a Far Side cartoon, a mummy-like bandage man, with two holes for eyes, a mouth and a big pink nose sticking out. The second week home, he switched to special Band-Aids which still covered most of his face and one of his arms. It was a debate whether he looked worse as a mummy or as a really tasteless commercial for Band-Aids.

Becky had been doing half-days the first week when he was the living mummy. She taught her knitting classes over in the corner behind the chainsaw display, and the dance classes took up most of the main showroom. Charlie tried to keep out of the action as much as possible, only coming to help when there was a technical question about carburetors or chainsaw tensioning.

On the second week, when he was Band-Aid Man, she walked in the door, stopped in her tracks and said, "God, you look awful!"

"Thanks," said Charlie, though she didn't seem to get the message.

"No, seriously. You really look terrible! Do you think you should be here?"

"Well, I was about to say that I'm feeling a bit better today, but...a little piece of advice: don't ever consider going into nursing. You're really awful."

"Well...you're not so hot yourself," she said, mostly on autopilot. "Seriously, are you okay? It looks like you'd be in mega pain."

"It's the price of being a hero."

"Okay, it looks like you want to run this into the ground. Okay, you're *not* a hero. You're not even close to being a hero. If a hero happened to wander into the shop, you'd have to fall on your knees and then genuflect."

"Let's see, I'm not that religious. That's when you cross yourself before you eat dinner."

"No. Man, you really aren't religious, are you?"

"I'm spiritual," Charlie answered. "So what's a genuflect?"

"It's when you do... It's sort of like a plié."

"Okay, now you're giving me a headache."

"It's sort of like a little dip, a little bow."

"Then why didn't you just..?"

"By the way, I signed you up for one of the dance classes. There's one tonight."

Charlie picked up a pencil and quietly broke it in half. "I *really* hope you're joking."

"Nope, this one's for real. A handful of the women saw you minding the store and...they think you're neat." She gave him a little cutesy smile just to make it more annoying.

"I'm neat? What? Did everybody suddenly get blind and stupid?"

"Neat," Becky repeated. "That and you saved half of Buckingham Township...because you're a... Gimme an "H" Gimme a ..."

"No way," Charlie said.

"Way," Becky countered. "Besides, I've been selling your stupid chainsaws and Whacky Blowers and...*stuff*. You owe me, buddy...big time."

And Then There Was Mom

Most of the time, eating alone in a motel room or a restaurant was not a big deal. When you're scheduled to pimp your book at one of the large chain bookstores, often there's a liaison assigned, usually a young woman, so as to insure no problems or misunderstandings.

The conversations are benign: how the weather is, who the manager of the bookstore is, or sometimes a run-down as to the style of the radio interviewer's personality. Sometimes a pamphlet of the better restaurants, sites to see, entertainment and such, and the conversation is terminated at the door to the motel or hotel where she'll be staying. She had learned quickly that there's a universal timing to swiping the magnetic card in the motel door to go from red to green. You have to be quick...but not too quick, and then there's the closing of the cold metal door behind you and facing rooms that are identically sterile and yet at the same time, comforting. There's a strange comfort in sameness.

The motel outside of New Hope was the first one in months where she was actually handed a brass key on a big plastic fob, *The New Hope Motel*, green letters on white plastic.

Tonight was a bit of a culinary splurge, not so much in quality, but in taste. Nothing was better than five pieces of Colonel Sanders' original recipe, with three biscuits and a six-pack of Genesse Cream ale from WaWas. It was a blast from the past, sitting in Becky's '55 Chevy and listening to what were now golden oldies.

She had discovered quickly that food and booze, music, stand-up comedy and even first-run movies on cable were pale versions of what they were like with someone with you. It wasn't so bad when you were in a strange town. Your mind accepted the loneliness as part of the deal.

But, being back to her old stompin' grounds somehow made everything even lonelier. She popped the tab on the Genny and took a long drink, pretending that Becky was sitting on the bed, flipping through the channels looking for some sexy R-rated movie to watch and chuckle at. *Oh, here's one we gotta see!* she'd say. *I think this is the one where the guy's got a great big dick and everyone always thinks they're turning him on.* And they'd giggle and snort beer out their noses. Well, that wasn't true. She'd never quite learned how to get the beer to go out her nose, like Becky did. She was a natural. Funny, to see a few grey hairs just beginning at her temples.

In a ritualistic way, she keyed the remote and clicked through fifty stations so fast, that even if there'd been something worth watching, there was no chance in hell she'd catch it. She took a large drumstick and went over to her laptop. At least there was a story to disappear into. Strange that the loneliest part of writing was also the one place where she wasn't alone...well, at least in her mind.

An old '60s song floated up in her mind from her extreme childhood. Sly and the Family Stone, singing *Stand*, a really upbeat song about a controversial topic. *Stand! Don't you know that you are Free? Well, at least in your mind if you want to be. Stand....*

She looked around the motel room, the shades pulled tightly shut, so there was no chance anyone could look in. *Stand*, her mind sang softly, and for a second, she actually considered standing up to make some kind of point. But there really wasn't much point when you're all by yourself. She took another sip of Genny and mimicked Becky's voice, "Yeah, but *you're* the one who got the hell out of here. You're our escapee! You're the *famous* one, being interviewed on Entertainment Tonight. Yeah, way to go, girl!"

"Yeah, if you only knew, Becks," she whispered, though she was glad that she didn't. At the very least, she had the reputation sewn up.

And then there was Mom. It was hard to tell just how bad it was. Most of the time, maybe 70 or 80 percent of the time, she was pretty much what you'd expect, a couple of cataracts that should probably be taken care of. She looked too skinny, though that was something she'd always strived for. Mom was a Jenkins and Dad was a Taylor. The Taylors were all skinny and the Jenkins were all buxom. You always want what you don't have.

But then, even in the couple of visits, there'd been moments where it seemed as if she didn't even know her. They'd just sit and look at each other, and there was an emptiness behind the eyes. *Anybody home?*

She took the last chicken leg into the bathroom and ate it while looking at herself in the mirror. It was a photo shoot, and cameras were clicking like baby machinegun fire. She posed with a hunk of chicken hanging out of her teeth. She growled and tried to look like a sex kitten. She opened her blouse and ran the chicken leg around and around on her breasts. "I'm not buyin' it," she said to her image. And then a different expression, the confrontational one with the pinched eyebrows. "What's the matter with you?" she whispered. "You're not a cold fish. You can slug a beer with the best of them. At the falls, you took your clothes off before anyone, even Becky. Cold fish don't do that...do they?"

One thing that the writing had done for her, because of all the plotting and chapterizations, she could run a scene in her mind, just to see how it would play out. And then she could compare it against another scene and then pick a winner.

    She pulled down the sheets on the bed and fluffed a pillow. The scene: Mom's house versus spending the night at the motel. Her house was three miles away, if that, and she could stop off at Wawa's again and pick up a half-gallon of Moose Tracks and some whipped cream. Mom had always loved ice cream, any kind, any time. It might help her get a little appetite going, too.

    They could talk about...God, what the hell could they talk about? There wasn't much talking anymore, not like it used to be. Now, Mom would share an anecdote and she'd nod and comment. And then they'd trade places. It wasn't really communicating, it was something else. She picked up the phone and stared at it for a long moment. "Hello, Mom?"

"Susan? Is that you?"

"It's me, Mom."

"Oh... Are you still in town, or did you fly off somewhere?"

"Still in town. New Hope Motel. Say, I was wondering, do you still like Moose Tracks?"

"Moose Tracks?"

"Yeah, the ice cream."

"Good lord, it must be close to a decade since I've had Moose Tracks."

"You up for some company?"

"That would be *wonderful*, dear!"

This time, when she came up to the door, she didn't ring the bell or knock. She opened the door a crack and stuck her head in. "Hello! Anybody home?" If things had truly been like the old days, she wouldn't think to do even that. Some things change forever.

And for a good ten minutes it was bustling time, bustling in the kitchen, getting bowls and spoons out the cabinets and yes, the dishes were exactly where they'd always been, soup bowls, second shelf on the right. "You want *the sauce*?" she giggled next to the fridge.

"Oh, my. Do you think we should? It's soooo..."

"Yummy," Susan said. "When's the last time?"

"Years."

"Well, that's too long!" she said, mimicking an old smoked sausage commercial, and the next five minutes were spent digging out the box of cocoa, a pinch of salt, a teaspoon of instant coffee, a splash of rum, two cups of sugar and a half-stick of butter. Slow heat for five minutes and...*heaven*.

Between the two of them, they polished off the top half of the Moose Tracks carton and for awhile things really were old times. She was sixteen again, and had her stuffed animals on the shelf over her bed, protecting her from everything.

"Sooo, tell me, dear...truthfully. What's it like being a celebrity?"

She looked at her mother's face. It was an easy read these days. Or maybe, it was the fact that she'd exercised her writing instincts so well, and so often, that she could just read people better...faster, more intimately. It was a blessing as well as a curse.

"Well, overall... I'd have to say that it's pretty damn good! It beats road construction or taking it to the streets!"

She could tell in a fraction of a second that her joke had completely missed its mark. "What I mean is, I get to jet around all over the country. They pick me up at the airport and take me out to dinner...and then the next day, I sit at a table and autograph my books about a kajillion times."

"That sounds like heaven!"

"Yeah, it sounds like it," Susan agreed.

Step, Step, Together

Charlie was the second to arrive. A dull orange lozenge of a sun had just drifted behind Holicong Mountain and the clouds looked like they belonged down in the Keys or maybe the Caribbean. Swirls of shocking pink blending into tendrils of the most subtle violet, and all laced and dipped in gold. It was almost worth pulling over and taking a picture. Almost.

    It was strange to see his shop lit up at night and it seemed like an orange light, not the utility bulbs he'd put in. It'd be just the sort of thing Becky would do to create...atmosphere. It was stranger still hearing Amy Winehouse broadcasting into the night air. He stopped to see if he could name that tune. It was an old hit, *You Know I'm No Good.* He smiled. He could just imagine Becky standing in front of her mirror singing along, *I told ya, I was trouble...*

    He managed to open the door without making the chimes clang at all. But, then he noticed that Becky had removed them entirely. Not a bad call, really. He'd never given it much thought, but they were annoying, and then there was the walking up and hanging them back up again.

    From the counter, she spotted him instantly and was over with a Loretta Young flourish, that was very fifties. *Nah, not*

Loretta Young, his mind corrected. Becky was wound too tight. More like, Sandra Bullock, only softer, and maybe a little less butch. He could tell, just by looking at her that she could climb on a Harley and do a proper job of burnin' out without looking stupid.

"Hey stud," Becky called, deliberately overplaying a role. "Don't you look...studly tonight!"

Charlie groaned, though he was almost getting used to it.

"Let's see now, black leather sports jacket. I give that an A. An A for the black turtle, and jeans that fit *just* right and a little tight...A+." She looked to the floor. "Theoretically, I suppose you can dance in engineer's boots. Theoretically."

"Too clunky?"

"Waaay too clunky. Plus, if you miss and step on somebody, you just might seriously take 'em out. Do you have any holes in your socks?"

"Uhmm... I don't think so."

"Okay then."

They had exactly enough time to confirm that his socks were not holey before the first couple arrived. Becky gave a micro-critique as each student filtered in. The first one, she whispered: "No problem here. If you combine their ages, you're probably up around a hundred and fifty. But they're dating, in there swinging. You don't have to do squat with them."

Charlie ventured a question. "Is there someone coming tonight that I do have to do squat with?"

She punched him on the shoulder and snickered. "Of course! Why do you think I snookered you into coming here?"

He managed to say, "Are you going to tell me, or are you going to make me guess?" but the next student was already in the door. She looked to be forty-ish and the word that came to mind, one of Charlie's words, was floozy. What made the whole thing interesting was, she must have been all of four-foot- ten, and that was in platform heels. She looked over at the two of them and walked straight over. "Is this the guy?" she called out from ten feet away.

"Could be," Becky called out. "It depends on how things..."

"Okay, I got dibs on him." She came over and had to look straight up to peer in his face. "This is your lucky night," she declared.

By seven forty-five, Becky was just putting on the first song of the evening. She walked out in the middle of the floor and made her welcoming announcement. "Okay, everybody! Here we are again and as usual we're gonna kick off with a song that you can do just about anything to. You can stand there, wave your arms and shake your booty. You can stomp around on the floor and sing along. Believe it or not, you can slow dance, Lindy, and if you're a flower child from the '60s you can sway around and pretend you're stoned out of your mind. There's no way you can screw up this song!" She retrieved a little remote control from her skirt and pressed a button. "The name of this song is....Dirty Water!!! Enjoy!!!"

A moment later, the heaviest bass guitar in Pennsylvania threatened to knock the socket wrench displays off the back wall. Then heavy simple drums pounding out the beat, followed by a completely raw harmonica, all welded to the same heavy four-four beat. Even the tiny bird-like couple that had been huddled near the weed eater rack got the message. The old man must have been eighty if he was a day, but they were chug-a-lugging out toward the center of the floor.

Charlie was the only one who seemed to be unaffected. He was leaning against the wall with arms folded and watching.

Becky caught his eye and waved for him to come over.

He just looked at her and shook his head.

She waved again...nothing. Then she yelled, "A deal's a deal! C'mon out or you owe me nine hundred bucks for five days working your shop!"

Charlie thought about it for a moment. He mouthed, *Nine hundred bucks?* And she yelled at him, "That's right, Studly. Nine hundred big ones. Make up your mind!"

Charlie came out with a weird expression. It was hard to tell if he was going to try to whack her...or more likely, walk past her and just leave, or... He came up to her, sneered at her nose-to-nose and then began a weird dance maneuver she'd never seen before. He was smooth, but in the middle of being smooth, it looked like he was crunching invisible barbells with his arms. Then a little dip.

"Well, okay then," Becky said as she instantly matched his moves. A minute into it, she called out, "I've never seen this before. What's this called?"

"Uhh... It's called Charlie at fifteen trying to figure out how to dance."

Two minutes and ten seconds later, Dirty Water faded to what was supposed to be a slow one. It wasn't a good idea to give your dance students heart attacks. But then, when the music stopped, half of them were still *groovin'* to the beat. She reached into her pocket and clicked a couple of times. The next song was called, *Tainted Love*, a song that truly lends itself to foot-stomping.

It wasn't until an hour later that the tempo slowed down to something a bit more romantic. Becky pushed a tiny button on her remote and then batted her eyes at Charlie.

"What? What is that supposed to mean?" Charlie grinned.

"Wow, you really *have* been out of the action awhile." A half-second later, Becky's four speakers began with a chorus of classical violins, followed by Etta James crooning, *At Last*.

"Yeah, well... And you don't play fair. Etta James is the

big guns."

"C'mere, sailor. You're new around here."

Charlie stopped. "Why do you always have to make everything into a joke? This is a serious song. It's a beautiful song. I don't understand..."

Instead of arguing with him, she covered the distance between them in three fluid steps. She was right in front of him now. He could feel the heat from her body radiating into him."You're warm," he said softly. "I can feel..." and then he stopped. "And please don't turn that around into something weird."

Awkwardly, he put his arms around her, as if she were a porcelain statue, about to break with the slightest touch. "Is this okay?" he whispered

She nuzzled into his shoulder and closed her eyes. "It's not okay...it's perfect."

Au contraire

Cubby awoke with a headache, which, in itself, wasn't terribly unusual. First off, Sluggo always managed to ooze up onto his bed at about one in the morning. For a morbidly obese bulldog, Sluggo was amazingly adept at not jumping on the bed. Instead, he moved his rolls of fat in slow motion as if a form of osmosis was taking place. Once up, he crept quietly under the covers using only his toenails to propel him. Unfortunately, the moment Sluggo, himself, fell asleep, two things happened: First, he began snoring louder than any human can snore. Second, his large and copious GI tract began to relax into its own meditative state. And with that came the farts, capable of emptying a room in ten seconds.

The farts were bad enough to cause a headache but other things were contributing as well. The blind date at Earl's Restaurant in Peddler's Village turned out to be more a major disappointment. Oh, Roy was a textbook beautiful Adonis, and it was common knowledge that he had done a photo shoot with GQ a bunch of years ago. This was entirely possible, though he also had an annoying way of smirking after sex, as if he were cutting you the big break. For a gay man, there was a certain point in your life where an invisible line in the sand had to be drawn. After that line reared its ugly head, Roy was "gone with the Schwinn" as Cubby liked to say. And then there were the tequila boilermakers. After four of them, he made a note to himself to do a special Bon Appetite Column dedicated to just how dangerous tequila was in general as well as how lethal tequila boiler makers (TBs) were, if taken in groups of four.

Cubby's head felt as if someone had thrown a cherry bomb

inside his head and then lit the fuse. Lastly, there was the story, which had started out as a little charmer of a melancholy puff piece and then proceeded to grow warts and tentacles. At the moment, he had no idea what to do and he'd used up about all of Sam's "extra grace time" to get the thing done.

Becky and Charlie...and perhaps even Susan would have been happy to help, except for the fact that they happened to be the focal points of the article. And then there were other complications, involving who actually owned Mrs. Davis's manuscript now that she was deceased. In the space of a few days, the world had grown uglier and certainly more complicated. And with all this in mind, he decided to drop in on Charlie for some man-to-man advice.

Entering the shop, his nose immediately gave him the first clue that things were different. No clanging chimes for one thing. Then he sniffed the air the way a master chef might sniff the nuances of a Chicken Cordon Bleu. *First sniff*...Pledge, 12-15 hours old. *Second* sniff, a complete lack of any underlying grease, gasoline or oil vapors. There was a strong aroma of Mop and Glo drifting up from the floor, and there was something else that was hard to pin down. He closed his eyes and sniffed again. Dust, a complete lack of dust. None whatsoever. *Becky*, he mouthed to himself. In a million, million years, Charlie would never dust anything. He'd even explained it to him long, long ago. He even remembered the words. *See, it's like this, if you start dusting stuff, it's never over. You're gonna have to go back every six months or so and do it again. It's a losin' game.*

"Hey Cub, what's up?" Charlie called from behind the counter.

"Hey..." Cubby called back. He looked over at his childhood friend/ dreamboat and saw, not a scroungy grease-stained man, but a man in a black turtleneck sweater with clean hands. His eyes drifted two degrees to the left and he noted a black leather coat hanging on a nail. And not a motorcycle or bomber jacket, but a genuine leather sports coat. He did a little quick calculation as to what to say. *A little good natured ribbing? This time...maybe not.*

Cubby pulled up one of the two barstools in front to the counter, slid on and nearly slid off again. Someone had Pledged that, too. He looked up, caught Charlie's eyes and for a moment they just stared at each other. "What's up?" Charlie said again, though in a softer voice.

Cubby groaned. "You don't want to hear."

"You get fired?"

Cubby looked slightly hurt. "No... Why would you think...? Actually, I had my first blind date in what must be a century."

"Didn't go well?"

"Oh, the guy was gorgeous, much better than you. You're kinda hunky, sorta like Wolverine in the X-Men. This guy was more like Rob Lowe. Almost pretty."

"Hold on there, Cub, you're already telling me way more than I want to know."

"Sorry. It wasn't just that, it was other stuff, too, but the reason I'm here is... I wish Mrs. Davis had just left the writing to the writers."

Charlie sat down on his slightly higher barstool on the other side of the counter. "I get it. So, what you're saying is, the writing stinks?"

"*Au contraire, mon ami.* If her writing sucked it'd be easy. We could just slide the thing in some desk drawer and toast her with a beer."

"I get it. So, what's the problem?"

Cubby looked at him in a way he never used on Charlie. It

was stern, business-like. "The problem is, it's just possible she's onto something."

"What? You mean us? Me and Becky and Susan?"

"Yes. Pretty much."

"Because Mr. Nichols died."

Cubby hesitated. He glanced at Charlie, but then he stared at his fingernails. They were a little too long, but then he glanced around the room as if there might be some answers hiding on the walls and ceiling. "I think this is where it gets a little complicated, or maybe a little muddy."

"Okay, Cub, it's not like I haven't thought about this. I have. I think all of us have. But the thing is, and the thing nobody's mentioned, is the fact that the three of us weren't the only ones on the bus. There were at least twenty or thirty other kids on it, too. They also crashed into the water. They could have drowned, too. They saw Mr. Nichols, too. Things happen, Cub. It's just a fact."

Cubby frowned through the whole sermon, though his eyebrows knitted together with every word. "Sure. And if that's how you choose to handle this, it sure-as-hell is your prerogative."

"I don't think anyone's choosing to handle anything. It's just what happened, that's all."

"I understand. So, when you and Becky and Susan were trying to save Mr. Nichols with that flute and the water kept coming up, and you saw him die, you're saying the fact that you weren't successful in saving him...that didn't have any effect on you?"

Charlie stood up abruptly. His eyes were already wet and trickling tears. His hands were clenched into fists. "Okay, don't fuck with me, Cubby."

Cubby raised his hand in retreat. "Hey, I'm sorry. You know me. In a million years, I wouldn't want to fuck with you, hurt you in any way. For one thing, you'd just kill me and then I'd be dead...okay?"

Charlie glared for another handful of seconds, but then he deflated back onto the chair. He even chuckled the world's tiniest chuckle. "Yeah, well, you're right about that."

Before any more time went by, Cubby said, "And with all that, I have a favor to ask. And I'm serious. Take a second to think before you say anything, okay? Promise?"

"What's the favor?" he asked, back on defensive.

"I'd really like to meet with you and Becky and Susan. I was thinking, The Gent. My treat. Order whatever you want. Could you do me this one favor?"

Charlie looked past him, out the front door window. A line of cars was stuck behind a truck pulling a bulldozer. The line was going about ten miles an hour. "I don't know. And I sure as hell can't speak for Becky and Susan."

"Would you, please, please, please ask them for me?"

"Why can't you do it?"

"Because you're the kingpin, Charlie. If you don't go, they won't either. You know that."

The line was still trudging by, though even slower now. "Okay, I can try...but no promises, okay?"

The Country Gent

As usual, Charlie made a point of arriving first, no matter where he was going. His big Dodge Ram pulled smartly into The Gent's tiny parking lot. It paused for a moment and then deftly backed up against the split-rail fence at the back of the lot. The day Charlie had joined Midway Fire he'd made a point of never nosing into a parking lot...just in case.

Becky arrived next in her cutey-pie pickup. She pulled in next to Charlie's Dodge, considered for a fraction of a second backing it up and turning it around, and then decided it wasn't worth it.

Cubby arrived in a white late model Audi and parked in the next row in front of Charlie. Susan was close behind in a silver Prius rental. She parked one space over from Becky.

"How long you been waiting?" Cubby called from 20 feet.

"'Bout forty minutes," Charlie called back.

Cubby looked suddenly panic stricken till he saw Charlie smile. "Did I say forty minutes? It was more like forty seconds, Cub."

Inside, some of the old props and ornaments had managed to survive from the *good ole days*. The lighting over the tables was still antiquey-clear bulbs with orange filaments dangling from spindly wires that looked like they were going to burn the place down at any moment. There were still a half dozen sepia prints of Lahaska in the '20s and '30s. It seemed like everyone wore hats and suspenders back then, and horses still had a place, pulling lumber wagons at Buckingham Lumber. But there were waitresses now, pretty and young, and in addition to the smell of stale beer, there was the smell of new carpeting and wood construction.

Over behind the bar, Lou Terkel, the proprietor, was washing dishes in his jeans and one of his ever present plaid shirts. If you were tallying the new and the old, Lou was definitely on the old side of the tally sheet. He spotted them in the mirror behind the bar and waved at them. "Hey there! You know the drill. Find a seat anywhere and make yourselves at home." Then he spied Susan. "Hey! Do my eyes deceive me or is it Susan Sorato, novelist extraordinaire?"

"Nice to see you, Mr. Terkel!" Susan waved back.

"Oh, Susan, please don't say that. Makes me feel like I'm a hundred years old. From here on in, it's Lou. Deal?"

"Deal," Susan called back.

Charlie spied the best seat in the house, the only bay window in the whole place, looking out on the new area for outside dining. The nice thing about the spot, was the chairs were in a semi-circle so everyone could watch what was going on outside.

Charlie pulled out a chair for Becky while Cubby did the same for Susan. A pitcher of Genny was ordered and delivered and the first order of the day was a toast. Charlie raised his mug and looked around the table. "Okay, we've got a famous novelist, a newspaper columnist, and a mad yarn bomber here. Somebody should be able to come up with a good toast."

They all looked around. "Toooo...getting laid in the back of a '57 Chevy!" Becky sang out.

"Perfect!" Charlie called out as they all clinked mugs.

Seven minutes after that, a bucket of barbecued wings arrived, still sizzling, along with a basket of warm garlic toast and four salads. And for at least ten minutes the conversation descended to grunts and *mmmm*s and proclamations that *The Gent* still had the best ribs and wings North of the Mason Dixon Line. And then slowly the tempo began to change. Susan pushed back from the table and declared that this was the first time she'd been able to let her guard down in a year...maybe three.

"Sooo, it's hard to relax when you're doing a tour?" Charlie asked.

Susan took a quick sip and considered the question. "I doubt that anyone's ever taken a poll, but, I'd be willing to bet that no woman who travels alone is ever completely relaxed. It might be hard-wiring."

"But then, it balances out, right?" Becky said. "I mean, how many people get to go on TV and be interviewed?"

"Yeah," Susan droned," but 90% of the time, it isn't TV, it's some radio station or some big bookstore."

"Yeah, but that's pretty damned big, too," Becky said. "Let's take a poll around the table. How many here have been interviewed on a radio station?"

Everyone chuckled, though Charlie's eyes were going serious. "Yeah, nothing sounds all that great when you describe it from your own viewpoint, but...would you want to trade? How'd you like to spend an hour under a car, replacing brake linings and getting brake fluid dripping down in your eyes?"

It was Cubby who interrupted the flow and not all that smoothly. "So, why do you think Mrs. Davis wrote the book?"

"Nice gear-shifting, Cub. I think you lost a couple teeth off of second gear."

"Sorry."

"I think she saw something going on with us. I'm not sure she even understood it." Charlie took a long draft and looked around the table.

"Maybe not a first," Becky said. "Or maybe not ever. I mean, how many people here have finished it?" She looked around the table. "Yeah, I figured. I haven't either, but I'm pretty far into it and I'm not sure what the hell she's saying. It seems like she's real proud of us, but..."

"But what?"

"I don't know. It's like she hasn't made her mind up which metaphor we are. In the beginning, she's leaning on the three-legged milk stool to describe us."

"Sorry," Susan said, "There's things I'm savvy about, but milk stools aren't in my stable of metaphors."

"The thing about a milk stool..." Charlie said, "Well, any stool that has three legs can never be wobbly like a chair or a stool that has four legs. And that's mostly because...well, it's really simple but it sounds complicated. If you remember your high school geometry class, with two points you define a line. But with three points, you define a plane. And what that means is, a three-legged stool will never be wobbly because with three legs, it'll always be able to hit the ground."

Becky batted her eyes at Charlie. "You would have made a terrific high school teacher. All the girls would've had crushes on you, and they'd study *real, real* hard just to make sure you gave 'em an A."

"Except for the fact that I hate kids, I might have been, at least passable."

"You hate children?" Becky said.

"Yeah, pretty much, though the way you say it, it sounds like it's a bad thing. Actually, I don't hate all kids, just little stinky squirmy, screamy babies. And I don't care what you say, they all look pretty damn similar, only when someone shows you a picture of their baby, you have to say, *Oh, your baby is the prettiest baby I've ever seen.* And every single parent will agree with you. C'mon, do the math. Every baby can't be the prettiest baby in the world. Oh, and teenagers. Now, there are a few exceptions to this.

Some teenagers have to grow up real early...just because."

"Like you," Cubby said.

"Yeah, pretty much. I had too much to do. Too many responsibilities, so I wasn't allowed to be a dumbass."

"Are there any little kids you like?" Susan asked.

"Oh, sure. Once in a while, maybe from four to twelve you can find a cute kid, smart, funny. And maybe the kid hasn't gotten jaded yet. But then, they hit thirteen or around there, and they all turn into assholes."

"Maybe *icks-naay* on teaching high school," Becky said.

Susan said, "You were talking about metaphors with Mrs. Davis."

"That's right. She starts out with a milk stool, and then for about twenty pages in the middle, suddenly we're oysters. That's a pretty big jump, and then on page 273, we're not oysters or stools anymore, we're... Anybody care to guess?" asked Becky.

"We're splinters," Charlie said flatly. "Yeah, I saw that."

"Okay, not to pull rank," said Cubby, "but from what I'm hearing, so far, I'm the only one who's actually finished the book. I don't think Mrs. Davis was calling anybody a splinter. But she was considering the way that each of you handled Mr. Nichols' death. I think she meant that, *That*...was the splinter."

For a long moment, no one said anything, but then Becky said, "Charlie, you okay? You're dripping blood on your plate."

Charlie looked down. "Oh. Sorry 'bout that. I must have bit my tongue. It happens sometimes."

Dessert was a bit more of a question than in the olden days. "Anyone for dessert?" Cubby offered. "It's on me." He looked around the table. "Oh, come on. Way back when every one of us would have been licking our lips. Did we all suddenly...grow up?"

"Warm apple pie *à la mode*," Charlie said, snapping the menu closed.

"Times two," said Becky.

Susan looked up. "You won't believe this, but I don't think I've had a dessert in all the time I've been on the road. Does anyone want to split?"

"I suppose that's s'posed to be me," Cubby said, "only, I happen to really like apple pie...and ice cream." He sighed and thought seriously about it. "I'm ordering four desserts. Everybody just eat what you want."

Once the waitress left, Cubby had one more issue to thrash around. "Considering that Mrs. Davis was a widow with no children, there's a little matter of what to do with the manuscript. I don't know if you read her preface or not, but she makes clear mention of the fact that this is *your* story, the story of the three of you, and I can't see anyone coming up and claiming it. On this topic, I think it's appropriate if I defer to you, Susan. Being as you're already a published writer, you have a lot more experience with this sort of thing than any of us. Any suggestions?"

Susan had been very much enjoying what was left of the melted ice cream. She'd switched from a fork to a spoon and was downing every last drop. She looked down at her spoon and thought for a moment. "It's true to some degree. I'm published. But, I'm published with the books *I've* written, no one else's. I have no idea what to do."

Becky caught her eye. "Do you think you could show it to your editor or something? Is that out of line?"

"I don't think it's out of line so much as...it's just plain weird. If we did get it published...what then? I wouldn't feel right getting the money."

"Since this is theoretical, would it be possible to split it up somehow?" Becky continued.

"Sure. I mean, I guess so. On the off-chance, what if it took off? What if it went viral?" Cubby asked.

Charlie was still dabbing his tongue with a paper napkin, but he managed to say, "I don't think there's much chance in that."

Out in the parking lot, everyone split off a little quicker than they had gotten together. Lots of waving and yelling from fifty feet. As Becky unlocked her little truck, she looked over at Charlie. "Say..."

"What?"

"About my scarf. When do I get it?"

Charlie had already opened the door to the truck. He looked inside and then debated whether to climb in, or walk around to where Becky was parked. After three seconds he slammed the door shut and walked around...leisurely.

"When we were in Carver's Mill Elementary, didn't we have some kinda term for when you give somebody something, and then ask for it back?"

"Indian giver. Yes, I think I remember that one. Only this is different."

"How's it different? You gave me a scarf, a scarf that you actually made for me. And now...you want it back."

"Yeah, well... I'm an Indian giver then. You want me to pick it up?"

"I can bring it in. It's no problem."

"Yeah, well... If you don't mind, I'd rather just pick it up and we'll be done with it."

"Fine. I did like the Morse Code that you wove into it though. Very...touching. I Love You. It's eight letters, but it's 24 dots and dashes. I even like the pattern you made out of them. If somebody wasn't looking, it'd be easy to miss the whole thing."

Becky's face changed instantaneously. "Hey--- We had a deal. You promised."

"Yup. And you promised not to go talk to Emmerling."

"That's different. You were..."

"Know what? *Everything's different in your world.* You never make a mistake, but everybody else..."

"Yeah, well, right back at ya, Skippy."

Charlie chuckled, but not in a particularly friendly way. "Yeah, ya know this is really funny. You send me a scarf when I'm in the Navy and you weave *I Love You* into the wool...and then you get all pissed-off when I finally figure it out. Tell me, what the hell did I do wrong?"

"Well, if you don't know... Maybe you're just a big dummy. How do you like them apples?"

"You might be right, "Charlie smiled, "But I'm a big dummy...that you're in love with. Heh, heh, heh."

"Well, maybe I just did that because you were off in some submarine or something, fighting to save the world."

"The USS Carl Vinson isn't a submarine, it's an aircraft carrier. You don't pay much attention, do you?"

"Sure I do. Aircraft carriers are boats that go on the surface and submarines just go under the water. It's something like that, right?"

Sooooo... Do you want to, stop by and pick it up, or what?"

Becky stood there, appraising him seriously. "Yeah, I guess I could stop by."

Manuscript of Alicia R. Davis
Susan

There's an old adage, As the twig is bent, so grows the tree. I looked it up so that I could give a proper reference, but apparently this old proverb has been batted around for close to 500 years.

Is it true? Is it false? And does anyone really know for sure what the author really meant? The adage came to me about a month after Mr. Nichols' funeral. It wasn't that anyone spoke it or brought it up. That took place somewhere in the ganglia inside my brain. To tell you the truth, I actually remember when the thought first asserted itself inside my brain.

It was the end of the day, and the kids were all at their lockers switching out books so they could go home and study. Right in the middle of all the hub-bub and lockers slamming, Susan showed up at the door and knocked to come in. Her knocking was so soft, it's a miracle I happened to look up and see her. I even remember what she was wearing. It was a blue-and- white plaid, like they wear in Catholic school, navy-blue sweater, white shirt, white knee socks and navy Mary Janes. She had her book bag in one hand and something tubular in the other. Her look was of someone in earnest. Huge, serious, and nearly tearful.

I put everything down and ushered her in. She came up to my desk, carefully placed what I soon discovered was her flute on my daily minder. "I'd like to return this," was all she said, and she stood there, staring at me. I remember saying, "Got sick of it?" and first she just shook her head. Then she said, "I can't play it anymore," and she was gone.

A moment later, it flashed into my mind, what the write-up in the paper had said that she and Becky and Charlie had tried their best to save Mr. Nichols, by helping him breathe through the flute, and that they had been unsuccessful. It didn't make a big impression at the time. But then, here she was, a month later...turning in her flute.

It had all happened so fast...I wonder now, if I handled the incident correctly. Maybe that was the key time for a little discussion about life. Maybe that was the moment that the twig was being bent, or did it happen that horrible moment during the storm? I guess no one can answer that one for sure.

I do know this much. It was right about this time that Susan and Becky and Charlie started hanging around with each other. I'd see them on the playground and I remember thinking, Now that's odd... None of them seemed like the type to be hanging with either of the other two. Charlie in particular. I probably noticed him first because, at that age boys don't hang around with girls...at all, but then there was a social distinction. Charlie was all blue collar, family, house, the way he dressed, and Susan was the quintessential good little girl. And Becky, bless her heart, was always the tomboy. I think in her year book she was the one most likely to have five kids and no husband.

And though it's more difficult to track the exact beginning, I believe that right about this time was when Susan began writing. She wrote an essay, which got picked up by the school paper. It was titled, "Why Do We Live?" and it seemed, at the time, to be unusually grown up. It was also a bit melancholy as I remember. And then she wrote a series of short stories. One of them, When Do Children Become Grown-ups? was picked up by Reader's Digest and she was actually paid some small amount for it. The kids at school teased her about suddenly being a writer and she'd *smile and say, "That's how I got my stereo!" and that seemed to make things okay.*

It was right about that time that Charlie had his growth spurt. In the beginning, I remember that it looked strange seeing two relatively tall pretty girls, with a short stocky boy between them and one step behind, looking like a body guard. No one messed with them after that. Charlie seemed to carry off his new role rather convincingly.

At the homecoming dance, everyone in the school was sure Susan would be nominated to be the homecoming queen. She was pretty, smart, and was beginning to wear her mantel as young female writer rather seriously. But then, she didn't even go to the dance, although she was asked. Strangely, Charlie didn't ask her. I know that much, and Becky did go, but she wasn't nominated for anything. She set the tone for the dance. It was a Halloween Homecoming Dance and Becky made a gigantic and very realistic spider for the center of the gym. It was about six feet long with sharp pointy legs and sharp fangs, all black. Somebody from the shop class wired it with red glowing eyes and nobody wanted to dance under it.

It was a strange triad for three teenagers to be in.

Transition

"Hello, Becky? This is Bert Emmerling. Sorry to bother you, but we're trying to track down Susan Sorato. I figured you might know where she is."

"Hi, Dr. Emmerling. Is everything okay?"

There was a short pause. "Actually, I'm sorry to say, no, it isn't. Somebody just called down to the fire department. Mrs. Sorato, Susan's Mom..."

"Is she all right? Did she die?"

"No, she's okay, physically at least. Someone saw her walking down Carver's Mill Road, actually down the middle of Carver's Mill Road. She was in her nightgown."

"Oh, shit."

"Yeah. It's a shame. Do you have any idea how I can find Susan?"

"Sure, I can give you her cell phone only... Do you think it might be better if I called her?"

"I was hoping you'd say that. I'd really appreciate it."

"Sure. I'm on it. Thanks for calling."

"Sorry to have to call you with such crappy news."

Becky picked Susan up at the New Hope Motel. She was already standing outside and smoking a cigarette, something she'd never seen before. As she pulled up, Susan stubbed it out in a low grey urn filled with sand.

She pulled right up to the entrance and Susan was already

walking toward her. She threw open the door and sat down hard. She didn't look over at first. She just looked straight forward. But then she did. They looked at each other and Susan said one word, "...fuck." Then they hugged, both in tears.

At the hospital, Mrs. Sorato was sitting in a small inner chamber with a nurse attending to her. She wasn't dressed in a gown; she was still in the bath robe she'd worn. They both stood up as Susan and Becky entered.

"Darling! I'm *sooo* sorry to bother you. I believe there's been a little misunderstanding. I hope they didn't frighten you."

Susan glanced past her toward the nurse. By the look on her face, there hadn't been any misunderstanding.

"What happened?"

"Well, to be honest, I believe I may have had my first *senior moment*, as they say. When you get to be my age, I don't think it's all that unusual. I am eighty-one years old, you know. I think that's appropriate, don't you?"

"What happened?" she repeated. "Were you hurt?"

"I wasn't hurt a bit. Not even a scratch. It was such a beautiful day, I thought it might be nice to go for a little walk. There's a chickadee family, I noticed in the pear tree. They're making the cutest little nest up in the branches...four tiny, perfect eggs. And then I decided to take a little walk down near the brook. Then I went up the bank to the road and...I guess I figured it was a nice day for a little exercise. That's not against the law is it?"

Susan was keeping watch on the nurse's expression. She just stared out the window looking sad. "No, of course not, Mom. We all take walks. But, then what happened?"

"Nothing, nothing at all. I just wanted to go for a walk."

Susan looked question marks over at the nurse.

"She walked three and a half miles down... the *middle* of the road, with her robe slung over her shoulder."

"Mom..."

"Oh, sometimes you're such a prude, Susan. It's a beautiful day and I was starting to get warm. I had my underclothes on. Tell her, nurse. Didn't I have my underwear on?"

The nurse breathed in and then shot a glance to Susan. "The bottoms. The *bottoms*, Mrs. Sorato. You were walking down the middle of the road, flashing your boobs for all the world to see."

"Good heavens. Have you never heard of nude beaches? And, we all have the same parts. Don't we, Susan?"

"There were four cars behind you, Mrs. Sorato."

"May I take her home now?" Susan whispered to the nurse.

The nurse nodded and quietly left the room.

The ride home was quiet. Susan watched the road. Mrs. Sorato watched it, too, and Becky stared out at some fields of cows on the way home.

Later still, Becky and Susan met at The Gent. It was only 9:30 at night, but for Carvers Mill, the dinner crowd was down to the last dregs. Lou Terkel was behind the bar as usual, polishing the glassware. He noticed the two of them head for the quiet section. He noticed the expressions on their faces and prompted Bonnie, who was on that night, to serve them, but keep a low profile.

This time, Susan ordered a dry vodka martini, only it was a double this time, and Becky went right to her Jim Beam/rocks, also a double. They toasted each other solemnly and without comment. For awhile they just nursed their drinks and stirred their swizzle sticks. Finally, Becky said, "How can I help? What can I do?"

Susan's eyes flared to over-wide for a moment and then she

took another large sip. "This is where it begins...today...right now. Things will never be the same," and then the tears began trickling down her cheeks.

    Becky squeezed her hand. "You don't know that. *We* don't know that."

    Susan looked up and stared in her eyes as if she were a stranger.

    "Okay," Becky said, squeezing her hand hard. "Let's say it is the beginning of *something*. Neither one of us is God. We don't know how fast or to what extent. We really don't."

    "We know that Mom walked three miles down the middle of the road...in nothing but her underpants. It's gonna go down from there."

    "Okay, what are your options?" Becky asked.

    Susan took another long sip. "Mom went through this, way back when with Dad's mother. It was *horrible*. At the time, Mom said *if this thing ever happens to me, just take a gun out and shoot me*. I was pretty little when it happened, but I remember, very briefly, Grandma moved in to the far end of the house. They had another bathroom installed, and a second doorway, sort of a big closet between the two rooms, only you could walk through."

    "Why was that?"

    "To cut down on the sounds, but also the smell. Grandma kept having accidents, sometimes horrible accidents. Sometimes I'd have to go out to Grandma's room and it stank so bad, I'd have to put my hand over my mouth to keep from throwing up. Dad had pledged to Grandma that he'd *never* put her in a nursing home. And he didn't. For two years, they hired two gals, it was a mother/daughter team and they'd take care of her, do the laundry, wash her, watch her from eight to five. But the nights..."

    "So, what happened?"

    "It got so bad, Mom finally had to put her foot down. It

was Mom...or Grandma."

"And, of course, your mom won."

"Yes. But their marriage... It seemed like they were always fighting after that."

"Sooo... after your grandmother went into a nursing home, what happened then?"

"Oh, every Sunday afternoon, we'd drive over to the home and it was just awful. The smell was always there. And it seems that all nursing homes have about the same smell, only some are worse than others."

"What happened then?"

"They were lucky. Grandma was old. She died."

Manuscript of Alicia R. Davis

Becky

"Where do I start? I'm not sure anyone will ever truly understand what makes up...Becky Pierce. There's a term, the girl with the curl, which comes to mind and I suppose it's good for a starter.

To begin with a physical description, Becky's hair is raven black. Her eyes are blue and look like tiny crystal images of the Earth as seen from the moon, twinkling, alive, sometimes cat-like, but always crazy. But then, cats don't grin at you, they just stare. Becky never stares; she looks you right in your eyes, ferreting out that one place in your eye where you exist and then she somehow focuses on that. Then she'll laugh, or giggle, or more likely, she'll cackle, which is strange for a little girl, or even a young woman.

Becky is a one-ten outlet hooked-up to two-twenty. If she's a car, she's a little English sports car, with a bored-out 289 plopped in, which is to say, she's an AC Cobra.

Becky is probably every other girl's worst nightmare.... except somehow, for Susan.

In high school, she was very good in all her classes except math. She HATED trig with a purple passion, asking her fellow students out-right if they had any idea what a cosecant or cosine was for. She passed trig, but just barely, and with her attitude, she came back a year later to state that she hadn't used trig once that year and probably wouldn't ever...not in her entire lifetime!

Strangely, she didn't date much at all. I heard one senior in the hall one time, talking about her. The term, "too *mucha* woman" drifted out of their group and no one didn't know what was meant.

To be candid, among the three of them, Becky is the enigmatic one. Susan and Charlie's wounds run deep, but only an idiot would fail to see how the wounds have manifested themselves.

On the surface, Becky never seemed to have changed that much, if at all. I imagine that twenty shrinks could devote their lives to digging into "What Makes Becky Run?" and it's quite possible that none of them would get it right. I could be out in left field as well, but when you quietly watch a scenario unfolding over years, you can't help but form your theories.

By all rights, Becky should have been the youngest mom and the first in her class to get married. And that hasn't happened. In fact, Becky is still single and I see those first layers of invisible armor congealing around her. It's as if she has a shiny, brittle glaze around her. Her eyes are ever-bright, ever-twinkling, but I can't help but wonder what's going around in that perky, shiny brain of hers...

Yarn-Bombing 101

When Susan pulled up in front of Becky's little shop, she was surprised to see so many cars parked in front. She was even more surprised when she got out and peered in the window.

Becky was at her little desk, with her business glasses perched on the end of her nose. She was wearing a navy-blue business suit and her hair was pulled back into a bun. She looked exactly like a before shot in a movie, where in the next scene, she's tossing her glasses and shaking out her hair provocatively. Only what Susan saw, was a generous handful of somewhat matronly-looking women circled around the room, sitting on folding chairs and knitting up a storm. From the looks of it, they were all knitting up the *same* storm. What was truly weird, was Cubby was sitting on a similar chair right in front of Becky's desk.

Susan opened the door quietly and peered in. "Uhmmm..."

Becky waved their little secret wave and grinned. "It's okay! Nothing *untoward* going on here!"

By the time Susan made it over to the little desk, Becky had already rounded up a chair and Cubby was standing, trying to look professional, but looking more guilty than anything else.

Susan half-mouthed and half-whispered, "I can come back."

"No, no, no. Nothing to hide, here. We're just ginning-up for a major-league yarn-bombing fest." She waved her hand around the room. "These young ladies are knitting 50 colorful gargoyle beanies to be sent directly to the senate chamber in Washington, D.C. ...to be worn by a certain faction of the US senate!"

Cubby looked up at her. "No, she hasn't divulged exactly who the lucky recipients will be. And yes, I'm here to get the quote-unquote, inside story."

"Yarn-bombing the US Senate. I'm guessing this is a first," Susan said with a smile. "So, what's the inside story? Who you sending to?"

"Sorry..." Becky said, grinning back. "It's a state secret...for now."

"Okay... Which side? Republicans or Dems?"

"Nice try. You'll find out." Then she flashed her secret smile and mouthed, *duhhhhhh*. She reached into her bottom drawer and dragged out a white paper bag stuffed with something black and grey, some green and purple trim and some tiny patches of red and orange.

"That's your template?" Susan asked.

"Yup."

"Is it okay to take a picture...uhmm...pictures?"

"Oh, I'm counting on it," Becky grinned. "And you'll get the inside story, only..."

"I know. The story can't come out before whatever you're planning happens."

"You got it, mister." Becky unfolded the black gargoyle hat. The design was clever. It wasn't a hat with a gargoyle on top. It was designed so that the wearer actually *became* a gargoyle.

"How are you going to get anyone to wear one?" Susan asked.

"Well, I think I've got that covered...but we'll see. Cubby, you set up for a group shot?" She swung around in her chair.

"Okay ladies! Here's your one moment of complete infamy! Hold up your gargoyles...and smile!"

Cubby shot twenty shots of a roomful of old ladies in about as many seconds, and then turned around and shot ten more of Becky...and then Susan, and then Becky and Susan together.

"What was that all about?" Susan asked.

"Nothing. When you work for a paper, it sort of becomes second nature. Oh, and 's'cuse me for the bad segue, but...how's your mom?"

"Remember, this is a small town," Becky said, anticipating the question.

"Yes. I hope this is off-the-record..." Susan said

"I solemnly promise."

Susan's stare became distant. She peered out the window, though there was nothing to see but the dusty grills of six cars in the parking lot. "I guess this is something that everyone faces at some point in their life. You're a child for what seems like an eternity. Then, at some point, you go away to college and start beginning your own life. And at another point...you return home, and you begin to sense that things have shifted, very subtly at first. But, it's there. And from then on, it's just a long gradual slope...downward."

"Do you have a plan?" Cubby asked.

"No... Do you?"

"Of course not. But, since we're grappling with the serious topics today, I stopped at Doubleday and picked up some books. One was a *Guide to Literary Agents*."

"Oh, you were serious about that manuscript..."

"Mrs. Davis was serious. And you're serious. And Charlie is serious."

"How 'bout me?" Becky asked.

"You...not so much," Cubby chuckled. "But, I opened the

literary guide and wished I hadn't bothered."

"Yes, it's a bit daunting to the uninitiated," Susan said.

"I'm surprised anyone ever gets published."

"Ninety-nine point nine-nine don't. And before we go waltzing down the bunny trail, I already called my publisher. I explained the situation. They offered to look at it...and, I already sent them a few chapters."

"What did they say?"

"Well, the good news is they want to see more."

"What's the bad news?" Cubby asked.

"The bad news is, Mrs. Davis was a helluva teacher. But, she wasn't what you'd call an experienced writer. It's rough around the edges. And there were two things they were candid about. First, they were pretty clear that if I hadn't been in it, they wouldn't even bother. Part of it is because people are curious about me. The other thing. They want to know how it ends..."

The gargoyle hat brigade broke up around 12:30 and suddenly Becky found herself alone, and for the first time since she could remember, she felt a wave of loneliness sweep over her. She pulled up to the entrance to Rt. 202 and put her turn-signal on to go left into New Hope for some McDonalds or some Chinese. It clicked about a dozen times while the traffic was clearing, and then suddenly at the last second, she turned right. It was so weird, that she said out loud. Hey-- *Qué pasa? Who the hell is driving this thing?* But then, there was an image of Charlie the other night, which made her smile and made her wet in equal amounts. "Oh, okay," she whispered. Her mind went right to a mental image. *Charlie was out in the woods, faded jeans, engineer's boots, orange helmet and chainsaw...lots of sweat trickling down his tan, hairy chest. Lots of noise, vibration, muscles clenched as he gripped down hard on that big orange machine.*

She turned right and coasted down the gravel path to Blair's Lawnmower Repair. To her surprise, Charlie was at the right side of the building with a tape measure and a little yellow pad. He had his Midway Fireman's hat on backwards. Normally, she couldn't stand backwards hats on men, but somehow, Charlie seemed to carry it off. He looked cute in them.

She pulled up right in front, slammed the door, harder than usual and walked over briskly. "*Hey, sailor*," she called from 30 feet. Her voice was taunting like a schoolgirl's.

He looked up. "That was a long time ago. And they don't really say that anymore, unless they're really looking to get laid."

"*Hey, sailor*," She called with the same taunt.

They did it behind the shop in broad daylight and on the hood of the Corvette. Technically speaking, it was a quickie, skirt was pulled up...pants were pulled down, zipper unzipped... But if it was a quickie, it was also a goodie and nobody was complaining.

Afterward, Charlie casually rubbed his hand over the hood.

"We do any damage?" Becky asked, trying to find where the front of her pants was.

"Naah. Everything's fine." He looked at her. "And...it would have been all right anyway."

"What, if I scratched your hood?"

"Yeah... No, actually, you could have blown up the entire car and it would have been worth it anyway."

"Really?"

"Yup."

"That's the nicest thing anyone has ever said to me. Sooo, what were you measuring when I drove down?"

Charlie smiled oddly and waved the question away.

"Oh. Now, I *really* want to know. What were you measuring?"

"It's stupid," he said, still grinning. "Next question."

"Okay. What were you measuring?"

Charlie took a big breath and made sure his zipper was all the way up. "Okay, but I told you already. It's stupid. I was doing a hypothetical measure of the store."

"Okay. For what?"

"Boy, you really are a pain in the ass, aren't you? Okay. You asked. But, don't blame me. I was doing a hypothetical measurement on the store. The whole left side of the store is some junk, and two old cars that have just been sitting there."

"Okay..."

"Well, I was just figuring...hypothetically, I could get rid of all that stuff. Fix a couple of windows, put in some insulation, a bit of paint and..."

"And what?"

"Well, hypothetically, it could be, sorta like a second business, a retail spot."

"I think that's great! What's the big deal? Do you have somebody lined up?"

Charlie looked at her seriously.

"What? Oh..."

"Yeah. I said it was just hypothetical. Please don't laugh."

"I'm not laughing, Charlie. It's extremely..."

"What? Stupid? Idiotic?"

"No. It's not stupid at all. It's extremely..."

"What? God, I hate it when you don't finish your sentences."

"Thoughtful," Becky said.

"Aw crap. That's the worst. That's as bad as it gets. Thoughtful...*fuck*... Just shoot me."

The Carver's Mill Patriot
(weekly brainstorming session)

At his end of the upstairs office (which had formerly been a twenty-by-forty, dusty hay loft) Sam Harper kicked off the Monday morning meeting of The Carver's Mill Patriot the way he always did, reviewing...eviscerating Cuthbert Miles' most recent restaurant review.

"Bon Appetite," he began, "so far, so good."

At his little desk at the backside of the room, Cubby sighed theatrically. "Why do you always do this?" he asked in what appeared to be the greatest sincerity.

"Why do I always do...*what*?" Sam called across the room. Sam's voice was truly easy to interpret.

"Okay," Delta Harper, Sam's wife interjected. "It's Monday morning. This can be the beginning of a good week...or a bad week."

Sam sat up taller in his five-way swivel chair. "What? What did I do? All I did was say two words, which, coincidentally, is the title of Cubby's column. I even said, *so far, so good*. How the hell can you take me to task for that?"

"Sam," Delta said, "you're so full of crap."

"Brava!" Cubby called out, "and points for speed!"

"Okay, on this last write-up for *Danielle's Bistro*, it seems like your main hard-on is against arugula, okra and kale. Do you seriously think it's professional to remove an entire *napkin-ring-point* in your rating?"

Cubby turned around in his chair to face Sam directly. "Sure... Danielle's serves food. Are you following me so far?"

"Cubby," Delta whispered, "I'm assuming you want to continue working here."

"No, I'm going to be a fair and dispassionate boss. Tell me, why the big bitch-fest over cilantro, kale...what's the other one?"

"Okra. Okay, let's take okra. It's not even how it tastes so much as the texture. When I eat okra, I feel like someone in the kitchen just blew their nose into a hanky and then rubbed it all over, whatever okra is. It's slimy, it's snotty, it feels like drool in my mouth."

Sam made a face. "Okay, what about cilantro?"

"Did you ever take a bite out of a bar of soap?"

"Can't say that I have."

"Well, then, I bet you've never eaten cilantro, Sam."

Sam gazed over in Delta's direction, "Have I ever eaten cilantro?"

"No."

"Why?"

"Because it tastes like soap."

Sam looked down at the mock-up for the front page of the Patriot. "Okay, moving right along, good write-up on Mrs. Davis's manuscript. It's a little long. Do you think you can cut it down a column or so?"

"I can, if you want. But in this one case, I think it's pretty important. I think the readership will find it pretty interesting. Besides, Mrs. Davis probably taught 90% of the people in this town how to read. Oh, and another thing. There's a distinct possibility that this thing might actually get sold."

"Okay, no biggie on the column inches. What else? What about the yarn-bombing with Becky?"

"Votes are still out. I got some shots."

"What's she gonna yarn-bomb?"

"The U.S. Senate, 50 members' worth."

Sam looked over to Delta. "This could be interesting. Are you thinking what I'm thinking?"

"Maybe. A bunch of years ago she made little sweaters and cozies for animals in the Bronx Zoo. How would we tie that together?"

"I don't know," Sam said thoughtfully. "But, right now, I'm picturing a double-truck shot. Some alligator or something with a sweater on, on the left, and on the right a row of senators with... What'd she make for the senators?"

"Gargoyle heads."

"Perfect! This'll be front-page! Maybe even viral!"

"Okay... I promised to hold off until things firm up a little. But she promised to give us an exclusive." Cubby looked up, his face downshifting to a more serious tone. "And there's one more thing. It's a little sensitive and, I've already seen a shot circulating around. It's of Mrs. Sorato. She's walking down the middle of the road in only her undies."

Sam inhaled deeply. "Yeah. Okay. I get it. We'll can the shot and go softball with it. Don't want to piss Susan off...and...it's a damned shame. She's been a pillar of this town. Alzheimer's, right?"

"Looks like it, but it could be dementia."

"What's the difference?" Sam asked.

"Dementia is the more general term. It's like an umbrella and Alzheimer's is under that umbrella."

"That helps me just about zero," Sam said.

"Everything is changing. Right now, they're looking for something that can dissolve the amyloid plaque that builds up inside the brain tissue. When they've got that nailed, maybe it'll be reversible. Right now, it's a long, slow, degenerative process. They call it *The Long Goodbye*. The only good news, and right now it's in its infancy, is using a specific kind of music to break through the barrier that Alzheimer's creates."

"It works?" Sam said.

"Yes. And quickly. The drawback is, it isn't a cure, but it's a window that a loved one can communicate through. It's complicated, but it's worth it."

A Short Conversation

"Mom..."

"Yes, Sweetie?"

Susan Sorato sat back in her chair and began searching for exactly the right words to say to her mother. "Mom, do you remember, way back when...when you'd tell me about your mom and how, one day you noticed she was, just a teensy bit different?"

"Oh, yes, I certainly do. I remember, there was a day and I remember that just the day before she was Mom, and then somehow the next day, she had changed, just the tiniest fraction. She was still my mom, in all her glory, but...something was different. And it never went back to the way it was. Uh oh... You just had that moment...with me, didn't you?"

"Mom..."

"Oh, shit... Damn... Fuck, s'cuse my French. You're right. I see what you're seeing. *Damn, damn, damn...*"

"It's not that bad, Mom. Not yet."

"Oh, my God. I walked three miles down Carver's Mill Road...in my robe. Wait a minute. Oh, shit, I was in my underwear, wasn't I?"

"'Fraid so. No one saw you, Mom."

"Yeah, right. Oh, shit, I wonder if it's going to be front page on The Patriot."

"I'm about a thousand percent sure it won't."

"Really? Why?"

"Because this town loves you...really *loves* you."

Mrs. Sorato's eyes were drizzling tears and her breath had gone ragged. "Shit. I always vowed, when I got to that point...correction...*this* point, I'd go out into the woods and...*do-the-deed*."

"Okay, Mom. C'mon back to reality. You're not even in the same county as what your mom went through. Seriously."

"Yes, I'm aware of that. But, how many days, weeks or months before I become a *thing* to be handled, not your mom, not the person who's watched you grow, watched you blossom..."

"That's not going to happen, Mom. I promise you."

Mrs. Sorato gazed deeply into her daughter's eyes. "Sweetie, I love you so much. But, you and I both know, that's a promise you can't make. I'm pretty sure I can...do-the-deed at this point. I've had a wonderful life, no regrets, at least no serious regrets. And I know how this thing goes. Very soon, there'll come a point where I don't have the focus or the ability to carry that out. I *know* that much. I researched it. Very soon, there'll come a point where I start saying gibberish things, and at that point, it'll be too late."

Susan was weeping openly now. "Oh God, Mom, please stop. You're killing me."

Got'cha

Becky drove quietly down the gravel drive to Charlie's place, made a K-turn and then proceeded to back slowly up to the shop.

By the time she opened the door and climbed out, Charlie was already out the front door. "What the *hell* are you doing?"

She looked at him seriously and pushed a strand of hair out of her eyes. "Well, I figured I just might have to make a quick getaway. Are you still pissed?"

There was something in her eyes, which, although stern, had a strange twinkle to them. "Well, that depends."

"It depends? It depends on what?"

"On why you came here."

"Oh... Okay. Well, the other day, you were talking about cleaning the crap out of your store, getting rid of the dead mice and possums...and so on."

"I don't have any dead possums."

"Yeah, well...you get my point. And the *point* is, would I have my own sign, or would people just have to read tea leaves to figure out where I am?"

Charlie thought for a moment. "You mean, you'd actually consider moving in?"

"Well...yeah. I'm assuming you're gonna give me some really *super* deal on the rent, considering all the dust and mold and dead animals."

"Geez... I hadn't even thought about charging you rent."

"Well, good! See, that's even better! I think this calls for a celebration!"

"What do you have in mind?"

"I was thinking, maybe could finish polishing the hood of

219

your Vette..."

"My... Oh... Oh!!!" As he was kicking off his boots and slipping out of his jeans he said, "Sooo...how does this work? Do we shake hands on it or...what?"

Becky was already down to her underpants, which now only had one leg inside. She grinned up at him and held out her hand. "Sure! We can do that too!"

At the Wookie Hole, Andrew, the head bartender nodded at Becky as she entered and sized-up Charlie in a tenth of a second. *Not only hetero, but very hetero and all business as far as gender is concerned.*

At the table, Andrew made a point of the whole thing. "Would you like the usual?" he asked Becky, and then he looked over and without blinking, asked, "First time in?"

Charlie looked up and then formed his own opinion. "Technically no. I used to come in a long time ago, before..."

"Yes, I understand. What can I get you?"

"Uhmm, I'll have a Dewars, rocks, just a splash of water."

"Very good, sir!"

After Andrew left, Becky leaned over, "Ooooooh, look at you! Dewars, rocks...with just a splash. You're sort of like Carver's Mill's 007."

Charlie thought for a long moment. "Ya know, when I start setting up the store room for you, remind me to put in a second wall, one with some of that high-tech sound insulation, just in case I can hear your voice somehow."

"Awww, that's not very nice. I just called you double-oh-seven. You should be grateful... You should be kissing my..."

"Okay, time-out. You're giving me a headache. Besides, I

already just did that. Is there anything at all we can talk about that's just the tiniest bit serious?"

"Sure!" Becky chirped as Andrew delivered their drinks. She took a long sip, flashed Andrew a thumbs-up, and said, "Okay then. So, when are you gonna make an honest woman out of me?" She peered closer into his eyes and began grinning from ear to ear. "*Oooooooh,* I got you on that one! You should see your eyes. You look like a mouse that just saw a mountain lion!"

"That's probably pretty close to how I feel right now. Do you seriously feel like you need someone to make you an honest woman?"

Becky's face changed once again as she began batting her eyes. "Oh, you ole Rhett Butler, are you thinking of making me an honest woman? I do declare..."

Charlie sighed. "Do you ever get serious? Or is this a topic that...scares you too much?"

"Ouch." She looked off toward the horizon and took another sip. "Okay, you want serious? You got it. I look around me and I see a divorce rate that's like 90%, pre-nups where you need a lawyer present, unpronounceable STDs, and hubbies with dinosaur tails and feet. And me... me left with six screaming babies to feed. Does that sound *groovy* to you?"

"*Groovy*?"

"That's code. I'm being ironic."

"I hate *ironic*," Charlie muttered.

"Well, okay then. At least we agree on something. But is that enough to base a relationship on?"

"What do you have for breakfast in the morning?"

"Mostly coffee. And the occasional chocolate bar...dark, of course, like your splash of water."

Charlie sighed and looked out the window. "I think I need a nap."

"Oooh, is that code?"

"NO! Enough already. You're wearing me out. From what I'm getting from this conversation, you're ready to move in next to me for 12 hours a day selling yarn-bomb thingies, but you don't want to think about the M-word. Is that about it?"

"M-word? What's the M-word? What does the M stand for?"

Charlie chuckled nastily. "Ohhhh, no. You're not going to sucker me on this one. I'm not going to be the first one to use it."

"Use what? What the *hell* are you talking about?"

Charlie looked at her seriously. "Marriage. I'm talking about marriage. What are you...?"

"Gotcha!!!"

Manuscript of Alicia R. Davis

Notes on Charlie

I'm sure you've heard the term, Napoleon Syndrome. It has a lot to do with little men, which is to say, men of diminutive physical stature, who consciously or sub-consciously attempt to make up for their small size by being overly aggressive or noisy, or pushy, or sometimes just obnoxious.

Before Charlie Blair went through his growth spurt, he was little Charlie Blair, though he never had a Napoleon Syndrome. He was never pushy or loud or even obnoxious. In fact, he was quite the opposite. Except for his size, Charlie would have been the quiet, but powerful captain of the football team, taking action only when necessary and preferring that people just minded their own business. Which is to say, Charlie went directly from toddler-dom to adult on one unmemorable day when no one was paying attention. One day, he was a baby, the next day, he was a man and in the part of his anatomy where it was most important...between his ears.

I also believe that it's important to make a point here that Charlie was not a carefree little kid before the incident with Mr. Nichols. He was already a serious little man. What happened afterwards is something else entirely, and it's important to understand that if you are to understand Charlie.

Without going into a full-scale psychiatric evaluation, I'd

bet dollars to doughnuts that Charlie was a mirror-image of his dad. I'm also betting that for some reason, Charlie had to seriously help out at his house, possibly be a second father-type when his dad wasn't around. I can't think of any other thing that would cause a young child to wear the mantle of responsibility so heavily.

I wonder if some of Becky's idiosyncrasies might stem from her crawling out to the far end of the seesaw to balance Charlie out?

The Conversion

Work began on "The Conversion" immediately. The following afternoon...after the M-Word had been used, Becky showed up in her little truck after work.

She poked her head in the door, yelled "Hi! It is okay if I go next door and start throwing away crap?"

She was dressed for work, and not in the cutesy-pie way. She wore what could best be described as combat boots, real ones, seriously ripped and stained jeans, which still managed to cling to her body as well as if it had been sprayed on, and an old, old navy-and-white Franklin and Marshall sweatshirt, which Charlie immediately noticed.

He said, "Where'd you get that?"

She said, "A guy." A moment went by as she swung a paint can around in circles. "It was a long time ago."

"What happened to him?"

"Oh, he was dropped...*summarily*."

"I see. Might I ask why?"

"Sure. He didn't know a good thing when he had it...until he didn't have it anymore."

"I see. Could you use some help?"

"You look like you're busy..."

"Doing what? There's no one else around."

They began by prying up the rusted roll-up garage door. It hadn't been opened in at least twenty years and one of the springs had rusted off. Then Charlie handed her a paper face mask. She was about to ask what for, but a moment later, he picked up a leaf blower and started it up. She wisely stood up-wind and then stepped back into the main shop as a hurricane of dust, dirt and strange objects began flying around the room. While they were up in the air, he deftly guided them out the door. The floor of the room was basically clean in three minutes, though it was going to take another hour to pick everything up outside.

Within an hour, they had the room downgraded from outrageously hideous to merely awful. They pushed the old Studebaker junker outside and around back with Becky steering when it got tricky.

Becky seemed to really be caught-up in the changes that were going on. Breathlessly, she climbed out of the car and said. "What's next?"

"Samey-samey," Charlie said.

"I have an idea!"

"What?"

"You know in those movies, when they push the car over the cliff and it crashes and burns?"

"Yeah?" He looked past her. Forty feet down a shallow embankment, Simmons Creek wound around past the property. "Are you saying you want to push it into the creek?"

"It's a thought!" She looked at his face. "But, not a good thought, huh?"

"Not particularly. Downstream, there are about 50 houses that get their drinking water from the creek."

"It might taste...a little bad..."

"Well...maybe a little. There's the brake fluid, the grease, oil, gasoline, five old tires, and 2000 pounds of rust. Would you want to drink that?"

"Okay. Maybe it's not such a good idea," she said, glancing around at anything but Charlie's eyes. When, she finally caught them, however, he was grinning.

The following day, Charlie spent the first half of it, moving little boxes of dusty junk from what was now, Becky's room, to his workshop at the back of the building. There wasn't time to sort through the fifty-some boxes and so they squatted there on the floor like patient toads; he stacked them on the workbench, sawhorses, and some shelves on the walls. Not a pretty sight.

When Becky came in that afternoon, she said a dutiful, "Wow!" Then she said, "Where'd you put them all?"

Charlie looked at her. "Don't ask."

She dragged six one-gallon paint cans from the bed of the truck, plus a quart can, a roller and an extension.

"You already picked the color?"

"Colorsssss," she said, dragging out the plural. "I always wanted to do this. Faux finish. It's gonna look just like a Spanish castle. A base color of tawny orange, only dabbed, so that it looks a hundred years old. Then, dabbing a dusty yellow-gold in randomly, spiking it with some hints of charcoal, like it's going back to nature. And then, finally, the piece de resistance, a metallic antique gold, that I'm going to smear around here and there, as if the wall is actually made of gold. What do ya think, huh? Pretty classy?"

"Sounds a little bit like a whore house...s'cuse me, a classy Spanish bordello."

She sang, "You say potato and I say pohtahto. You say, *Clamato* and I say, *Clamahto*... I saw it on one of those Discovery Travel thingies. It was *nice*! Besides, if the business tanks, we can always subsidize our income. We can call it, *Just a Gigolo!"*

Charlie frowned, "What about you?"

"I'll be... let's see... a Gigolette?"

"Okay, now you're getting *weird*...even for you."

An hour later, a brand new Lincoln Mark LT truck trundled down the driveway. It was shiny black and looked like it hadn't worked a day in its life. A trim man in his fifties with short salt-and-pepper hair, new jeans and new sneaks hopped out rather youthfully. He looked around as if to make sure he was in the right place and then walked in the front door.

Charlie peeled off his disposable gloves, which were now Tuscan orange and walked back to the counter. "What can I do for you?" he asked with just the right amount of friendliness and aloofness.

The trim man gazed around the room at the chainsaws, weed eaters and the handful of lawn mowers and garden tractors. "Do you sell garden tractors?" he asked seriously.

Charlie suppressed the urge to laugh, but only partially.

"No, what I mean is, do you sell the good ones, you know, the modern ones, the ones that can spin around in a circle."

"Zero-radius," Charlie said.

"That's right. Now, you're cookin'," the man said. "The good ones. Do you sell any of the good lawn mowers?"

"Yes, we do!" Charlie answered cheerfully. "Okay, to begin with, how much land do you have? How many acres?"

"Why do you need to know that?"

"Well...the good tractors come in different sizes depending on..."

"Oh, I understand. I want the largest one they make, and with all the bells and whistles."

It was at this moment, that Becky came in from painting.

She had cobwebs in her hair and smudges of orange paint on her left cheek, a strand of orange paint and orange gloves. She looked at the man and said, "Hey..."

"Uhm, hello," the man replied, suddenly flustered.

"This gentleman would like the biggest, zero-radius lawn machine they make...with all the bells and whistles," Charlie said.

"Of course! Nice truck by the way!"

"I only buy the best."

"Well, you've certainly come to the right place," Becky said. She gazed over at a green-and-yellow John Deere that was up against the front window. "John Deere has the best performance record. You can check out Consumer Reports. Kubota is really good, too, but...it's an import and when you buy a tractor, it's best to stay American..."

Fifteen minutes later, Mr. Jason, R. Welton handed Charlie his American Express Card. "Oh, you'll be delivering it," Mr. Welton added.

Charlie opened his mouth to speak but Mr. Welton was way ahead. "I don't want to risk scratching the bed of the Lincoln."

"Of course not!" Becky chimed. "Of course, when you demand the best, there is cost and time involved. How far away are you?"

"I live in Doylestown."

"Oh... Well, that's not too bad. What is that, Mr. Blair? Is it $150 or $200?

"Two hundred."

"That's fine. No problem."

After Mr. Welton pulled out onto the road, Becky raised her hand for a high-five. Charlie did so...reluctantly. "Ya know, that guy could have gotten away with a smaller model and saved about two K. And it would have fit in the back of his...*truck*."

"It's not a truck, it's a Lincoln Mark LT. They're a little different."

"Yeah. You're right."

The two of them were just getting around to pulling on new disposables when another truck rolled down fast into the driveway. It pulled right up to the window and you could hear the emergency brake being yanked up from 50 feet.

Bert Emmerling climbed out in his navy-blue Midway Fire windbreaker and then he walked around to the passenger's side, opened the door and pulled out a basket with a grey horse blanket tucked inside. There was a tiny black head peering out solemnly.

Inside, Bert walked up to the counter, looked around and said, "What'cha doing?"

Charlie looked around, trying to see things through Bert's eyes. "I think it's in my lease. Every twenty years, whether it needs it or not, I have to wash the windows, shovel out some shit...and stuff like that."

Bert stared Becky right in the eyes. "I get it."

"Who is this?" Becky asked, staring down into the basket containing a black-and-white Boston terrier puppy. Her right hip was taped-up from her tail to half way up her spine and she was looking up at them as if she were about to be excommunicated from planet Earth.

"That's...the puppy with no name. She got hit by a car. The owners came in and I did four hours of surgery. And then the goddamn sons-of-bitches decided not to pay and to boot...they wanted me to put her down. It was all I could do to keep from..."

"So, you're stuck...again. How many animals do you have over there?'

"Too many. That's why I'm here. You don't have any pets,

nothing at all, and you'd be a natural."

"Uhhh...that's okay. She'd have to be alone all day and that's not fair to the animal."

Bert's eyes drifted over in Becky's direction. "How 'bout you?"

Becky leaned over to the mournful pup and looked at her. The puppy raised up as far as she could from the blanket and began licking Becky's nose. "Sold! This is a new world's record. How long did it take me to cave? Did I make it to a quarter of a second?"

"But you have the same problem I have," Charlie said. "You have a shop to run. It's not fair to...little Foofey here to leave her home all day."

Becky began batting her eyes in earnest. "Have you forgotten something?"

"Aw shit. You mean you're going to be bringing her over here?"

"Well, there'll be two of us."

Bert perked up. "Oh! Are congratulations in order? You two getting hitched?"

"Oh, hell no," Charlie said. "She's just moving her yarn crap into the storage room, that's all."

"For free!" Becky giggled. "Oh. Now that we're talking dollars. What was the cost of the surgery?"

Bert smiled at Charlie. "Zero. It'll be my, *I'm not getting married, I'm just moving in present.*"

The Gent Revisited

Becky and Susan swung into The Gent's parking lot and pulled up to the first position by the front door. Becky looked at her watch. It was only 11:18. They weren't even open yet, at least not officially.

Inside, Lou Terkel was behind the bar, like a captain of his ship, making sure all the glassware was clean and stowed, the olives, onions, cherries and orange slices were all prepped and ready for action. The bar top had received its final swipe before the lunch crowd began filtering in.

Lou looked up and his craggy face instantly crinkled to a smile. "Heyyyy! How are the two prettiest damsels in Buckingham Township?" He thought for a moment. "I hafta admit, that's not much of an accolade, but...sometimes ya gotta take what'cha can get! Would you like your usual tables, ladies, or are you gonna play it wild and free up here at the bar? I promise I'll protect ya if anything...*untoward* arises. That's the right word, isn't it? That's one of those words that doesn't sound like what it means. Ya gotta admit, it sounds a little like...going *backwards* or something."

Becky and Susan looked at each other like they were still in high school and then saddled up, front-and-center. Becky thought for a moment, "Do you still make those weird things you used make? Carver's Mill..."

"Special. Carver's Mill Specials. I sure do, only I don't get a whole lotta call for them lately. Let's see... that was red wine, a bloop of honey bourbon, Jim Beam as I remember, and a twist of lime...on the rocks. Did I get it?"

"You sure did!" Becky declared. She glanced at Susan. "Two?"

Forty seconds later, two new Country Gent coasters were slid onto the bar, adorned by two Carver's Mill Specials. Lou took a quick glance to make sure everything was in order and then stepped back. "I guess the question *du jour* is...well...I hear that congratulations just might be in order?"

"That's right!" Becky said brightly, her face with a nearly invisible glaze. "As of Monday, my little shop is moving up to...just a half-mile down the road. Very soon, you'll be able to pull in, get your lawnmower blades sharpened, buy a weed eater...and some skeins of yarn, and maybe even learn to swing dance!"

With timing that only bartenders know, Lou processed the information, and then backed way off from asking about any pitter patter of tiny feet. "Well, that just sounds fantastic!" Lou said, pouring some tonic water in a shot glass to toast with.

They clinked glasses and toasted and then Lou put his shot glass in the sink. "Dare I ask? How is our infamous Mr. Blair handling all this? I'm guessing he must be pretty darned happy. It's no secret that..."

"Charlie is Charlie," Becky said. "Right now, we're just taking this one step at a time...seeing what's amicable for everyone."

"Well, I personally think that's a *fine* idea! Amicable is always a good place to start."

A moment later, a family with two teenage girls slipped in the door. Lou disappeared around the counter to seat them.

"Sooooo," Susan said.

"Yup, that about sums it up," Becky agreed. "Charlie is

Charlie," she said again. "I have no friggin' idea where this is going to go. How 'bout you and your mom?"

"I have no friggin' idea either. Would you like to trade?"

Becky examined her drink more closely. She held it up to the stained glass light hanging down and looked at the different colors through the bourbon and wine and then took another sip. "Do you remember a time...I don't know how far back you have to go, but...wasn't there a time when everything was carefree and the only thing you had to worry about was getting good grades...and getting asked out on a date? How long ago was that?"

"I think that was pre-Revolutionary War," Susan said. "I think the Indians were still circling our wagons."

"That's right. I think I've still got some scars on my ass from getting shot with arrows."

"Yeah, well, that *sounds* good, but I don't remember anyone ever shooting arrows at you. You have an arrow-free ass."

Becky laughed hard, perhaps a little too hard. "Yeah, that's right. I forgot. They can chisel that on my tombstone: *Becky Pierce, the gal with the arrow-free ass.*"

"Sooo, what's up with you and Charlie?"

"Well... we did the deed, if that's what you mean."

"Are you prepared to supply details? Number one, was it good?"

Becky took a moment to bask in a tiny victory of sorts. Susan had always been the pretty blonde with the smarts...mildly annoying. "It was... I was going to say, *unbelievably outrageous*, but, I think it would have to be Zorro in a cape and a sword for that. After all, *Charlie is Charlie.* I think I'm gonna have to get that tattooed on my butt. He's a terrific guy and he's one thousand percent in the sack. And with time...I think he'll get even better!" With that, they grabbed arms and gave each other a good old high school hug.

"Details?"

Becky wrinkled her nose. "I guess I'm not a big kiss-and-tell sorta gal after all. Go figure... Okay, I'll tell you this much. If things keep on going the way they're going, I may have to spring to get a new paint job for his Corvette. I think it's getting worn down a little. And...moving right along, where are you at with your mom?"

Susan flinched visibly. "God, it was horrible. I can't imagine anything worse. She'd had a bitch of a time with her mom. And then, the other night, she wanted to talk to me while she's still sort of coherent. She truly gets it that she's losing it. And somehow, that's making it even worse."

"I can't even comprehend what that must have been like. So, what do you do?"

Susan just shook her head and looked off into space. "I don't know. Maybe it's a little like that old poem about the definition of what *home* is. Home is the place, where...when you *have to* go there, they *have to* take you in. Only it's with your mom. Mom *has to* have a care giver...pretty much for the rest of her life. And I *have to* make sure she has it."

Becky nodded her head, but then she looked at her point-blank. "Or else..?"

Susan shook her head again. "No, that's not on the table."

"Okay. I get it. But it sounds like, what your decision is now is, do I hire somebody? Or do I put her in a home? Or do I take care of her myself? There aren't any good options."

The Name Game

Charlie chucked a 36" mower blade into a vice and eyed his rotary grinder on the wall. He could easily sharpen both sides in under two minutes, only the problem was, Becky wanted to keep him company while he worked.

Actually, she wanted to try out names for what was going to be her new store. Charlie was a good one for bouncing ideas, because he didn't get swayed easily. Anyone else and she could get them to agree with her in under a minute. But, when Charlie was tasked with the same job, he took it *very* seriously.

"Okay... How 'bout *Knit-Purl, Cha Cha Cha*?"

Charlie squinted as he lined up the file at exactly 30 degrees along the blade. "I don't know, he said. "And why do they call it pearl?"

"I don't know. All I know is, it's one of the stitches."

"Did they used to string pearls in the yarn or something?'

"No. It's not that kind of pearl and it's spelled P...U...R...L..."

"Well, even that's kinda stupid, don'tcha think?"

"Okay, scratch that. How 'bout "*Knit by Day, Tango by Nite*?"

"Are you planning on being open, like eighteen hours a day?"

Becky watched as Charlie carefully filed the edges of the blade. "How sharp are you going to make it?"

"There's an optimum sharpness. Too sharp isn't good. Hey,

how about "*Dance and Knit Instruction*?"

"That's pretty good, Sweetie. But, do you think it might be just a little too straight-forward?"

"How can something be too straight forward?" He looked over at her. "Sweetie?"

"It's a term of endearment and it's kinda short...like a nickname."

Charlie counted on his fingers. "They both have seven letters. Charlie...Sweetie. Charlie is already a nickname."

"Okay, Charles...that's also seven letters. How 'bout...*Spinning Yarns*?"

"Actually, that's not too bad. But what about the dancing?"

"*Spin your Yarns. Spin your Partner.*"

Charlie made a face. "I don't know. It seems like it's getting kind of long and...something or other." He unchucked the blade from the vise and tightened up the next one.

"Okay... How 'bout, *Lawnmowers and Yarn and Tangos...Oh My*?"

Charlie looked at her. "Now, you're just getting goosey. I can tell. Nobody's going to go into a shop named..."

"Okay. I got one! How 'bout, *Wanna Fuck*?"

Charlie put the file down on the counter and scratched his head. "Now, you're *really* confusing me. You really want to name your side of the shop..."

Becky's eyes were huge and dazzling now. "Nooooooo. One last chance, *Skippy*. Pretend I'm a wealthy heiress, drop-dead wealthy and drop-dead gorgeous. Your goal is to convince me to set up in this shop so you can have unlimited sex and unlimited money...*forever*!" She looked at him more closely. "Ooooooh, you're blushing! I've never seen you blush before. Do you blush all over, or just your face?"

Charlie tried to hide his face. "I wouldn't know."

At that precise moment, Foofey woke up in her basket and began whining. "Hey little puppy, you really have piss-poor timing, you know that?"

"I'll take care of Foofey. Can you find some place better than the hood of your Corvette?"

The second Becky closed the door behind her, Charlie raced around the shop looking for anything that was soft, comfortable and clean. Things were beginning to look bleak. A bale of bubble wrap promised to be noisy if they did anything at all. And an old awning promised to be just that...old and with no padding whatsoever.

Finally, on top of the big grey metal shelves on the back wall, he spied a large cardboard box that had been duct-taped over. He ran to the shelves like a basketball player and swiped the box off the top. It hit the floor and opened up half way, just as Foofey and Becky were coming in the door.

"Lock the door and put that back in ten minutes sign up."

"Oh, he's a tennn-minute...mannnn," she began singing. "Not five, not six, not seven....he's a tennn..."

"Okay, you keep singing like that and we're gonna be zero minutes."

"Oh, he's a zero minute..."

"Enough already!" Charlie yelled, genuinely pissed.

They found a dark quiet place at the end of the hallway. Charlie threw down the sleeping bag along with all the chair cushions he could find.

"Where do you want to put Foofey?" she asked.

Charlie looked up, still pissed. "I don't care. Just anywhere but here."

In fifteen seconds, Charlie was down to his black t-shirt and his new red underwear. Becky had her blouse unbuttoned and was trying to gauge what to do next.

Charlie looked over. "How expensive is that brassier?"

"My bra? Oh, I don't know. It's pretty old. I got it at..."

"I'll buy you a new one," Charlie said, yanking the bra into two pieces with one yank.

"Oooh, I like it when a man..."

"Shut up," Charlie commanded. "Just shut the fuck up."

She began to call, "Ohhh..." but then her mouth was covered by his. Ten seconds later, she was without underpants.

Ten minutes after that, a couple of very rare things happened. With their clothes back on, Charlie stepped out behind the shop and pulled the tarp off his robin's egg-blue Corvette and tossed it off to the side. There was a twelve inch stripe, where the tarp had slid down and that part was dusty. He rubbed it clean with one of his old t-shirts and yelled into the shop. "Leave that back in ten minutes sign up!"

"Okay!" she yelled from two rooms away. A minute later, she showed up at the back door and looked around. "What's up?"

Charlie did a quick spritz of the wheels with a hose and threw it off to the side. He smiled oddly at her. "What's up is...you and I are closing shop for an hour or so, and going down to Colonel Sanders. How do you like your chicken? I'm guessing extra-crispy."

"Well, then...you would be wrong! Way down deep, I'm an old-fashioned girl. Original recipe or *die*."

"Wow... I didn't know you had such strong feelings about chicken."

"Or we could go to that Chinese place. That's good, too!"

Although they were dressed country-casual...very casual, Charlie walked around to the passenger's side and held the door open for her. And for reasons unknown. Becky suddenly got southern-belle-dainty and waited till the door was completely open. She sat down, graciously and then batted her eyes at him. "Thank you," she murmured.

For the next ten minutes they were the *cool people*, tooling past tiny towns and quaint clearing toward New Hope, PA. The KFC was located on the edge of a shopping mall and they pulled up to the window so they wouldn't have to sit...with the *peons*.

They parked at the far end of the lot and then walked down to a farm pond where a dozen Canada geese were diving for their lunch.

After dividing up the chicken and the biscuits, Charlie said, "Damn. I should have brought some wine or something."

Becky looked over with a dreamy look on her face. "Not necessary. I'm already...*high*."

"What? You toked-up?"

"No, silly. So far, this is the best date I've ever had in my life."

Charlie was just about to say, "*Gee, you don't get around enough,"* but then thought the better of it. "Me, too," he said instead. Faraway, he heard an unfortunately familiar sound. It was the twin sirens of Midway Fire taking turns, howling at the sky. A second later, his cell phone went off. "Shit..." He looked at Becky as he answered. "Where?" was all he said. Then... "Yeah, I'm on my way," followed by "New Hope."

Becky stowed the chicken and fastened her seatbelt. "What happened?"

"Accident. 413 and 202. Somebody ran a stop sign. If you don't mind, I'm goin' straight there. You can drive the Vette, back?"

"Sure."

"The shift pattern is a little different, but if you can drive stick...you can drive stick."

Idiots...

(What's black and white and orange all over?)

It was drizzling when Bert Emmerling's truck coasted down the drive. But instead of parking, he pulled in next to the Charlie's shop. For a long minute, the truck just sat there, windshield wipers swiping time, and then Charlie hopped out and gave a wave as the truck idled back up toward the highway. A moment later, it was streaming back up 413 and was gone.

Charlie was still in his fireman's yellow slicker and boots, his jeans and flannel shirt were stuck in an Acme bag. He entered the show room and looked around. Things didn't look bad, but they didn't look quite right either. Something looked weird.

There was a crash, followed by Foofey, their new pup, racing down the hall, flapping and shaking. In the middle of the showroom she stopped to give a really good shake and began racing around. Foofey, who was normally black with a white throat and tummy, was now black and with an orange tail, orange tummy and feet, dripping orange water.

Becky was ten steps behind, yelling "*Bad dog!!! Bad Foofey*!" but Foofey seemed oblivious and began racing wildly in circles around the store.

Becky raced into the showroom, still yelling, *Bad dog*, when she spied Charlie. She stopped. "Oh... You're back. Sorry 'bout that."

Charlie looked around. There were tiny orange footprints going everywhere and splashes of orange on the door and on two of the lawnmowers.

They looked at each other. "Don't tell me," Charlie sighed, "let me guess."

"Yeah, well... I had the roller pan on the floor, so I could use the extension to make it more efficient."

Charlie looked around. "All in all...how much more efficient do you think it was?"

"Not all that much," Becky agreed. "I'll get a mop."

"No, I'll get a mop. See if you can get Foofey back in the sink. I'd rather not have to do this twice."

Three minutes later, Becky returned with a squirming furry creature wrapped up in a towel. She rubbed vigorously and finally Foofey leaped onto the floor and resumed racing around. Charlie watched and then resumed mopping up orange dog footprints.

"How'd it go?" Becky said, pouring out two coffees.

Charlie stopped mopping so he could think better. "Idiot," he said matter-of-factly. "Complete effing idiot. Ding bat. Two cars. A big ole Chrysler heading south on 202...minding his own business. And this BMW runs a stop sign, doesn't even slow down, and t-bones right into the side of the Chrysler. By the time I get there, you can hear the ambulance coming, sirens a-blazing. The guy in the Chrysler was hurt, but he's over trying to see if the gal is okay. The gal in the BMW...nothing, only she's on her cell phone...apparently *still* on her cell phone. Never gets off for the whole time."

"How could you tell it was her fault? Maybe it was..."

"Nope. It was her all right. When somebody plows into the side of a car...from a stop sign, there's only one way it can happen. But, the funny, stupid, idiotic thing about it, is when the cop arrives...she's *still* on her cell phone...won't get off. Just unbelievable. People think they can multi-task...and they can't. They just can't."

"So why did you have to go?"

"When there's a bad accident, there's always a chance there'll be gas leaking. At that point, you've got seconds. She was lucky, damned lucky...and the guy gets hurt, just driving down the road. I *hate* cell phones...*hate* 'em. And every single person I've ever met agrees with me. Then they say, *"yeah, but I'm safe when I do it. I've got a system.* ...Yeah, right."

Becky looked over at him. "You know what a mirror ball is...right?"

Charlie looked back at her. "What does that have to do with cell phones?"

"Uhmmm, nothing. I'm changing the subject."

"Okay, fine. Yes, I know what a mirror ball is. It's like what Lawrence Welk used to use. Old farts slow-dancing around in the dark and little lights whizzing around the room. I'm surprised it didn't bring on epileptic fits or something. They were sorta like the precursor to strobe lights...which also brought on epileptic fits."

"Wow, you really are a buzz-kill on certain topics. Sooo...*icks-nay* on the *irror-ball-may.*"

"Why? What do you want to do with mirror balls?'

"I was thinking of installing one in my new dance studio. Kinda spice it up a couple notches."

"You do know, don't you, that you can't just hang a mirror ball. First you gotta attach it to a little motor that turns it at about 3 rpm. Then... then you gotta buy a spotlight to shine at it. Better yet, two spotlights, so you have the whole room covered from every angle."

"Wow! You're kind of like a mirror ball guru!" she said,

twinkling at him.

"You're settin' me up, aren't you?"

"Big time! But just think, after work, we can close the doors and turn on the music...and *then*...turn on the mirror ball!"

"Yeah, but it only works with slow, old folks music."

"Says who? What kind of music do you like?"

Charlie sighed. "I don't like much of anything new. I'm an oldies kind of guy."

"Me too! Can we get a mirror ball? And some lights and motors and stuff? During the day, we can park some of the garden tractors under them. It'll look like they're moving around!"

Time and Money

The following day, Susan checked-out of the *New Hope Motel in the Woods* and quietly checked-in to the place where she'd learned not to pee in the bed as well as how to write her first novel. It was with extremely mixed emotions that she carried her bags upstairs to that now tiny room which had once been her sanctuary in the early years, the years when all she had to do was write a two-page term paper or pass a test on who the Green Mountain Boys were and why the Declaration of Independence was important

It was a sanctuary back then because no one ever came in uninvited. That, and she could hear mom and dad, down in the kitchen, making dinner or clinking coffee cups and grinding the captains' chairs around on the old wooden floors. Captains' chairs had an unmistakable sound. She could tell when Dad was pushing back from the table whether he was hungry or angry or just getting comfortable.

The sound of the screen door slamming told reams of information as to the emotional climate of the house. The sound of the old lawnmower cranking up. It sounded one way on the first rebirth after a winter of discontent, different in mid-summer and different in late autumn where its chief chore was moving maple and oak leaves...somewhere else. There were the sounds of the robins in spring, the red-winged black birds, the crows two fields over in the summer, and the sad litany of crickets chirping their lonely goodbye to warm weather. It was all comforting back then.

But now, decades later, though there were much the same sounds, made by the great, great, great grandchildren of the robins and crows, red wingers and crickets, now they provided little comfort. They were just sounds. And Mom had somehow found a way of sitting in a captain's chair without making any sound at all. It seemed like it was some kind of show of respect to Dad, as if he were still sitting there now...only invisible. All the sounds seemed quieter now, and more ghostlike in her declining years. As she got older, it was as if the volume of life had been turned down, the dimmer switch slowly rotated until at some point....*poof.*

That evening, when she was certain that Mom was asleep, she saved the e-mail message she had going on the screen to the publishing house and Googled: *Assisted Living, Rehab Facilities and Nursing Homes,* already knowing, at least in theory, the hierarchy of the horrors.

Assisted living was something you did for yourself...or perhaps to yourself, when you no longer wanted to have to do much of anything. Always hated shoveling winter snow? You're done! Finished! Hate mowing? Raking leaves? Washing windows? Cooking? Driving? Making your own bed? Washing clothes? It's all over! You've graduated! For a *small* fee, any or all those things could be put aside *forever,* allowing you to now do only the fun things in life. The only trouble was: *What exactly were those fun things?*

Rehab often resembles a nursing home, and there is a lot of overlap. The main difference is, theoretically, you can get better, rehabilitated and eventually leave a rehab facility. A nursing home is the end of the line. It is where mature adults place their parents when they can no longer take care of themselves. Down the corridor from Rehab and across the hall is Hospice, which doesn't last so long...

In a half-scroll of the computer screen she had summed up humanity. *And behind which curtain do I get my final reward?*

She scrolled down two pages to the relative pricing. Here is where life and time and money and quality of life fight it out to see which is more important. And even if you're truly wealthy, there are decisions which must be made. *How much time is worth how much money?*

The following morning, Susan was down in the kitchen early. She had already scrubbed the sink to a shade it had been two decades ago. She poured an entire can of Comet cleanser down the garbage disposal and flipped it on. For three minutes, a noisy war took place 12 inches below the sink before settling into a quiet *humm*.

The refrigerator from her childhood was now in the process of shedding two inches of white ice as she sat at the kitchen table making a list of how many light bulbs had to be replaced. She figured at least nine. She had scrubbed out the coffee pot so you could now see how much coffee was in it and the garbage can was filled with all manner of half-opened jars of things with a dubious vintage. As far as the ice box was concerned, there was nothing that could be trusted.

When Mom came down, she didn't seem to notice anything, or if she did, she chose not to say anything.

"Looks like a *lovely* day!" Mrs. Sorato sang, pulling back the blue and white curtains. "Aren't we blessed?"

"Yes, we are," Susan agreed. "I brewed some coffee. Can I interest you?"

"Oh, that would be *wonderful*!" Mrs. Sorato effused. She looked at a large hunk of ice in the sink which was a perfect impression of the inside of the icebox. "Oh, good. I can't remember the last time I defrosted the fridge." She hesitated a moment. "Sorry, I'm having a bit of a senior moment, Sweetie. Am I defrosting or are you?"

"I am, Mom."

"Oh *good*, because I can't, for the life of me, remember doing it. You'll see when you get a little older. Things start to get a little muddy...a little blurry. Old Age ain't for sissies, ya know! In fact, I remember my mom telling me that when I was...oh...about your age, give or take."

Susan rotated in her chair. "Mom, is that about when you had...*your talk*?"

"Which talk?"

"You know. The one we had the other night."

"I'm sorry. I think I'm getting a little dotty. We've talked about a lot of things, Sweetie."

"We were talking about getting older and how you had a talk with your mother..."

"Ahh, yes. Well... You may not believe this, but when I get to that point, I have a plan. I'm going to walk out into the forest and...*do-the-deed*."

Susan looked at her differently this morning. "I'm sorry, but I really don't understand. What does *do-the-deed* mean?"

"It means, *do-myself-in, end-it-all, take-the-long-walk*. Choose whatever metaphor you like."

"How exactly are you planning on doing this?"

"Oh, I don't know. It doesn't really matter. At some point...I'll just *do it*." Mrs. Sorato looked around. "Are we out of English muffins? I like to have a muffin or two to get the day going." She stood up in the kitchen and opened a cabinet door. "You want one, too?"

"Sure. That'd be great!"

Over breakfast, they talked about birds and how the bird population had changed over the years. "Remember what I used to call you?" Mrs. Sorato asked.

Susan smiled and took a sip of coffee. "Yes, I remember it well. You used to call me your *accidental birder* because..."

"Yes, but do you remember how you came to have that name?"

Susan opened her mouth to speak...

"It was because at first you weren't even interested in birds...not at all. Not no way. Not no how. You were completely oblivious as if they were just large insects or something. And then one day you spotted..."

"A pileated woodpecker. Yes, I remember. He was large and colorful and kind of *funny*. He looked like he should be on one of those cartoons."

"That's right, dear, though at the time you didn't know anything about them, not the name, not their habits, what they eat...nothing. But slowly, very slowly, I brought you along, bird by bird."

"That's right, Mom!" She took another long sip of coffee and then placed it carefully in the saucer. "I don't know if you noticed or not, but I moved out of the motel. I brought my bags up to my old room...just temporarily, of course."

"Oh! Do you remember when you spotted your first rufous hummingbird? You were the first one. No one around here had ever seen one before. Do you remember what color it was?"

"As I remember, it was sort of a burnt orange."

"That's right. And we looked it up, right on the spot."

"Yes... About my moving in."

"And then the funny thing about that rufous is, we saw him that one time, and then, never again. Oh, and do you remember that one time? It seemed like a million male cardinals descended into the back yard? I think Daddy even got a picture of it. It's around here somewhere. I could go through some boxes. I know it's around here somewhere."

Susan poured another coffee and looked out the window at the bird feeder. Nothing much to see, a dove, a tit mouse and two chickadees. She turned around and looked at her mom. "So, tell me, have you spotted any new and exciting birds recently?"

I wouldn't be very good.

It was just quitting time for pretty much all of Carver's Mill. At five thirty, the *Open* signs all get turned around in the windows and the lights go out...with the exception of the restaurants, gas stations...and the fire department.

    Charlie had turned his sign around and flipped off the circuit breakers for the lawnmower side of the building, while Becky was up on a ladder adjusting the speed of the new mirror ball in what she was now calling *The Ballroom*.

    "I need some help!" Becky called down from the ladder.

    Charlie came in, sized up the situation and walked over to the base of ladder. Becky looked down. Charlie looked up...smiling.

    "You do know you're a perv, don't you?" Becky said.

    "No. But it's only lately that I've come to realize *exactly* why I love ladders!"

    "You're still a perv," Becky said, still trying to adjust the speed. "I don't know why, but this stupid motor doesn't want to change its speed."

    "Are you sure?" Charlie asked.

    "Am I sure? Sure I'm sure. It's still slower than hell."

    "Yeah, but you gotta remember, it's geared-down. If you go from six rpm to 10 rpm, you can't really tell till you wait a minute. They're both pretty slow."

    "Okay...gotcha." She climbed down into Charlie's arms

and received a quick feel. "Sooo...what do I do if I want to dance fast, I mean really fast?"

"I think you can do whatever you want. But, if you have the lights going round at 50 rpm, I think it's just gonna be a big blur. And, you might see people looking around for a barf bag."

A second later, Dr. Bert Emmerling cleared his throat in his best, most-unconvincing way. "Uhm, hey guys, you're just the two people I want to see!"

"How long you been standing there?" Charlie called over.

"Just exactly the right amount of time! When you're all through playing grab-ass, do you think we could talk for a minute?" Bert made a point of watching the lights zooming around on the walls, while Becky pulled her skirt down and straightened her hair. "Is that the right speed for dancing?" he asked after a minute. "It looks a little slow."

"That's what I thought," Becky said. "This reminds me of those old Lawrence Welk shows."

"Fine. I'll just take the gearbox off and they'll be spinning at 5000 rpm. How's that?"

"Sounds like somebody got up on the wrong side of the bed," Bert said, "but while we're on the subject, it's that time of the year again and I was wondering if *this* year, with you two sprucing up the shop with mirror balls and lights and stuff, whether you might want help out with the Midway Firemen's Annual Fundraiser. It goes to a good cause, and...you kind of have a vested interest already. If we could have it here, we could have some actual dancing, music, maybe a raffle or two, barbecue... What do you think?"

"Done and done!" Becky said before Charlie could get his mouth open.

Bert and Charlie exchanged glances. Both were smiling though the smiles were slightly different. And then they were different again.

When Bert left, Charlie walked him out to his truck, something Becky wasn't expecting. She went back to the counter, but she couldn't see anything so she quietly meandered closer to the door to see and hear better. She still couldn't hear anything but now she could see Bert's face fairly well. He was serious now; not angry but seriously serious. He wasn't wearing his veterinarian clothes or his fireman's uniform either. Right that moment, he was just Bert dressed in Bert clothes. Old jeans that had been worn down the old-fashioned way, by years spent milking cows and loading hay or fixing the occasional broken water pump or circuit box.

He was wearing his usual black crew-neck t-shirt which seemed to be the official gear for upper-level working men in Carver's Mill, and an old olive-drab pea jacket which looked like they'd actually been through a war. The only thing that didn't match were the shoes, which were a herringbone of medium brown leather. They told of some other life, some other story which she wasn't privy to.

He had his foot up on the front bumper and as he talked to Charlie, he kept looking around, at the trees, the mountains. It was obvious he wasn't looking at anything, just blanking out his mind as he spoke, which he did for at least fifteen minutes. And when he left, he gave Charlie the usual handshake of men who are also friends. But then he gave him a quick hug and a slap on the back.

When Charlie came back in, he was different...more somber. He caught her eye as he passed but it was a weird expression and then he disappeared into the bathroom. When he came out, he was drying his hands and it seemed like he was determined to change the subject from whatever it had been.

He looked up at the mirror ball on the ceiling and said, "I

think I have a solution. I can just put a second rheostat on the wall down here. That way, you can piddle with the speed on the mirror ball to your little heart's content...even in the middle of a song."

"What were you gentlemen talking about out there?"

"What? Oh. Nothing. Nothing at all. We were just shootin' the shit."

"Bullshit. You were talking about me, weren't you? He thinks we're moving too fast. Or... No, I got it. He thinks I'm too *something-or-other* or other for you. He's like your big brother now. Did I guess it?"

For a long moment, Charlie just looked at her like she was crazy. "No," he said, "Actually, the conversation wasn't even about you. You weren't even mentioned."

Becky's right hand shot up. "Okay, then swear to that. Swear that Bert doesn't think I'm too something for you. Swear it."

Charlie frowned at her, and it was clear that he was suddenly annoyed. "Okay, I swear it. We didn't talk about you and we didn't talk about me...or us, for that matter. It was something completely different."

"Good."

"But, I gotta tell ya, when I say something to you, I'm telling you the truth, the whole truth and nothing but the truth. And I kinda resent having to swear to you like I just did. It tells me that you don't trust me, and I haven't given you one goddamn reason to think that."

"Oh, shit. I'm sorry. I really am. It's just that..."

"It's just that...what? You think I'm a liar?"

"No, not at all. I trust you more than anybody on the planet. I trust you completely...more than I trust myself."

"It sure as hell doesn't feel that way," Charlie muttered. He walked over to the amplifier that was sitting on what was still a workbench. He turned it on and, as if by magic, the mirror ball began rotating as well. Pale fireflies were swooping gracefully along the walls, only hiccupping slightly when they got to a corner. "Nice touch," he said. "You're gonna have 'em all connected."

He pressed random and a song came on that made him smile. "*What's your name?* Let's see, I actually remember who sang this. It's a real oldie, but they used to play it at the very end on the Friday night dances at the high school. It's the song that...if you hadn't danced all night, you had your last chance to ask somebody."

"*Don and Juan*," Becky said. "Do you remember?"

"Yup. That was me in a nutshell. I waited the whole damn night, just staring across the floor in the cafeteria, trying to get up enough nerve to ask you to dance. As I remember, you started making faces at me across the room. I'm not sure I would have had the nerve."

"I wasn't going to take any chances," Becky said, stepping closer to him. "Wanna have an instant-replay?"

Charlie smiled, but wrinkled his nose. "I think I'll have to take a rain-check, least for the moment."

Becky came even closer. She gently lifted his chin so that he couldn't look away from her. "Okay. I'm sorry to have to do this, but now you *really* have to tell me what's going on with you and Bert."

"Nothing. Nothing's going on between me and Bert. He's just down, that's all. He doesn't have a lot of people to talk to so...sometimes we talk, that's all."

"About...?"

Charlie side-stepped the question. Instead he said, "Bert Emmerling is a really good fire chief. He's got his priorities straight. He puts the lives of his men, as well as the lives of the families he visits above stuff...and it doesn't matter what kind of stuff or how much it costs. He's just really good that way."

"And as a vet?" Becky asked.

"As a vet, it's different. He isn't just good. Good isn't the right word. Sometimes, when it's necessary, he has to take the place of a god. He has to make really, really tough decisions based on..." Charlie sighed. "I don't even know what they're based on, he just does it. He doesn't shy away from those decisions, because they have to be made. *Someone* has to decide. But, with Bert, it's like he never got a thick skin. It takes it out of him, just the same. And today he had to put an old friend of his down. His decision point isn't based on whether he's blind or deaf or whether he looks good anymore. It's whether or not his little furry buddy wants to go on living. And that's a hard decision for a human to make for...well...anyone. He takes it *that* seriously."

"Sounds like you've been through this with him," Becky said softly.

"Yeah, you could say that. And more than a couple of times."

"Did you know the dog that he had to put down?"

"Yeah. It was an old Basset hound named Buck. He'd been treating him since he was a pup. He was a good dog. He was just...mellow. He kinda moved in slow motion. Even when he was running, he ran in slow motion. And then. Buck just ran out of steam. Doing anything...anything at all made him yelp, so he just stopped doing anything. Sooooo..."

"Bert did what he had to do."

"That's right. Down beneath that tough-guy exterior, he's really soft when it comes to animals. He just wanted to talk to somebody."

"Maybe he relates to you. Maybe he sees you sort of like a son?"

"Nah, I don't think so. I wouldn't be very good."

The Wookie Hole

"I'm drowning," was all Susan had to say.

"The Gent?" Becky said into her cell phone.

"Yeah, that's fine, I guess." Susan said too fast. "Or..."

"Or?"

"Is there any place where we could meet and not have it go right to a page-three story in The Patriot?"

"Sure. If you wanna go ultra-clandestine, we could go down to Newtown."

"It's not *that* hush-hush, I just need some...perspective right now. I think I'm down a quart...maybe five quarts."

"The Wookie Hole."

"Right. That's good. Let's do it. You free in twenty minutes?"

"I'm free right now."

"Okay, see ya in a few."

On off-hours, the Wookie Hole could easily be mistaken for a normal restaurant. There were no overt signs on the outside nor any erotic paintings on the inside to suggest that as soon as the sun went down, better-than-average-looking guys would be Frenching, glued to each other on a tiny, dimly-lit dance floor or playing pocket-pool in the booths. The food was good...better than good, and the wait-staff was as attentive as anything on the Upper East Side.

When Becky opened the door for Susan, Andrew, the head waiter did a quick double-take, thinking perhaps Becky had suddenly gone to the other side. Becky noticed the look and shook her head. "Just friends," she called across the room.

Andrew nodded and snickered. "That's what they all say."

They walked to the back of the restaurant and chose a booth that was remote, but facing the bar so they could keep track. Susan sat down first and looked around. "I feel like I should have a Beretta stuck in my purse," Becky chuckled.

"Godfather, Part One," Susan said. "Once you watch one, you'll always have to sit, facing the door. Or Jaws. When's the last time you did any actual swimming in the surf?"

"Uhm, that would be never. I was scared of the ocean before it was in fashion. ...So what's up, Suse?"

Before she could answer, Andrew showed up. "Usual?" he said to Becky and then he turned to Susan as if he sensed that she had some sort of horsepower. "And you, Mizz....."

"I'd like a vodka martini, up and as cold as you can make it. By any chance do you have Greek olives?'

Andrew smiled appreciatively, "One or two?"

"Two, please."

Andrew stepped back and nodded in what seemed like deep appreciation.

"You've got to hand it to the gays," Becky said. "When it comes to sticking their pinky finger out, you can't beat 'em."

After Andrew left the second time, they toasted quietly and Becky repeated her question. "So...?"

"It's my mother."

"She go off the deep end?"

Susan took a long, histrionic sip from her martini before answering. "If that were the case, it might actually be easier." She tasted her martini and thought about it. "No, that's probably not true. That'd be a nightmare. But the thing is: right now, she'll be fine. It'll be just like old times and we're talking with some pretty sophisticated nuances. But then, right in mid-sentence, I can tell her mind has just gone off the rails, and I have no freakin' idea where she is...or even *who* she is. And then, thirty seconds later, she's back to being her old self."

Becky looked at her point-blank. "Okay. How can I help?"

"I'm not so sure anybody can help with something like this. If something got tight on the book-scheduling, maybe you could drop by for an hour or so...see how she's doing." She thought for a moment. "I'm not even sure that's a good idea. It's a helluva lot to ask."

"It's nothing," Becky said. "Your mom probably made as many dinners for me as my mom did. It's the least I can do. Uhmmm, having said that, she doesn't have any really whacko tendencies does she? Do I need to bring a knife...or a gun?" A second later they both broke into hysterical laughter and then they hugged, hard and strong, like the old days...sort of.

As they broke away, Becky noticed a long, pristine, baby-blue Lincoln convertible pull up in front. The top was down and two men in matching sunglasses were just sitting there. The driver was tall and wearing a blue-and-white polo shirt. You could tell he was handsome just by the way he carried himself. The man in the shotgun seat was...Cubby! "Sonofabitch," she whispered past Susan's ear. "I didn't think he came in here anymore."

Susan turned around. "Oh... Who's the other guy?"

"Okay, that's Jonathan Wilder. He's a real estate agent with Caldwell Banker. He's also Cubby's on-again-off-again hot fuck. They used to come here a lot until Cubby did one infamous restaurant review on the place...a quarter of a napkin ring for the rating. Didn't go over very well."

Susan looked question marks at her.

"Apparently they rubbed Cubby the wrong way. Or maybe they just didn't rub him the *right* way. It's hard to tell with the gays. But that quarter of a napkin ring was like bombing Pearl Harbor. Sam Harper made him go back and re-rate the place to something not so nasty, but the damage was done. There's been bad blood ever since. I don't know what's going on."

They watched as Jonathan and Cubby came in the front door. Jonathan led the way and flashed a combination salute and peace sign to Andrew. Cubby waved as well, though it was half-hearted. And it was Cubby who spotted the two of them in the back. "Hey strangers!" he called from across the bar. "Is that a private party or could you stand a couple of crashers?"

Becky didn't miss a beat. "I don't know. We're pretty expensive..."

"For what it's worth, if we all sat together, we'd look like two straight couples!"

"Works for me, Cub!" Becky sang back. "Only I've got first dibs. You're gonna be *my* date...and we're gonna have...*funnnnn*."

As Susan was being introduced to Jonathan, Cubby noticed the obvious. "You know, you two could actually pass as a couple. You're both tall, blonde, good-looking. You *look* like a couple."

"Well, I used to be married," Jonathan said, pulling up a chair.

"To what?" Becky asked.

"To a woman. Five years. We just...drifted apart. Hard to explain."

"He took one look at me," Cubby said, "and she was toast."

Andrew showed up with two more coasters and some napkins. "Oh, one thing," he said to Cubby. "Is this *on-the-record*?"

Cubby sighed in annoyance. "No, it's not. But I've answered that question about forty-five times now. Right now, you're getting a solid three-and-a-half napkin rings."

"Deserved napkin rings," Andrew countered.

"Okay, fine. They're deserved. The place looks great. Food's great and the service is great. But, annoying your local restaurant critic... Do you really think that's wise?" he asked, batting his eyes, though not in a friendly manner.

"How about a round of drinks...on the house?"

After he left, Susan asked, "Do you have to go through this crap at every restaurant you critique?"

"No. At different restaurants I have to go through *different* crap. At Fran's Pub, in New Hope, they didn't even want to serve me, at least not until somebody told them who I was. Then they got all weird, trying to figure out how to wait on a gay person."

"How do you wait on a gay person?" Becky asked.

"Carefully. Very carefully."

Susan looked across the table at him. "I don't want to pry," she said."

"Uh oh, here we go," Jonathan said.

"Oh, I'm sorry...really sorry. I'm just curious by nature. Just cancel that last transmission."

Cubby reached forward and squeezed her hand. "Don't be silly. Jonathan just doesn't know you, that's all. When you're gay you get all kinds of questions come across the bow. "Most of them are fairly innocent."

Jonathan wrinkled his nose. "Speak for yourself."

"Really, it's just that I've never written about a gay

character before. My brain was just in writer's mode."

Cubby sat back in his chair, took a large sip and then sighed. "I'm gonna take a wild guess and say... You'd like to know when I first realized I was gay."

"Wow, you're good," Susan said.

"No, it's just what everybody wants to know, that's all. And, I actually have an answer for you. I was about three and a half, and I didn't have the slightest idea was gay was, or what sex was, none of that stuff. I was just a little, slightly chubby kid. The family that lived next door to us had two kids, a boy and a girl. The boy was about my age and the girl was older, maybe a year or so."

"And you were attracted to the boy?" Susan said.

"Nope, it's not what you'd guess. I wasn't even thinking about sex or love. I really wasn't. But when it came time to play, Kenny was all about his Tonka toys. He had a great big dump truck that neither of us could even pick up, and there was a road grader, a bulldozer...all this stuff. And Kenny wanted to go out to this one sandy place move stuff around."

"Yeah?"

"Yeah. Only Tina had her dolls. She liked to dress them up and change their clothes, have tea parties and little conversations. She had little dishes and shoes and... Well, I just thought that was the greatest thing! Much better than plowing dirt with a Tonka truck. I also remember my parents trying to guide me back to the straight and narrow Tonka truck side but...I just wasn't interested."

"It's not all that straight-forward," Jonathan added, "...no pun intended. I had my regulation kid toys. I even built model airplanes and hung them up in my room."

"What was your first recollection?" Becky said.

"It was more...overt. High school. First time we had gym

class. I got a hard one in the shower with the other guys. Fortunately no one noticed. But, that one experience seemed to wake something up inside me. And I was smart enough to hide it."

"When did you realize you were hetero?" Cubby asked.

"Wow. I never even thought of it that way," Becky said. "It was just a gimmie. I know I paid more attention to the boys. I kind of teased them, flirted with them. I liked to get them to react, chase me, and flirt back. The girls...were just the kids I hung around with in between flirting with boys."

Noble Gas

Susan let herself in the front door and saw that the computer screen in the den was on. Out of deference to her mom, she called out, "Hello! It's me. Anything going on?"

She watched the screen instantly switch to another image and there was something about the timing that clicked in her mind. It had switched just a little bit *too* fast. It reminded her of a couple of TV shows where the naughty teenager in his bedroom also clicks just a little too fast. She was 99% sure her mom wasn't watching porn, though, these days, she couldn't rule it out completely. "May I come in?" she called outside the door.

"Of course, Sweetie! I'm here in the den. *Entre vous!*"

Susan peered in and looked around. The lights were all off, but she couldn't remember if that was something Mom usually did. "What'cha doing?" she asked breathlessly.

The screen was now tuned to the home screen with 25 tiny icons staring out at her. Clearly whatever she'd been watching before was something she didn't want her to know about.

"Oh, nothing really. I just like to use Google to look up things I don't know about. I can't even fathom how smart I'd be if I'd had a computer when I was growing up. I'd know about every country on the planet, every recipe for *chicken paprikas.*"

"Oh, I know one," Susan chuckled. "It was from Dad's mom. *"What's the first step in making chicken paprikas?"*

"First, ya gotta steal two chickens!" Mrs. Sorato cackled.

"That's right!" Susan cackled back. "Lemme see what other recipes you came up with!"

Mrs. Sorato looked up at her daughter. Her eyes had changed. "Daddy and I always thought you'd have made a good prosecuting attorney. Usually, it's a good thing. But, *sometimes* it can be just a tiny bit irritating."

"Sorry, Mom."

"Oh, that's all right, dear."

A moment went by, and then, "But, I can't help notice, you're still dodging the question. Do you have some...*significant other* you're writing to? It's allowed, you know. It's been years. You can pretty much do any damn thing you want. The world has changed, Mom. It's changed a lot."

Mrs. Sorato considered the words. "Well, I suppose you're right. But, try to keep in mind, you pushed for this. I just don't like having anyone in on some things...and I think this might be one of them."

"Sounds...*juicy*."

"Believe me, Sweetie, it's not." A long moment drifted by. Okay...have you ever heard the term, *noble gas*?"

"I think so. It might have been back in high school chemistry, I think. I just don't remember why."

"I just looked it up. There's helium, xenon, argon, and a couple others. Your father mentioned them a long time ago when he first ordered his MIG welder. I never quite understood the concept. Apparently, the MIG is an electric thing. He had to have an electrician come out and wire a 220- outlet in the basement. But for some reason, I don't even understand, he also had to get a big tank of some kind of gas so that the welds would be better...cleaner, I think. Not exactly sure why. Why would welds have to be clean? They're just...welds."

"I think when you use tanks, it's called gas welding, Mom."

"No, I know it wasn't for that. With the MIG, the gas cleans the welds somehow. I think he said it keeps the oxygen out of the welds."

"Are you thinking of getting into welding?"

"Oh, good Lord, no. What brought it to mind...there was an article I was reading. It was written for the elderly in nursing homes."

"They use helium? I bet they blow up balloons and launch them. Either that, or they do it to make their voices sound funny."

"Sorry, dear. It's not for blowing up balloons. Or, maybe it is. But, it's becoming popular for something else, dear."

"For what? I don't get it."

Mrs. Sorato sighed and then looked at her daughter oddly. "I have to warn you, you did ask, dear."

"You're beginning to scare me, Mom."

"Well, I'm truly sorry about that. But, the world is changing, even for us cranky old senior citizens. Senior citizens are looking for uhmmm... Oh, gosh. For alternatives to spending the rest of their lives staring out the window of a nursing home."

"Now I *really* don't get it. Are you talking about assisted living?"

"No, dear."

"Well, if they're not blowing up balloons, I don't..."

"It's the gas, dear. You can breathe it. Did you know that helium and nitrogen are in the air we breathe? In fact, they make up *most* of what we breathe. For us, it's just air. But it's only the oxygen in the air that keeps us alive. The other gases are just...filler. They don't do anything."

"Uh oh, I don't think I like the way this is unfolding."

"Sweetie, you've always told me to keep an open mind. Maybe it's time for you to take a teensy-tiny bit of your own advice. By the way, I don't think they actually use helium, though I s'pose you could use it. I did my homework. The interesting thing is...none of these gases are poisonous at all. Not at all! But it's only the oxygen that actually keeps us alive."

"But if you were to breathe just argon..."

"Yes, well that's the point, dear. The good side of it is, you don't have to worry about messing up using a scarf or your belt in a doorway... too many things for an old person to screw up. Or anybody for that matter. And personally, I always thought that blowing your brains out is kind of barbaric. I don't think I could stomach that. And to be honest, I think it's a bit inconsiderate as well. You leave a big mess to clean up and I don't think that's considerate at all.

"With argon, or nitrogen, you can just keep on breathing the way you normally do. You don't gag. You don't suffer at all. I understand it's just like having a drink or two. And after a minute or so you just pass out. You just drift off. And personally, I think that's *much* more considerate."

"This entire topic is sick, Mom. I'm surprised you're even considering it. Besides, what about the fifty years you've been going to St. James Episcopal? I'm pretty sure that what you're considering is a sin."

"Oh, yes, I suppose it is. In fact, I'm pretty sure of it. But...this may come as a shock to you, but in living on this wonderful old planet for all this time, I'm about 99.99% sure that I've sinned myself into a corner at least fifty times over. The God I believe in is a kind and loving...and most of all, an *understanding* God. I think He'll understand. ...Besides, when you get to a certain age, you begin to see things a little differently. I'm just not as afraid of dying as I used to be. And...tell me the truth, in your quiet moments, aren't you wondering what you're going to do with me once I'm a full-fledged vegetable?"

"Never, Mom."

"Oh, that's sweet. But it's also bullshit, Sweetie. Bullshit. You and I both know that."

Preparation

Charlie slipped into what was now Becky's official dance-and-yarn studio and walked over to the back wall, the one that used to house his work bench, trash cans and drill press. Now, it was stippled Tuscan orange-and-gold paint and housed furniture that was pretending to be antique.

    Becky watched him from her little work area on the other wall, but decided just to watch him, see what he was going to do.

    He examined everything, opened a few cupboards which now held skeins of colorful yarn, and then made his way over to her iPad which now straddled an amplifier and two huge Akai speakers. He peered down into the tiny monitor and began scrolling. "This is good," he said softly enough that she couldn't tell if he was even talking to her. "Yeah... This is really good. I like this."

    She finally made a point of looking up from her knitting. "Okay, *what* is good? *What* do you like?"

    Charlie continued scrolling. "Yeah, this is a really good idea. With these playlists, you've sorta made your own private juke box, only you've got it loaded with stuff people might actually want to listen...or even dance to." He looked at her. "It's really good!"

    "Why thank ya kindly, Mr. Blair!" Becky said in her best Southern belle's voice. "We certainly aim to please!"

    "You even named the playlists with...your own sense of

wry humor. *Oldies, Serious Oldies, Ridiculously Old Oldies. And then, Elegant Slow Dance, Slow Dances to grab ass to* and this last one, *Modern Crap.* Who's that supposed to be for?"

"Anyone who wanders in who's two or more generations younger than we are. I did it so they can't peg us as old fogies."

He smiled knowingly at her. "Tell me that you actually give a shit."

"I don't, but I'm also trying to make sure we don't turn into old fogies ourselves. It happens ya know."

"Sounds like you give a shit. By the way, what constitutes modern *crap*?"

"Anything I don't like."

"Fair enough." Charlie flipped through the playlists and came to rest on *Slow Dances to grab ass to.* He went quiet for a while and then pressed the fifth one down, his mind half-expecting to hear the sound of a forty-five dropping on a turntable and a needle lowering into some static. "This is a good one," he declared. "It's timeless. A hundred years from now, people will still be grabbing asses to this song."

Becky gave him the tiniest twist of her head. It was a question mark nod, that only lovers use.

"*At Last.* Etta James. Yup..."

"She was great. I wonder how many babies have been born because of this song."

Charlie's face changed fractionally.

"What?"

"Nothing."

"It's not nothing. What are you thinking?" Becky said.

"Okay. Ever since we all found out about Mrs. Davis's book, I've been going over it in my mind. And I guess I kinda get it with the conclusions she came up with. I mean...I *know* I'm serious," Charlie said.

"*Way too* serious. I think that's the point she was trying to make."

"Okay, I'm not trying to arm-wrestle you on this. I plead guilty, guilty of taking things maybe a bit too seriously."

"Make that, *waaaaay* too seriously and we got a deal."

"Okay, got it. I'm too friggin' serious. I understand...done and done."

"Good! That means you're making progress. You have to admit what's wrong with you if you're going to heal."

"Fine."

"Fine."

"Sooo, with that in mind, my question is: What's *your* splinter?"

"Who said I have a splinter?"

"Well, Mrs. Davis for one. Or maybe you think she was mistaken...for all these years."

Becky put down her knitting and took a long sip of coffee. "You really wanna go into this?"

"It's not my job, and it's not my goal to back you into some kinda corner. Answer it, don't answer it, that's your business not mine."

Becky listened to the words and then went quiet for long enough that Charlie just figured the case was closed. "*Maybe* not a splinter," she said finally.

"Huh?"

"Three-on-a-metaphor. Maybe that's too much. Maybe mine wasn't a splinter so much as a..." She paused again, thinking. "Maybe mine wasn't a splinter so much as me building a thin, invisible shell around myself. Thin and invisible, but tougher than steel. Yeah, that's me, armor-plated Becky. Let's see you figure that one out!"

When he looked over at her, her eyes were twinkling, but

they were also glassy. "Hey... Okay, this discussion is over. I never ever, *ever* want to make you cry."

"Too late," Becky called out. "And you can never, ever, ever do that again. Do you understand?"

"Yup. From now on, your nickname will be, APB, Armor-Plated-Becky."

"No! I don't want you joking about it, either. Just......case closed. Next topic..."

They were quiet for about an hour after that. Charlie finally came over with a peace offering of a question. "Soooo, with this party. We're celebrating your grand opening, right?"

"Yup."

"But we're also throwing the annual party for the fire department."

"Yup to that, too...and thanks for the *we're*."

"You're welcome. And, correct me if I'm mistaken, but aren't you also throwing your big, gala, extravaganza for your dance students?"

"Uhmm, when I think of it, the words gala and extravaganza don't exactly come to mind, but yeah. I figured we'd knock-off three birds with one stone. At least there should be enough people that no one's sitting there keeping the seats warm. Oh, also..."

"There's an *also*?"

"Yup! Apparently every year Bert also has a raffle to gin-up money for new goggles and helmets and stuff. I'm already throwing in ten tickets to be raffled off for free dance instruction. Not sure if anyone is sucker enough to fall for it. Oh, and, I'm gonna knit one custom crazy sweater for the pet of whoever buys a ticket. Oh..."

"There's another *Oh*?"

"Yeah, but I wanted to talk to you first. Do you think you could raffle off...like one of those zero-turn lawnmowers or something? I bet those tickets would sell like hotcakes."

"Do you have any idea what one of those babies costs?"

"Okay. Could we raffle off a free mower blade sharpening? Or maybe whatever it is you do with chainsaws. You could sharpen the blades on those."

"Chains. They're called chains. I could do that. In fact, I could probably go a little better than that. So we're gonna have a gala grand-opening, with a chainsaw raffle and all do *slow-dancing-grab-ass*. What would be the dress-code for something like that?"

"I'm not sure. I haven't worked-out the details."

"I understand. No problem. And...I'm not stupid. I know we touched on a sensitive topic just now."

"What topic? I don't remember any topic. I think you must be confusing me with someone else."

"Becky."

"When does No not mean No? I thought we had an agreement."

"We do. I promised not to hurt you and I fully intend not to do that...ever. But, if we're going to be serious with each other..."

"And why the hell do we have to do that? Can't we just dance and play grab ass and have the occasional fuck on the hood of your Vette?"

"We can do all of that, and more. But, if we're going to be close, really close, I think I have a right to know a little bit about how you tick."

"Okay then, fire away, Sparky. What do you wanna know? My cup size? It's 34 B. Last time I checked, my waist was 22 and my ass is 38. That's pretty intimate, isn't it?"

"I guess. When did you start constructing barriers around

you? First grade? Third grade?"

Becky's eyes went hard and she began staring hard at a spot on the table. "Okay. I guess you really want to do this. When I think about it now, I can't remember a time when I didn't have some kind of shield up. I just didn't think of it as a shield...more like my warm and fuzzy security blanket like that Peanuts kid."

"Who were you trying to shield yourself from?"

The question seemed to have the effect of a stun gun. Her eyes suddenly drifted off to someplace far away and just stayed there. "I don't know," she said finally. "I was going to give you a quick answer... I was going to say, *adults*, although I remember that I didn't think of them as adults so much as just *big people*. Big people were scary for me. I felt like they could see into my brain and see what I was thinking."

"And you didn't like that."

"No, I didn't. Did you?"

"I don't remember thinking that they could read my mind. I just knew that they could make me do stuff. So I just stayed away as much as I could. And when they'd tell me to do something, I'd just do it. It was easier that way."

Becky began smiling a funny kind of smile, only it wasn't that funny. For the first time in his life, Charlie recognized it for what it was. It was her armor-plated smile. "Yeah, but...I'm a girl. I learned that you can be a little crazy and bat your eyes and no one has any idea what's going on. Maybe I would have been a great actress. Maybe I would have been *famous*," she said with that same smile.

"I see it now. I can hear it in your voice. You're acting right now, aren't you?"

"Uh oh. You know this means I have to shoot you, don't you?"

Charlie didn't laugh. He looked disgusted.

"What? What happened?"

"Nothing."

"Bullshit. You have to tell me what happened."

Charlie looked at her. It looked like he couldn't decide whether to stomp out of the room or spit at her. "Nothing. It's just that right now, I can't figure out if I've been dating you, or some character you play...for fun and profit."

"Ouch."

"Okay. Poor choice of words, but you know what I mean. How much of you...is actually you?"

Becky went silent and then sullen. "Ninety-two percent," she said, finally.

"What? Great another tight-assed fast-mouthed joke. You've just been screwin' with me all this time. Tell ya what. You can keep your shop and everything, but you and I are through."

"Jesus Christ, Charlie..."

"No. This is just one long eternal joke for you..."

"No, it's not! I love you, Charlie! I've always loved you. Always. You're the only one I'm ever myself with, but, I gotta be honest. I'm so used to acting that it's almost automatic now. Sometimes it just flashes up. But I try to never do it with you. I try as much as I can."

What Kind?

Charlie had spent the last twenty minutes eavesdropping on the speaker-phone conversation going on between Becky and Susan about what to wear that night.

It was strange to hear the strange girl-logic going back and forth between them. In a quadrillion zillion years, no two guys could possibly have the conversation they were having. It was fifty percent amusing and seventy-percent scary, thinking that otherwise normal, logical, human women could form the thoughts they were forming.

Twice he mimed that he'd be happy as hell to leave the room if she wanted, but twice Becky wrinkled her nose that it wasn't a big deal.

"It always comes down to this," Becky said after the first ten minutes. "You don't want to be too whorey, but you also don't want to come across like you're out shopping for a cat."

"Do you think I've been coming across like a lezzie?" Susan asked.

The fact that Becky took five seconds to answer said something in itself. "Not exactly, "she said finally. "But you know guys. They add two and two and two...and then they come up with six."

"But, two and two and two does add up to six," Susan said.

"Yeah, sweetie. That's kinda what I'm saying."

Charlie looked at her like she was crazy, like she was speaking in tongues, but Becky just ignored him. "See...here's the thing. First off, you're smart so that's...not *exactly*, but it's kinda like your first strike against you. Keep in mind, we're talking about a regular normal guy. Now, I'm guessing if you were fishing for a Princeton or a Harvard guy working in Manhattan, that would be different. But, we're talking Midway Fire and somebody who lives within ten minutes of Carver's Mill.

"Next thing, you've published, not just one but a whole slew of books."

"Three," Susan corrected. "Is three a whole slew?"

Becky went patient with her. "C'mon, Suse. In Carver's Mill, three is an entire shit-load. Soooo, you've kinda got a handicap just walking in the door. And you're pretty, too. Classy and pretty and beautiful."

"You make it sound like that's a handicap as well."

Becky looked at her like she was trying to teach trig to a hamster. "C'mon Susan, get real. You're classy and pretty and smart and you've got a shitload of books out. Most guys are gonna wanna crawl away and hide. And the ones that don't. The ones that figure, *what-the-hell,* they're the dangerous ones anyway. You probably want to stay away from them. Am I right?" she said to Charlie.

"Hey, Becky," Susan sang out, "Who else is over there with you?"

"Oh, it's just Charlie, but he's like family."

"Hello Susan!" Charlie called out in his least intimidating voice. "It's your Uncle Charlie..."

"Hi Charlie. Sorry, I didn't know you were there."

"I can be outta here in four-tenths of a second..."

Susan thought for a moment. "No, I guess it's okay. Besides, it's a little late for that. Tell, me something, Charlie, being as you're already here. Does what Becky's saying make sense to you?"

Charlie looked over at her. Becky was now glaring ominously. "Uhmmm... I think it would depend on who's there at the dance. I don't want to get in trouble, but I think Becky might a little bit right that some men could be..."

"Scared off," Becky said.

"They might be a little bit *intimidated*. I'm not saying it's definite, but it's *possible*."

"Okay, so from what you two are saying, I don't have a chance in hell of even having someone ask me to dance."

Charlie and Becky glared at each other. "No, not at all" Becky said. "These are just factors to be considered."

"Okay, this sounds like it's almost hopeless. Is there anything at all I can do to send the odds over the other way?"

There was a long silence and then it was Becky who spoke. "Now, this is kinda weird, what with Charlie here, but he can't really bow out now."

"Sure I can," Charlie said.

Becky kicked him hard under the table. "He's just joking. We're both here for you. What you do have going for you are the same things you have against you in that Zen kind of way you like to talk about. Bottom line is, you're smart, pretty, successful, and sexy. By all rights, you should be a big catch. You're just, a little *too* much of a catch..." Becky's mouth began lifting into a slow, wide smile. "Consequently, we have to trash you up just a teensie weensie bit. Chippy-fy you, make you just a little sleazy, or easy...something like that, but just a little teeny bit. Do you get it?"

"Sounds like you want me to change my name to Trixie and leave my underwear home. I'm not bringing a cot to this thing."

"No cot necessary. I think they just need to think that

there's *some* chance in hell that you might actually like them."

"God, this sounds like a total disaster," Susan muttered. "Sorry, Charlie. Sorry to put you through this shit."

Charlie's eyebrows raised high on his head in agreement.

"You're completely 100% wrong," Becky said, giving him a jab in the same spot on his shin. "Isn't that right, Charlie?"

Before he could answer, Susan said, "What kind of guys do you have in the fire department?"

Charlie's eyes went blank. *What kind?* he mouthed, and then gave an astonished shrug. "Uhmm... They're just regular guys, Susan. Two legs, two arms..." He was going to say, *They're a lot like me*, but then he thought the better of it. "They're all pretty healthy...pretty good shape, pretty smart. I'm pretty sure all of them have gone to college."

"Really?" Susan called out.

"Yeah. Of course. Now, it may not have been Princeton or Harvard, but...I'm pretty sure they went somewhere."

On her end of the phone line, Susan stared out into space. "Okay. It sounds like I have to get into some specifics with the floozy wardrobe department. Do you think we could go off the speaker-phone communication now?"

"Absolutely!" Charlie said. "It's been...nice talking to you."

"Yeah, you, too," Susan said. "See you tonight...maybe."

Parties 101

Elite institutions of higher learning have devoted entire psychology courses to the nuance and symbolism of throwing a party. Apparently, *how* you throw one, *when* you throw one and *why* can divulge as much as a year lying on the psychiatrist's couch.

At one end of the scale are those whose goal is complete and utter perfection and with that, complete and utter control. The food and spirits are meticulously chosen to make a specific impression on the guests. Usually, the desired impression is: I am wealthy and powerful...and you are not, though there are twelve to fourteen subdivisions of this syndrome.

And it doesn't stop with the food or booze. It goes on to what music is chosen, as well as what music for what period of the party. Lighting is of the utmost importance. A single misplaced fluorescent light can take a party down from five stars to two. Are your automobiles washed and waxed to perfection and your tires sprayed with something to make them shiny? Good show! That might garner you an extra half-point...*though you might ask yourself, do I really care about someone who's impressed by my shiny car?*

Smell is, obviously, important as well. You can't really garner any extra points to speak of. Your place is *expected* to smell perfect. But, your lovable dachshund or pussy cat can take you right out of the competition if you're not careful. Yes, for a good pie-section of the country, throwing a party screams one thing and one thing alone. ME!!! ME!!! Look at ME!!! Ain't I great?

This is, obviously, a really easy subset to spot. Look for

the still-wet asphalt driveway when you're driving up. Only a pristine black drive is acceptable, though a circular drive at the entrance automatically gives you an extra point.

Enough with these people. You will probably never invite them to your house. And they will never have as much fun as you at any party.

At the opposite side of the spectrum, some notable party throwers make a concerted point of being in the shower when the first guest arrives. They listen for the knock on the door or the sound of the chimes, and then call out, "Make yourself at home, I'll be down in a minute!" while still others do nothing at all and enlist the aid of their guests to get all the drinks served and the spare ribs on the broiler, the whipped cream whipped, and so on.

Artists and some of the extremely wealthy may have a similar *modus operandi* because, they have one thing in common, little or no regard or concern for how the rest of the world is doing much of anything. This group of people is called the X-Class. Although they may be hugely wealthy...or not, you can't go by what an X-Class person drives. Rather than a Mercedes or Jaguar which the moderately wealthy people drive, an X-Class or an artist may very well be driving an old Morgan, a froggy-looking Saab, a weird little Citroen 2CV...or even an old milk truck. It just doesn't matter. All bets are off for artists and the eccentrically wealthy. They are flying by their own individual freak flag.

Bert Emmerling was still another subset on the spectrum of party throwers. Bert essentially never threw a party he didn't absolutely have to throw. If Bert had his way, he'd only invite his furry and feathered patients, and have their owners just drop them off. He often smiled, just thinking about what that sort of party would be like. Definitely more fun than a people party.

Sam and Delta Harper, the twin pistons of *The Carver's Mill Patriot*, didn't throw parties per se, though on special occasions, Sam and Delta were capable of throwing potentially lethal extravaganzas...and then viciously critiquing their own parties the very next day.

You could conduct a psychological study as to whether Lou Terkel, the owner of *The Country Gent*, or Andrew McAllister, the owner of *The Wookey Hole*, never threw parties or threw one every day of the week. It's quite likely that neither gentleman could answer the question.

As far as Charlie and Becky were concerned, it had never occurred to them even a single time to throw a party for people. The very word, *party*, had never crept into Charlie's lexicon...ever, nor did it crawl into Becky's brain, though some would argue that.

Becky had an inherent flair for getting people together to dance, but it was a logical culmination of getting people together to dance all the time. It was work. It was her living. Every get-together looked a helluva lot like a dance, until Becky would pause the music and have to show fifteen couples how to execute a proper *coco rolla*, or a *rhythm bounce* for a samba.

So far, Charlie's main contribution to the party had been making his workshop bathroom look like a place that no one would be afraid to pee in. He had scrubbed every square inch of the room and fixtures with Clorox, cleaned the mirror and then assumed he was done. But then Becky flitted in, sized-everything-up and congratulated him on a terrific beginning to prepping the bathroom. For one long moment they stared at each other in the small bathroom mirror. They looked like Bonnie and Clyde posing for a mug shot. All they needed were the words, *WANTED, DEAD OR ALIVE* printed below.

Both the good and bad potential about the party which was just about to start, was that no one had mentally taken responsibility for it. And with no one responsible, all of the governors that most people put on parties, quietly dissolved into the vapors.

The only thing that Becky noticed at first was that each of the volunteer firemen had arrived...in their yellow plastic coats, helmets and fire axes, along with shopping bags crammed with their civilian clothes. Something registered in her mind, she just couldn't place it.

It was Charlie who noticed the second thing that didn't add up. The folding card table that was set up to hold the refreshments was now stocked so well, that a second table had to be brought in to handle the overflow. Apparently every invitee had had the same concern.

The third thing was a happy surprise. Becky's homemade juke box had become an instantaneous hit and Bert was drafted as the watchdog to make sure everyone got their turn.

It couldn't have been more than fifteen minutes into the party that Becky took it upon herself to make the official welcome. She thanked everyone, beginning with Charlie and Susan who had helped the most, followed by her dance class, and then the entire Midway Fire Department, commencing with Chief Emmerling.

What she hadn't noticed was the remarkable speed with which half the women in the room seemed to be getting blotto. One of them, who shall remain nameless, tried to play Patti LaBelle's infamous hit song, *Lady Marmalade*, only the woman in question could only remember the one famous lyric, *Voulez vous coucher avec moi, ce soir?* Which loosely translated means, *You wanna go to bed with me?"*

Bert managed to cut the power to the amp in time, but the woman, who appeared to be three drinks ahead of everyone else, began calling out, "C'mon! I know you guys got nothing on under those jackets! Let's see some skin!"

There was a small quick conference, with Bert acting like the coach on a football team. The yellow-slickered firemen finally gave a little cheer, fist-bump and retired to another room. When they came back, all but one had changed to civvies, under the strong suggestions of their wives. Ronnie Blasser, however, the only bachelor and the wildest part of the team had taken a couple of quick tips from Becky and came out, ready to rock.

Dressed in a yellow slicker, yellow boots, and not much else, Ronnie appeared on the makeshift stage, called out, *"Ladies!!! Voulez vous coucher avec moi???"*

Completely out of character, it was Susan who pressed the first wad of dollar bills into Ronnie Blasser's jockey shorts.

The party broke up at 1:30 in the morning, a new, all-time record for what were usually, tepid Midway Fire parties. Although it had been only six hours long, it seemed like it had gone on for a thirty-hour evening. By the end, Susan had to really concentrate to verify in her mind that she had really stuffed dollar bills in some guy's underpants.

When things were over, Susan began to mouth, "Did I really...?" to which Becky replied, "Oh, yeah, that was you all right. Carver's Mill finally has its first official hussy." But, then she gave a wink and a twinkle to make sure everything was all right.

Strangely, the hard core at the end turned out to be four people...no more. Becky, Susan, Charlie and Bert. And Bert turned out to be a really good guy on pretty much all fronts. He could gather up paper plates and slam-dunk plastic cups while eyeing the room for more serious atrocities. At the end, Bert came over and whispered to the three, "We made enough tonight to maybe even upgrade the masks. They're making new ones now that are just better across the board. Nice work... Thanks."

The Day After

Charlie was in extra early the next morning. He rinsed out the coffee pot and started a fresh pot. Then he walked around, sniffing, half-expecting the place to smell like stale beer and cigarettes. It didn't. It wasn't even that bad when he stepped out into Becky's studio. All the trash was wrapped up tight and put outside. Bert had seen to that, and the only thing that resonated in his mind now were all the songs from the night before and played at 500 db. His ears hurt just from the memory.

Becky pulled in twenty minutes later, looking for the first time that he could remember, like her Energizer Bunny Rabbit's battery had gone flat. He watched her step out of the truck and then pause to take a long deep breath. By the time she made it to the counter, Charlie had already poured a cup and slid it toward her.

She took a long deep drag of coffee and then sighed, "Bless you my child."

"You play...you pay," Charlie said trying to crack a lame joke.

Becky ignored it. "It wasn't the party," she said.

"Crap. What'd you do, have *another* rendezvous after you left?"

Becky listened seriously to the words. "Yeah. In a way, only it wasn't much of a fun rendezvous. More like...I can't even think what it was like... Out in the parking lot, I was saying goodnight to Susan."

"Uh, oh. Did one of the firemen rub her the wrong way? Did someone piss her off?"

"No, not at all. In fact, it had absolutely nothing to do with the evening. She actually had a pretty good time. Somebody asked if she'd like to go out for coffee sometime, and she said, 'yes'".

"Well, that sounds pretty good. So, what's the problem?"

"Susan wanted me to ask you a question."

"Great. I'll try my best to answer it. Shoot..."

Becky held his eyes for a long moment. "Okay. She wanted me to ask you what you know about nitrogen."

"Huh?"

"Apparently her dad has some kind of MIG welding thing in his studio and apparently you need a nitrogen tank to make it work?"

Charlie frowned. "Not exactly. You can weld with a MIG; the welds just aren't as good, that's all. Is Susan looking to learn how to weld?"

"Uhmmm, no. Apparently her mother brought up the subject and..."

"Okay, her mother is thinking of getting into... Aw shit, I bet I know where you're going with this. Is she looking to take herself out?"

Becky looked at him.

"Shit..."

"I don't even know what to do. Should we sneak in and steal the tank? Or maybe open it up and just let it leak out. That'd work, right?"

"*No!* That's a really *bad* idea! If you don't know what you're doing, you could fill the whole basement with nitrogen and if someone...say, Mrs. Sorato went down there, or anyone else, for that matter, they'd fall asleep and never wake up. It's insidious. No one would know. There's no smell, no nothing. They just get a little woozy and then...nite-nite."

"Okay, then. We'll get Susan to take her mom out to lunch or something and then we go in and get the tank out of there."

Charlie went over to the window and just stared out, looking at nothing. Becky came over next to him and looked at nothing as well. "What?" she said after a long minute.

"Nothing."

"Bullshit. What are you thinking?"

Finally, he turned to her. He smiled. He said, "You know that I love you. You also know that I'm deeply *in love* with you."

"Wow, how did I screw up? We were talking about Susan's mother. What's the problem?"

"The problem is... The problem is, you ask questions, but you don't really want answers...or to be more accurate, you want to hear answers that agree *exactly* with what you think. And sometimes there are shadings to questions as well as answers. And sometimes, you're not going to like the shade you're hearing."

"Okay. I'm listening. What do *you* want to do with Mrs. Sorato?"

"That's just it, Becky. You put your finger on it. It's not up to me to decide how...or when...or even if Mrs. Sorato should live or die. That's up to Mrs. Sorato, not me, not you...and for the most part, not even Susan."

"I get it. But... What if Mrs. Sorato isn't playing with a full deck?"

"Okay. Now, that's a good question. But once again, who is it that decides if Mrs. Sorato is sharp enough to make that decision? You? Me? Are we qualified? From the things you've told me so far, Mrs. Sorato has been thinking about these things for a pretty long time. And she has her own perspective...which she's entitled to...we're all entitled to."

Becky's face changed. "I have to say, I'm a little surprised. Make that a whole lot surprised. I thought you liked Mrs. Sorato."

"I do like her. In fact, I like her enough to respect her. Please try not to make this about me. It's not about me...or you. It's about each of us having to decide how we manage our lives."

"I gotta say, I'm a little disappointed. Make that, a lot disappointed."

"That's your right."

"Damn straight, it is."

"Well, guess what. I'm disappointed, too. Can I make a point?"

"You're a big boy. You can do what you want."

"Okay. But, you sound like you've already tried and convicted me. Can you keep an open mind?"

"Sure."

"Okay, the other day you were asking me about the conversation I was having with Dr. Emmerling. I told you that he was down in the dumps because he finally had to put Buck down. Do you think he was wrong to do it? Do you think he was evil or wicked? He killed an animal...cold-bloodedly."

"Yeah, but now you're stacking the deck the other way. From what you said, Buck was in pain and there wasn't any chance of his getting better or getting over the pain. In that case, what he did was humane."

"Right. That's exactly right. And if you have a horse or a cat or any pet that's suffering badly, you make that decision...because you love them."

"Yes, but we're talking about animals now, not people."

"Okay. So, here's the 64,000 dollar question: What's the difference? Seriously. As far as suffering goes, people are animals, too. We eat, we breathe, we get old, we get sick and eventually, just like every animal...we die. Should we have to suffer, sometimes for months, years, because we're people? Don't we deserve at least as much consideration as a guinea pig or a mouse?"

"It sounds like you're saying we should go over and hook her up to a tank of some kind of shit and gas her."

Charlie was glaring now. "You really don't get it, do you? In your world, everything is coal black or pure white. No greys whatsoever." He looked over behind the counter and spied Foofey sleeping in her bed. "Okay... Okay... What if Foofey got hit by a car and she was in extreme pain and was going to die in a day or a week...but you knew for sure she was dying...and in incredible pain. What would you do? Seriously. What would you actually do? Let her suffer for the rest of her life, because you didn't have the guts to do the right thing? People deserve at least as much consideration."

Becky looked him right in the eye. "Right now, I don't think I like you very much."

Charlie stared in her eyes. "Right back at ya."

The Carver's Mill Patriot

Something for Everyone
by
Cuthbert Dixon

Dear Reader, as you know, I periodically do a review of some new restaurant, bistro, or coffee house. And at the end, I give a rating of anywhere from zero to five napkin rings.

Some of you may have noticed that I've eased-up just a bit on some of my favorite haunts (at the advice of my wise and most gracious boss, Sam Harper). His reasoning is quite straightforward and I quote, "Carver's Mill ain't Manhattan" which, of course, is true, though I do think it could be argued that there's no reason why Carver's Mill can't have food as good or better than Manhattan. But that's a fight for a different day.

Today, I'm here to give you a first. I'm writing up Midway Fire's Annual Fund Raiser. Why? Because, this year, it truly deserves it. For its culinary excellence? Oh, good gracious no. There are only so many napkin rings that can be accorded bags of Fritos and Korn Doodles.

Is it for its free beer and barbecue ribs? No, but you're getting closer.

The truth of the matter is, Midway Fire's Fund Raiser now has something for Everyone! I'm not exactly certain whose brilliant idea it was to have it at Becky and Charlie's new section, including all forms of dance instruction from samba to tango to boogie woogie, but you can also buy a shawl, a sweater, some yarn, or even commission a secret yarn bombing. And...Becky and

Charlie have set up the ballroom with magical mirror ball extravaganzas, plus a cleverly designed juke box which only has great music!

Is that all? No, it is not! Last night, we had a fairly close reenactment of the movie, *The Full Monty*, featuring Midway's finest. Whether you're a little old lady or a little young lady, or...well...whatever, there was something for everyone. I give Midway Fire a full FIVE NAPKIN RINGS based on spirit alone! Whether you were there last night or were busy, I hope each of you will support your local fire department. They put their lives on the line for you. Put your wallet on the line for them.

Truce?

When Becky pulled into the parking lot the following morning, a long green-and-silver semi was backed up to the front door of the lawnmower side of the shop. Charlie had both doors propped open and was pulling cardboard boxes down a long silver ramp that looked like it had a hundred roller skate wheels welded to it.

Charlie had noticed the first second she pulled off the highway, but he made a point of being extremely busy as she walked by. Even so, their eyes connected for a second and he gave her a gruff nod as if she were the termite inspector. She gave him a little neutral wave and went directly to her side of the shop. And for the next four hours Charlie cleaned out carburetors and sharpened chainsaw blades.

Becky, for her part, was in the middle of knitting a sweater she'd started two weeks before. It was blue and white and the entire sweater consisted of tiny dots and dashes. It was meant to be an in-joke between the two of them. But once she'd started, she knew Charlie would do whatever it took to translate it, so she had to go back and make sense of the whole thing. Although Becky was adept as hell at expressing herself with her mouth, putting it into Morse Code...or even words was proving to be a challenge, and right that moment, she couldn't think of anything very gracious or romantic to say.

At lunch time, Becky took out a large paper bag, stuffed with the usual things she brought in to share. She stared at it, trying to decide what to do. If she brought it over to share with Charlie, it was...sort of an olive branch, which she had mixed emotions about. And if she broke with the way things were going, that would definitely prolong the argument, at least till dinner and maybe beyond, which she really wasn't up for doing.

Finally, she tromped into the shop and threw down the bag. "Okay, what's it gonna be?" she asked in a surly tone. "Are we gonna go on like this forever? Is this how you fight? You just do the freeze-out treatment until you get your way?"

Charlie looked up from an old Weber four-barrel carburetor and promptly dropped a tiny brass nut on the floor the size of a flea. He peered down, didn't see it, and said, "...fuck."

"Okay, that's great. Fuck you, too, Mr. Blair."

Charlie looked up. "What? I just dropped a little part on the floor. Are you still pissed?"

Becky glared at him. "Okay... I'm gonna go down on the floor and look for that little thingie. And if there isn't a little thingie down there, you, my friend, are in deep doo doo."

Charlie watched her go down on her knees and crawl around. When she turned, her ass in her jeans stretched a bit, presenting possibly the world's best jeans' ass he had ever seen. Embarrassing to get a hard-on in the middle of a fight.

When she finally stood up in front of him, she had a tiny hex nut between her thumb and forefinger. She said, "This damn well better be the part you dropped," and dropped it daintily in his hand.

"Are you okay?" Charlie asked seriously.

"*Am I okay?* Don't pull that shit. I'm not in the mood. If you're pissed, I'm twice as pissed."

"My dad used to say, *If you're gonna dish it out, you have to be able to take it...*"

Strangely, this was a phrase she had heard at least twenty times before. She sighed. "I brought in some roast beef sandwiches with the kind of mustard you like."

Charlie was going to say, *I forgive you*, which would have

started round three, but the sandwiches she pulled out were really thick and rare. "I was just trying to give another perspective. It's a really, really serious topic...and people don't talk about the serious stuff...ourselves included."

"Okay, it sounds like you've still got a burr under your saddle."

"Why does it have to be *my* problem...*my* burr? I don't think I'm the first person to ever wonder about things. My grandfather was a surgeon. But when he was practicing, it was a different world. Everything was different. He rode a horse in the early years and the medicine, well, it was crude by today's standards, but he told stories. Sometimes, on rare occasions, he'd run into a situation, where there just wasn't anything he could do and the guy, or sometimes the gal, would be lying there dying, but it was gonna take an hour for them to die. Soooo..."

"So, he'd put them out of their misery."

"It wasn't just my grandfather. That's what they did back then. If someone had truly had it and they were in horrible pain..."

"Still... It sounds like they were playing God. Doesn't it to you?"

"Sure. No argument. But that's exactly what takes place 24/7 at *every* hospital, every doctor's office, *every* vet clinic, not to mention all of our armed forces, our policemen, firemen, and whole shitloads of senators and congressmen...and even our farmers. Playing God isn't the rare thing you're making it out to be. And just to make my point, we all play God with our own lives every single day we're alive. It's what we do. Susan's mom isn't some rare exception from Mars. She just doesn't want to spend the last part of her life like a wounded animal. She has that right....and to tell you the truth, you are playing God *exactly* as much as she is, telling her what she can and can't do. How are you any different?"

"Well, for one thing, there's a pretty big difference between trying to keep someone alive, and allowing them to do themselves in."

"Yes, there is. But I wonder what you'd want if you'd just been burnt over 100% of your body and were going to die...and were in the most hideous pain in the universe. Not to make a point, but I've gone through something close to that just a few weeks ago. It's no effing fun, even if you're pretty sure you're gonna survive. If I knew I wasn't, I'd find a way...*real* fast. Just in the for-what-it's-worth department, I'm guessing Susan must be weighing-in on this some way."

Becky looked at him, and then she squeezed his hand. "It's hard."

"Yeah, no shit."

"When you go out on a call..."

"Every time. It's always on your mind. If there's a wreck and there's three people in trouble. There's triage, but things aren't always that neat and tidy. And if you think about triage, you're playing God big time. That's exactly what it's all about. You're deciding who you're going to let die so that you can save someone else. It's there. It's always there. It's just, nobody wants to talk about it. Nobody wants to admit it." He looked over at her and noticed that her eyes had changed. They weren't tight anymore. They had softened. "What are you thinking now?"

Becky grinned but it seemed a bit wistful. "I was remembering back to grade school, when all I had to worry about was passing math in Mr. Daniels' class. Imagine that. And now, here we are...together, and talking about all this heavy-duty stuff. When we were little, I used to secretly watch when you'd come up at bat. You'd get really serious and you'd stare right at the pitcher like you wanted to kill him."

"You watched me?"

Becky laughed. "You were always serious weren't you?"

Charlie smiled. "Not always. Two minutes ago when you were crawling around on the floor trying to find that carburetor nut I thought... I thought your ass should get some kind of medal or something. You have a perfect ass, little skinny waist and then it just curves out and comes right back, like an apple or maybe a peach. It's perfect."

"What's the worst ass?" Becky asked.

"Well, I want to say having no ass is pretty bad, but then...I've seen some asses that were big, but they were flat. It's like looking at a great big hamburger patty and just flatter than hell."

Cubby's car coasted down the driveway and pulled in exactly in front of the front door. They watched him get out and look around, like a newcomer. He was in plaid shorts, black socks and a black t-shirt and he had on some police-style sunglasses perched on the tip of his nose.

"Five napkin rings!" Becky sang out as he came through the door.

He paused and bowed graciously. "Well earned."

"Soooo, I guess you have the hots for Ronnie Blasser? I gotta agree with you. He's kinda cute."

"Nope. That had nothing to do with it," Cubby countered. "Well, not much to do with it. If he were the last man on Earth, I wouldn't throw him outta my bed."

"Please, Cub. You're searing terrible images into my brain. And the question is, is this an official call or are you looking for some garden shears or something?"

"Well...I've been threatening to buy a chainsaw for two years now and...today's the day!"

"Do you have a budget in mind?" Becky asked.

"Icks-nay on the budget," Charlie said softly. "I got this."

"Oh? Do I hear somebody setting me up? Is business that

slow?"

Charlie chuckled. "No, Cub. It's kinda the opposite. First off, let me guess. Some big branch fell down on your house or maybe some old dead tree fell over. Something like that?"

"Well, sort of. There's this old tree that's been leaning over more and more for months. And you can tell just looking at it that something is going to happen soon. I'm guessing it's better to do something now than wait till it falls over. Am I right?"

"It depends on a whole lot of stuff. First off, from our previous conversations, I'm guessing your prior knowledge of chainsaws is...a bit limited."

"Make that zero and you'll be pretty close."

"Okay. You're making this easy."

"Little teeny chainsaw," Cubby said.

"Close. You don't even have to buy a chainsaw at all. How's that?"

Cubby thought for a moment. "Okay...unless you have some kind of disintegrator ray you can shoot at it, it's not going to just disappear on its own."

"Well, in a way it is. If you just stay inside your house tomorrow morning, I guarantee the whole thing is gonna just disappear."

"I get it. You don't trust me with a chainsaw."

"Wow, I was thinking I was doing a good deed."

"Is it the fact that I'm gay?"

"No. Not at all. It's the fact that you're Cubby. Besides, have you ever seen anyone screw up with a chainsaw? It's pretty friggin' ugly."

"Okay. I guess I forgive you...this time."

"Thank you, Cubby. I really appreciate it."

When he left, Becky came over and squeezed his hand again. "You're really into this playing God, aren't you?"

Throwing Out Crap

The following morning, when Susan went downstairs, she was surprised to see that the coffee was already perked, and it was cappuccino, no less. She saw an empty yogurt cup and the remnants of an English muffin on the counter and looked around for her mother. She was nowhere to be found. But then she heard some moving of boxes out in the garage and saw that the light was on. She fought the urge to run out and make sure that she was all right. She was bustling and that meant it couldn't be too dangerous.

She followed suit with the breakfast and ate as she checked the e-mails on her iPad. It was junk, as usual, but then sandwiched between a flyer from some Vermont bookstore she'd lectured at and a sale from Home Depot, she noticed Jason Caldwell's name and she stopped. Jason was her latest, newest contact at Connifer Publishing. He had recently replaced Maia Gregory, the old warhorse who had gotten her started in the first place. From the little she'd gleaned about Jason, he was the diametric opposite, all new, all business, all streamlined. And it made her worry as she booted up the e-mail. As usual, Jason was all business, no rounded edges at all, only as she read, she was surprised.

Good News! Thumbs up on The Milk Stool, though the

powers that be are holding back on the title. Not a deal breaker, they just want to see if you can punch it up. Also, your name has to be prominent on the cover and you'll have to have a pretty meaty forward...and that IS a deal-breaker. Soooo....Congratulations!!!

    She closed the iPad and poured a second cup. It was good news, but not without some caveats. Technically, this book would have to come in under her name, though the style was completely different...not bad, just not her. Second, human nature being what it is, there was a possibility that Becky...or Charlie...or Cubby...or all of them could suddenly go mercenary and it could turn into a huge mess. Even if she walked away from the money aspect and did it *gratis*, it could still backfire. She imagined the conversation: *Who the HELL do you think you are, just tossing the money away. Are you all that wondrous?* Or, it could be fine. *Have to keep your guard up though.*

    She trudged out to the garage with that very thought in mind, keeping your guard up. It occurred to her that, probably from now on, there would always be *some* form of guard up, waiting for Mom to walk naked down the road again, or leave the stove on or take a bath with pills...God knows what. It was there. The image of Mom sauntering down the road in her undies was now indelibly tattooed into her sub-conscious.

    She knocked politely on the garage door, a strange thing to do and then called out, "Helloooo! Anybody home?" When she peered in, her mother was sitting on a large cardboard box and going through another cardboard box. There were two green trash bags on one side, stuffed to over-full, and a third one about two-thirds.

    "Wow, someone's been busy," she said with cautious cheer. "What'cha doing?"

    Mrs. Sorato looked up and for a moment she seemed to be

in another world. "What? Oh...hi, Sweetie." She peered back down at a box filled with papers and littler boxes and widgets she could no longer even recognize. "I'm throwing out crap. Or at least I'm trying to. It's time."

Susan's mind raced. "Is there any possibility there are some important papers in there?"

"Not to worry. The boxes that are out here have been taped shut for at least twelve years. No bills, no IRS crap, no mortgage papers, the house is long since paid for. This is mostly just *stuff* that, at the time, we had to hold onto. Now...now it's just crap."

She picked up one of her father's old sweaters. It was green with some tan horizontal stripes around the chest, only it looked like the mice had made a nest in it. She remembered it from when she was in grade school.

Her mother picked it up and buried her nose in it to inhale. "Whew," she sighed. "Mothballs and mice." She gave it a last look and tossed it into the trash bag.

"How do you decide what to keep and what to throw?" Susan asked. "I imagine some of that stuff has memories for you."

"Some of it does," she agreed. "But Daddy and I had more than a couple of discussions about this...when we were younger and full-fledged human beings. Everything's a little different when you're younger, but we ironed it out pretty well. And now, I'm abiding by his wishes, and our decisions. Daddy wanted to make a point of telling me that his clothes were just that, clothes and not to mix them up with who he was. He said that the two sweaters that I'd made for him, I should keep, just because, but, his underwear was from Hanes and Jockey and his jeans were just jeans. I told him the same goes for me." She looked up at Susan. "And it does, dear. He didn't want me to get stuck with mountains of...*stuff*. We decided to keep all our old letters and the jewelry and watches we'd given each other, but for the most part, stuff is stuff is stuff.

And I don't want you to get stuck with the horrible job of having to sort out who I was from old cardboard boxes of crap."

"Ohhhh, Mom," Susan whispered. She went over and knelt next to her mother and hugged her for a long time. When she let go, they were both in tears.

"I'm defrosting a London broil for lunch and I was thinking we could split a yam, and top it off with some Moose Tracks. You interested?"

"Sounds perfect, Mom!"

Later on that afternoon, Susan rounded up the usual suspects for a little celebration get-together. She picked The Gent this time. In the back of her mind, The Wookey Hole was a place to get away to, a place to lick wounds, but The Gent was only one removed from a backyard barbecue.

When she pulled in, everyone had dutifully waited in the parking lot though they'd all found a shady spot so that they wouldn't roast when they came out again.

"Sooo, good news, eh?" Cubby said as they walked in.

Susan smiled at them. "As they say around these parts, good effing news!"

"The book?" Becky said.

Susan just gave the brightest smile she'd ever given. "Inside," she whispered.

As always, Lou was behind the counter, doing what he always did, polishing glasses and making everyone who came in feel a little more special than they'd felt five seconds before.

"Wow! We've got the whole crew here today! By any chance are we celebrating something a little special...or maybe a little new addition to Carver's Mill?"

"Whoa, there Lou," Becky grinned. "We're celebrating but nothing that extreme. Besides, if and when I finally do get knocked-up, I want it to be because we came up with the idea...not you."

"Well, I think that's the very best strategy of all. You folks want your special table in the back?"

Susan nodded in his direction. "Yup, and two things. First, this one's on me."

"Objection," Charlie said.

"Sorry. Objection over-ruled. Secondly, I don't know if you can do this or not, but we would all very, very much like it if you can have a celebratory drink with us. Doable?"

"Very doable," Lou said. "What are doing? Wine? Champagne? Scotch! Bourbon?"

"What kind of champagne?" Susan asked.

"Well..."

"Okay then, what's your best scotch and what's your best bourbon?"

"I got some 18-year-old Macallan, single-malt."

"Done and done!" Susan sang out.

The shot glasses appeared on a dainty silver tray less than a minute later. "What exactly are we toasting?" Lou asked as he raised his glass.

"To...The Milk Stool," Susan pronounced. "Oh, I'm sorry, Lou. That's the working title of a new book that's coming out. With a whole lotta luck, maybe somebody here may even get to star in the movie, if it happens. Right now, it's a long shot but...who knows?"

"To The Milk Stool!"

Twenty minutes later, four filet mignons were being sliced and eaten amidst a barrage of questions. "If there's a book tour, who would go?" Becky asked.

Susan was expecting this. "To tell you the absolute truth, we're on completely new territory now. I don't think anyone has the complete answer, though I can tell you this. With this type of book, if it takes off...and it could, without having the original author around, they very well might want as many "characters" and you are characters you know, to come out and push the book. And...right now, we might as well dream. If they did a movie on it, I'm thinking maybe a Sundance film, who knows where it could go? Just keep in mind, this is all fantasizing right now. All we know for certain is we're getting a book...and some money. How much money depends on good old-fashioned luck and how much you guys are able to go out and pimp it. Believe it or not, that makes all the difference. Oh, and by the way, I got another e-mail from Jason regarding the advance. The advance is the money they send you just to let you know they're interested. When you accept it, that's pretty much the deal."

"How much are you getting?" Charlie asked.

"Well, all things considered, and I've been thinking about this awhile, we...which is to say, all four of us are getting $2500.00...an even split."

"Are you sure you aren't gypping yourself?" Charlie asked.

"This is the *only* way this whole thing is going down. Also, just so you know, there's one small catch and it's pretty common. They *like* the title as it stands, and they may run with it. But they want me to see if there's anything punchier, and they have a whole crew at Connifer Publishing devoted just to this kind of thing. Oh, and once the movie rights are sold, it's a little like selling your newborn baby to gypsies. Once they give you that big check...and it's pretty damn big, then they can do whatever they want with it. In the end, we could all be Indians or live in Tahiti. Characters can get added...and deleted. Or, as I said, somebody will probably come out and study Carver's Mill as well as you guys. And, who knows? Somebody here could be the next Brad Pitt."

Susan's cell phone began playing the first bars of Moon River. "Oops, bet you fifty bucks it's Connifer with some more words of wisdom. Truth is, they get excited, too, when a new book is chosen." She keyed the phone and put it up to her ear. "Ohhh, hi Mom! We're over at The Gent just celebrating The Milk Stool. Would you like to come over and... What?" Her eyes darted around the table. "No, Mom. NO! You can't do this! NO! I love you, too Mom. How 'bout I come over...right now! I can be over in five minutes. I need to talk to you. Seriously. No, you can't... I love you, too but... Hello? Mom?"

She dropped the phone and thought for a second. Then she looked at Charlie. "Mom's about to kill herself."

"When?"

"Now. Right now."

"Do you know how?"

"Yes, I think so. She said she's going out nobly. That's code. Dad's got a nitrogen tank in the basement."

"Shit..." Charlie keyed his own phone. "Bert-- Emergency, Mrs. Sorato's got nitrogen in her basement and... Yeah. I'm on it. Ambulance...and they'd better do frickin' wheelies. Nitrogen will take her out in... Gotta go..."

Charlie was still sprinting out to the parking lot, when Midway's two sirens began spooling up to a howl. Charlie burned out of the parking lot and disappeared. Susan, Becky and Cubby were twenty seconds behind.

On the way over, Charlie's phone went off again. He keyed it. "What?"

"It's Bert. Be fucking careful running down into the basement. If she's already turned the main valve full on...you wouldn't even know it. Do you get me?"

"Got it."

"HEY! CHARLIE! DO YOU GET ME?"

"I got it, Bert. I'll be careful," and then he hung up. A second later, he rekeyed the phone: "Becky. I know you're behind me. When you get there, do NOT go into the basement. None of you. You do, and you're dead. You hear me? That's an order!"

By the time he got there, the ambulance was just pulling in. Charlie pulled up in front of them and jumped out. "Stop! You don't know what you're up against. You go down there, you're dead. You got it?"

"Poison gas?"

"Sort of. Just wait. Stay back. And trust me." He opened the back of the ambulance and took out a small oxygen tank. He disappeared down the back basement steps and threw the doors open. It was dark inside. The only light bulb on was the one over the workbench and for a long minute everything was just dark. "Hello?" he screamed through is mask. "Hello? Mrs. Sorato? Hello?"

He looked around again. His eyes were adjusting to the darkness. "Hello?" he called, and then he saw Mrs. Sorato over against the far wall, sitting in what looked like her wedding dress. It was all lacey and frilly and she was just sitting there on a plastic chair.

He trotted over as fast as he could and kneeled down next to her. He turned her face around...and saw two eyes peering back at him. "You're alive? Please say something. Tell me you're alive." He pulled her facemask off and looked at her. "You okay?"

Mrs. Sorato yanked the facemask back and put it on her face. Then she removed it for an instant. "The write-up on Google is bullshit. I've been on this nitrogen for five minutes and...I'm still here. Please, just go away."

Charlie looked at her face mask and then at the green tube leading down from it. Then he saw the large green tank it was attached to and he started laughing.

"This isn't very humorous Charlie," she said, removing her mask a second time. "I think it's a bit untoward, if you ask me."

Charlie took his mask off and hugged her hard. Then he turned her head toward him. "Mrs. Sorato....you're breathing oxygen."

The Wookey Hole Revisited
(two weeks later)

Charlie looked around the inside of The Wookey Hole. He looked at the dartboard, the table they used to sit at and bang their beer mugs to the Moose song. He looked over at the bar stool at the far end of the bar, the one some old guy had fallen off and right then and there, it became apparent that none of the gays sitting at the bar had the slightest idea how to get an old guy onto a stretcher and off to the hospital. It all seemed like decades ago. He looked over at his friends. They were all sort of the same, and yet they were all different.

Lately, the foggy images from his childhood were fading more and more into the background. Becky and Susan were women now, full-fledged women with serious full-fledged adult problems. Even Cubby was a man now. He drove an Audi and made grown-up decisions. He'd never actually thought of himself as a man, at least not objectively. In his mind, he still felt like the Charlie he'd always been. And yet...

"Well..." Becky said, "I'm glad I didn't suddenly pin my lifetime's hope on being the star of a movie, cuz...that's not gonna happen."

"You're too perky," Charlie said with a grin. "Perky isn't "in" anymore. Maybe back in the days of Mary Tyler Moore. Now... not so much."

"Well, don't all fall on your swords at once," Susan said. "The fact that they're going to spend the week here, doing test shots and looking at buildings, that's a terrifically good sign.

Imagine having your story, *our stories* up on the big screen."

"Yeah, but not Hollywood. We're not talking a big movie."

"Geez, guys, are you familiar with the term, *ingrate*?"

"It'd be cool if they could use my shop for something, but I'm guessing it's a little too..."

"They might use it," Susan said. "Maybe they'll let you do a cameo. They might have you in the back room working on a lawnmower or something." She picked up her martini glass and made the third toast of the day. "To life, even with all its twists and turns..."

"It's friggin' weird," Charlie added and they all toasted. "By the way, how's your mom?"

"Ooooh, *really* bad segue," Becky groaned.

"No, it's not," Susan said, "It's extremely appropriate. He's the one who threw everybody out and went down into...what he thought was a room full of deadly gas, for the express purpose of saving my mom. At this point, Charlie can do no wrong...zero. Charlie walks on water."

"Well, in the wintertime," Charlie murmured.

Susan leaned forward and poured the rest of the martini carafe into her glass. "Okay, I think I have a little tiny confession to make to all of you. It was necessary, and there wasn't any other way I could do it but. Well, as a writer, sometimes you have to do certain things."

"What the hell are you talking about?" Cubby asked. "I feel like I'm getting set up...retroactively. What did you do?"

Susan took a second long sip to bolster herself. "Okay, it's like this. Bankers bank. Painters paint...and writers write. It's what we do. We take something out of nothing, an idea, a dream, sometimes just an image, and we try to shape it into something that will sell, something that will entertain a reader. That's the deal. But, having said that, there's a myth that every character in every novel just materializes out of the ether...and it doesn't. With the situation with Mrs. Davis's book, it wasn't a novel really, it began more like a diary, only a diary chronicling you three."

"You're in it, too, remember?"

"Yeah, fine. Only when Connifer read it, they had to read it like what it was, a book that they might want to publish. And to do that, you two, and I include myself as well, had to get shaped a little."

"You changed us," Charlie said.

"No. I didn't change you, but in some instances I had to make you more you than you really are. Does that make any sense?"

"Not to me," Charlie said.

"Me either," Becky agreed. "How did you make me more me?"

Susan sighed. "You, grasshopper, required the very least. In fact, I had to tone you down a bit. But even that is a change. And what I'm saying is, it was necessary to get the book accepted."

"Am I still a guy?" Charlie asked.

"Absolutely."

"And I still fix mowers and am a volunteer fireman?"

"Pretty much," Susan said.

"What does *pretty much* mean?"

"Let's just leave it at that. But, I'm not completely finished with my confession. Like I said, writers write. We make up characters out of a whole bunch of things...people and suddenly they're real, really, really real. But, my brain, or my muse, whatever you want to call it, sometimes, it takes real people and turns them into characters. When I do that, I can let my characters solve problems for me when I can't figure out the answer myself."

"You're losing me," Charlie said. "*Who* solved *what* problem for you?"

"All three of you. For weeks now, I've been wracking my mind what to do with Mom. And the more I thought about it, the more I realized that there just isn't, or perhaps *wasn't* any solution at all. I can't leave her home by herself, particularly now that the police and firemen know what she tried to do. So that's out. I can, if I have to, move in for pretty much the rest of her life, and maybe my own, and that works in a way, except..."

"That's a rough call," Becky said.

"Yes, it is," Susan agreed, "though many families have done it."

"Nursing home? Assisted living?" Cubby said.

Susan inhaled deeply and let it out like a stale balloon. "Yeah, only both my mom and dad hated that with a passion. They said they'd rather take a long walk off a short pier, which is where we're at now. But then..."

"Then what?" asked Charlie.

"Then I did a naughty thing. I wrote a scene in my mind, with all three of you and you were all trying to figure out what you'd do if it were *your* moms."

"Who won? Who had the great idea?" Becky asked.

"Well, I wish I could say it was you, because you had some interesting ideas, but, once again, it was Charlie."

"Figures."

"What great idea did I come up with?"

"You said, and I quote, 'Make yourself a commune.'"

"Huh?"

"Hold on. It's not a bad idea. In fact, it's being implemented even as I speak. Way back when, whole generations of families would live under one roof. And everyone took care of each other. That's all changed, but...with the way things are right now, young families are going broke, just trying to buy a house and raise a family. I put an ad on the internet. *Family wanted to live in quaint rustic house in the woods. Housing and food are included, but at least one spouse must be capable of taking care of an elderly person.* Know how many responses I got? Thirty-one, and that's just in five days. I think I have a live one, from North Carolina. They've been taking care of their grandmother for forever. They're used to it."

"It could work," Charlie said, "if you get the right people. So, when you make me into a character, do I still look like me? Do I still talk like me? How does that work?"

THE END